Wants and Needs

By the Same Author

As Young as This

Wants and Needs

ROXY DUNN

FIG TREE
an imprint of
PENGUIN BOOKS

FIG TREE

UK | USA | Canada | Ireland | Australia
India | New Zealand | South Africa

Fig Tree is part of the Penguin Random House group of companies whose addresses can be found at global.penguinrandomhouse.com

Penguin Random House UK,
One Embassy Gardens, 8 Viaduct Gardens, London SW11 7BW

penguin.co.uk

First published 2026
001

Copyright © Roxy Dunn, 2026

The moral right of the author has been asserted

Extract on p. 20 from *Worstward Ho* by Samuel Beckett, published by Faber and Faber limited, © Samuel Beckett, 1983. Reprinted by permission of Faber and Faber limited; extract on p. 148 from *The Crucible* by Arthur Miller; extract on p. 173 from *Song of Myself* from Walt Whitman; quotation on p. 241 from Apolo Ohno in the documentary *The Weight of Gold*, HBO Max, 2020.

Penguin Random House values and supports copyright. Copyright fuels creativity, encourages diverse voices, promotes freedom of expression and supports a vibrant culture. Thank you for purchasing an authorized edition of this book and for respecting intellectual property laws by not reproducing, scanning or distributing any part of it by any means without permission. You are supporting authors and enabling Penguin Random House to continue to publish books for everyone. No part of this book may be used or reproduced in any manner for the purpose of training artificial intelligence technologies or systems. In accordance with Article 4(3) of the DSM Directive 2019/790, Penguin Random House expressly reserves this work from the text and data mining exception.

Set in 12/14.75pt Bembo MT
Typeset by Falcon Oast Graphic Art Ltd
Printed and bound in Great Britain by Clays Ltd, Elcograf S.p.A.

The authorized representative in the EEA is Penguin Random House Ireland, Morrison Chambers, 32 Nassau Street, Dublin D02 YH68

A CIP catalogue record for this book is available from the British Library

ISBN: 978–0–241–63275–8

Penguin Random House is committed to a sustainable future for our business, our readers and our planet. This book is made from Forest Stewardship Council® certified paper

For Jim

The afternoon Barney broke off our engagement I was watching *Newsround* on CBBC while eating a box of mini raisins. He walked into the living room where I was sitting on the sofa with my post-surgical knee encased in its leg brace and asked, 'Why are you watching that?'

He was frowning as he said it and I could tell he disapproved. I told him I was curious to know what was going on in the world but that I was finding the adult News overwhelming and that this was my temporary-slash-potentially-long-term solution.

'That's just called the News,' he said, sounding embarrassed even though there was no one in the room with us. 'Not the adult News.'

I said if we were rating offences then my extra word insertion scored pretty low in comparison to present war crimes, and asked him to pass me my glass of orange squash, which was slightly out of reach.

As he handed it to me he frowned again and said, 'I think you need to grow up.'

This wasn't the first time he had said this. Ten months earlier he had said the same thing, although that time he had said 'we' and referenced the fact we often spoke to each other in a cartoon voice that had begun as ironic and sporadic and at some point had stopped being ironic and sporadic, and that we now had so many bits and skits and in-jokes that it had started to feel as though we were children and maybe we ought to see someone, like a couples therapist.

I had laughed out loud and said, 'But that's what grown-ups

do.' In that moment I felt he had a point, but pointed out that neither one of us had any spare money to pay a professional to essentially teach us to be less fun. I had thought the matter closed, but now here it was, rearing up again.

I paused putting a raisin into my mouth and asked, 'In what way specifically do I need to grow up?'

He looked down, kicking the toe of his sock into the corner of the rug and said, 'Pretty much all the ways.'

I muted the television then and turned to look at him because I understood there was something he wasn't saying.

'I don't think I can marry you,' he said, still not looking up. 'Or be with you,' he added, in case this needed clarifying.

I suddenly felt light-headed and started putting the raisins into my mouth very quickly. 'But you asked me to. Why would you ask me to marry you and then not want to marry me?' My body was churning and panicking but my voice sounded too flat, as if it hadn't yet caught up with the situation.

'I thought it was what you wanted.'

'Well, duh. Only if you meant it.' I actually did say 'duh', and felt myself go hot with shame.

He said he was confused, that he thought it might make things clearer inside his head if we got engaged, but that it hadn't and how could he join himself to me when he wasn't even joined up inside himself?

I shouted at him to stop talking like he was a dot-to-dot and for him to bring me a bowl because I thought I was definitely-maybe about to be sick.

When he came back from the kitchen holding the bowl, he started saying stuff again about not knowing who he was and needing to figure it out because he was fractured and needed to feel like one complete whole, but I had stopped listening a) because I'd heard all the fractured whole stuff before, and b) because I was trying to remember how to breathe.

'I think you might be hyperventilating,' he said, alarmed.

He put a hand on my shoulder, and I heaved at his touch, jolting forwards.

'It's all right,' he said. 'You're all right.' He held the bowl with one hand and me with the other as I dry-retched over it. 'You're going to be all right,' he said. But I was not all right. I was the absolute opposite of all right. I wasn't crying just from sadness; I was crying from fear. It was so frightening to suddenly be this alone.

'How come it's all so big for you?' he asked. I was still crying but by now had transitioned to the juddering hiccupping stage.

'But how could it be any smaller?' I said, amazed.

He raised his shoulders up, and then dropping them, said, 'I guess just because it's not actual life and death.'

But short of physically dying, being left by the person you loved was the hugest, worst thing I could think of – almost the same amount of bad and terrifying as death.

I kept crying into his navy fishhook jumper and he said, 'Yeah, get it all out,' working on the unlikely assumption that my tears would have an endpoint. But he was right. Eventually I cried myself dry and fell asleep.

When I woke my throat was sore so that it hurt to swallow. My body felt worn out and crumpled, as though it had been scrunched up and folded out again lots of times. I heard the hum of the fridge and saw the sun through the kitchen window was red and low in the sky. For a tiny moment I couldn't work out why I was on the sofa and why I had been asleep when the clock above the microwave said it was only eight o'clock. And then I remembered that it was because Barney had broken up with me and all the pain – but also the fear – came back in one big whoosh. Ow. Oh wow, oh ow.

*

I moved out three days later back to my mother's house in Brighton. I took all the house plants and left him our four-month-old bed we hadn't yet had sex in. We had been together eight years and nine days.

A week into living with my mother I got a call from my friend Erica who announced that by sheer miracle both her twins were napping – warning me that at any moment either one of them might wake – before offering her shocked and aggrieved condolences.

I brought my shoulder up to my ear to hold my phone in place as I hobbled into a patch of shade on the patio, out of earshot from my mother, who was kneeling on the lawn breaking up a bed of soil with a trowel. 'I know he hasn't died,' I said. 'Logically my brain knows that. But as far as my body's concerned, he might as well have done.'

'Well, yeah, of course.'

'And I'm still wondering whether there's been a kind of weird mix-up with reality and I've entered some form of alternate universe that I'm going to eventually pop out of and get back to my old life.'

'Again, of course.'

Listening to Erica affirming each of my statements – even the infeasible ones – made me feel fractionally less awful and alone. I told her it was mildly comforting to hear her confirm that along with my world imploding, I wasn't also going insane.

'You're definitely not. Do you know what is insane? My dentist, who's married to another dentist, told me that *three* out of their four children are professional clowns.'

'What's the fourth one?'

'Obviously a dentist.'

I harped on some more about my shattered life until after nearly an hour she informed me with regret that she ought to wake the twins.

'It feels like such a masochistic act but otherwise they won't want to sleep tonight and losing my evening isn't worth staying on the phone to you now, no offence.'

I assured her none was taken and asked if I should stay on the call to briefly say hello to them. She said that while that was a sweet offer, I would likely get embroiled in the retelling of their dreams, which would be long and tedious for me, and difficult to extract myself from.

'They have no innate sense of storytelling at this age; they don't know how to set things up or get to the good bit. It's just *and then and then and then*.'

'You're looking for causality from a dream?' I asked.

'At least a build and then a climax.'

Erica's high conversational standards meant she prioritized telling the best version of a story, rather than its factual accuracy. Just before she hung up I reminded her of the time she had told me about a woman she vaguely knew who had been diagnosed with colon cancer and whose partner had been planning to leave her but then had stayed nursing her until she died, only later admitting that the woman hadn't actually died, but that 'until she lived' just didn't have the same ring to it.

'I still maintain it doesn't,' she said, putting the phone down.

'Who was that?' asked my mother, looking up from the flower bed, her trowel still in motion.

'Erica.'

She frowned and said, 'I hope you're not being too sad with her. You don't want to exhaust her goodwill entirely.' She stressed 'entirely', as if to confirm I was already on the cusp of this.

I reached my nose up to the magnolia tree to sniff its giant vanilla horn and told her, 'That's precisely what friends are for. If they were only there for the good times they would have checked out years ago.'

'I'm just warning you, her tolerance is going to have a cut-off point.'

'What do you suggest I do? Pretend to be OK even though some hours it physically hurts to breathe?' What alarmed me about this statement was that I was not exaggerating.

'Use me instead,' she said matter-of-factly. 'My capacity to listen to you is limitless.'

I felt my eyes start to sting and began to blink quickly, but it was too late. She had caught me off guard with her tender pragmatism. I hobbled to hug her but she had already turned back to the flower bed, pressing down on the earth with vigour.

I had torn one of the major ligaments in my knee the previous Easter, preparing my annual chocolate egg hunt for Barney. He claimed to partake in this ritual solely for my sake and was always dismissive when I told him to close his eyes so I could hide the eggs, but when he opened them again I'd see the glint of relief and excitement at the prospect of some tangible gratification, after hours spent toiling away at his desk rearranging the word order of a sentence, only to wonder if it was better the original way around. Only that year, we never got to the hunt part because when I jumped up to position the final egg on top of the bookcase, I landed weirdly and heard my knee make a loud popping sound as it buckled. When I tried to stand up I found I couldn't put any weight on it and so lay on the sofa whimpering while Barney got a bag of frozen berries out of the freezer. But even after icing it, it swelled and went so bulbous that it looked like an elephant leg and so we took an Uber to A&E.

The consultant who looked at my X-rays was initially confident the injury would heal without surgery, but after two months of crutches and wearing a leg brace, followed by half a year of physio, my knee still wasn't working properly and so this same consultant decided I did in fact need to be operated on. To her regret (I assured her it was even more so to mine), there had been a further complication when the material she'd used to stitch me up had caused some sort of allergic reaction and so she'd recently gone back in to retrieve it, meaning for the last couple of months I had been back on crutches and inside a leg brace for the third time in two years. She had referred to it as 'just a quick little op this time around', making me wonder if she herself had ever been operated on. Arguably, I now had more first-hand experience of the procedure than she did. But I liked her because she seemed genuinely invested in the outcome of my knee, and I found the way her trainers always looked brand new very endearing.

Thanks to the cocktail of drugs I was on, low-level nausea became my new norm. Hobbling around the garden in a stupor, I'd do three laps of the lawn before queasiness would take over and I'd have to change direction. My mother said she didn't think that was a thing – getting sick when the circle was as large as a lawn – but I said, 'Trust me, when you're on Cipro it's a thing.' I thought the fact I was now abbreviating drug names made me sound either like a doctor or like one of those perpetually ill people who are always in and out of hospital, and since I didn't have a medical degree only one of these categories was available to me.

I wore a rucksack around the house to transport my things because the crutches had taken away the use of my hands. For some reason the rucksack made me extra sad and protective over myself and so I stopped wearing it and took to carrying things in the pockets of my pyjama shorts or underneath my armpits, but they often slipped out because I was sweating so much from the drugs and the heat. (It was unseasonably hot for June and my mother classified fans in the northern hemisphere as an unnecessary use of the world's resources.) She had given me a small brass bell and told me I could ring it if I needed something pressingly but took it back after two days, saying my ringing was too liberal and that she felt she was living with a town crier.

In the evenings after dinner – normally a proteinous salad, as my mother deemed cooking 'frivolous' – the two of us would watch an episode of a documentary series about the lost railway lines of Great Britain. I got tired of this show halfway through the first episode and would gladly have stopped watching it, but saw the uncustomary morsel of pleasure my mother got from it and this gave me a morsel of pleasure, and as I was not in a position to turn down morsels . . . on we ploughed with those branch lines. Sometimes pleasure can feel a bit teeth-gritty.

Often my grandfather would call while we were watching the show and my mother would reluctantly pause it so he and I could compare notes on our ailments, while she caught up on her WhatsApp correspondence. I told my grandfather that my thigh had shrunk so much from inactivity that I could now reach both my hands around the widest part of it and my fingers would touch but that I didn't like to do this because it made me squeamish. He said to make sure I did my physio exercises so that the skin didn't get saggy or else I would end up like him, looking like a turkey that nobody wanted, not even really at Christmas. I adored my grandfather and said of all the people I might resemble I would be honoured to resemble him. He put the phone down shortly after this because he mostly disliked sincerity without wit and I hadn't managed to think of a joke in time.

'It'd be nice to get through an evening without that man interrupting us,' said my mother, tersely, picking up the remote.

'Why are you so anti Grandpa? I like talking to him.'

'I'm not anti him, I just find his attentiveness ironic.'

'Why? It's not like he abandoned you. He just worked a lot to earn money so you could have a nice life.'

'Oh, so you're the authority on my upbringing now, are you?'

'Well, didn't he?' I was impatient with her cryptic and dismissive remarks about my grandfather that had peppered my childhood. Either she could be specific about her grudge or she could get off her hate train. But she just hovered her finger over the play button and said, 'From now on, you two can play happy families on your own time.'

My mother is a retired GP who administers injections casually and owns a toolbox. I am the least hardy person I know and wept when my patients died playing *Theme Hospital*. 'Your suffering is not unique' is my mother's favourite aphorism, of which I am the primary recipient.

A few years ago, I read an article about Love Languages and understood that all my life my mother has been giving me acts of service while what I've wanted is physical touch and verbal affirmation. When I told her this discovery, she said, 'So I should have spent less time bleeding the radiators and more time stroking you, is that right?'

'Maybe tried splitting the difference?' I said, and then felt thick with guilt.

She was forty-one when I was born. She had been working for Voluntary Service Overseas, training local doctors in a town outside Java, where she had met my father – a VSO employee and Glaswegian engineer – and had by her own admission tricked him into impregnating her, telling him she was on the pill when she wasn't. What with her specializing in sexual health and family planning, I imagine from his point of view it seemed reasonable to have believed her.

On learning she was pregnant she moved back to Sussex and installed herself in a three-bedroom end-of-terrace house in Preston Park – the same house where I grew up and where I was now currently living again.

She had written my father a letter on her arrival back in the UK explaining the situation and that she had no expectation or wish for any financial or emotional involvement on his part, that she understood the importance of his fieldwork and didn't wish to disrupt it in any way, and that the greatest service he could do would be to allow her to raise their child alone with the knowledge that his efforts were being more effectively used overseas. She has been open about this narrative with me since birth.

I met my father only once, when I was seven, inside the café of BHS in Glasgow. He brought me a shadow puppet which I had pretended to play with while watching him and my mother sip black tea and reminisce about old colleagues. They had started speaking Bahasa Indonesia at one point and my mother had become animated and uncharacteristically soft. It is the only time I have ever seen her do what I think was a version of flirting.

He had elderly parents he visited every couple of years but otherwise didn't come back to the UK. I had never met these grandparents and my mother told me she had no intention of us meeting them as they were evangelists. My mother distrusts anyone with devout faith, believing they lack autonomy and self-sufficiency. I hoped we might see my father again on his next visit but this coincided with a Eurocamp holiday to Brittany my mother had already booked for us and would lose the deposit on if we didn't go.

The next year she received a letter from an old VSO colleague telling her that he had died in a moped accident, that because of the state the body was in, his parents had been persuaded not to fly it back to Scotland. We didn't go to the memorial, which was held at a Reformed Presbyterian church in Glasgow. Apparently he hadn't left behind a will and we were not short of money anyway, thanks to my mother's salary and the fortuitously timed sale of my grandfather's photographic business which he had worked in since the age of fifteen as an apprentice, before later inheriting it from the owner.

My mother let me cry as she told me the news. I said to her, 'You can cry too.' She said, 'I have no need to do that.' She has never once let the wall between parent and child slip. No, that's not true. She did cry one time, when she read me *The Railway Children*. When we got to the end bit where Bobbie is reunited with her father at the train station my mother shook the bed with her tears and I said, 'Mummy, stop it, you're scaring me.' 'Sorry,' she said, tipping back her head and shaking her hands. 'I'm sorry.' At the time I interpreted her sorry as an apology for frightening me, but I've since wondered if it might have been her saying sorry for not giving me a dad whose arms I could run into. She tells me my father's ashes are scattered in a paddy field in Java, the precise location of which she is unaware of.

The middle Saturday in July my old school friend Beth and her husband Jon visited. They lived in Bristol but were spending the weekend in Hove with Beth's parents, who were celebrating their wedding anniversary. It wasn't a big one but Beth's mother liked to mark any kind of holiday or festival or celebration – even Bastille Day, despite their lack of any French heritage.

Beth and Jon were both doctors. Whenever anyone asked Beth how she got into medicine, she always said, casually, 'Oh, I just fell into it.' When I told this to Erica, she rolled her eyes and said, 'Please. People fall into accountancy or someone else's vomit, not saving lives in exchange for respect and a six-figure salary.' I thought dermatology was pretty low on the life-saving scale and I knew for a fact that Beth didn't earn six figures because I had asked her this outright, but didn't say this to Erica because I got the point she was making and didn't want to be pernickety.

I led the two of them into the living room, where the curtains were still drawn from my sitting in the dark.

'Let's let some light in, shall we?' said Beth, enthusiastically moving to pull the curtain cord.

I asked if they wanted anything to eat or drink and added if they did they would have to get it themselves because I was presently incapacitated, gesturing to my crutches. They said they were fine, that they had each just drunk a full glass of water before leaving the house. They were both keen cyclists and fanatical about their health. Ordinarily they wore Lycra as their everyday look, although today Beth was wearing a floaty dress that looked very tent-like and swamped her lithe frame.

They sat next to each other on the sofa opposite me and I felt their nervousness at not knowing what to say. Beth's engagement ring seemed particularly glinty in the sunlight, as if it was doing a little dance for me that I hadn't asked for or wanted to sit through. She must have seen the way I was looking at it because she suddenly reached with her other hand to cover it, which I thought was a gracious, albeit irrelevant, gesture since her husband was sitting live on the sofa in front of me.

'I like your plait,' she said, and asked if I had done it myself. I confirmed I had, and she said, 'That's clever. They always look rubbish whenever I do them.'

'Yeah, I could never do a plait,' Jon added.

Yikes, I thought. We really are scraping the barrel in terms of my accomplishments, but I thanked them, because I knew how hard they were trying and I wanted to see if I could be stoic and dignified – traits that felt perpetually out of my reach.

'How long does it take?' asked Jon. 'To do a plait.'

'That depends,' I said. 'Normally about a minute and a half but this one took longer.' And I went on to explain that I had intentionally spent thirteen minutes doing this particular plait that morning because I had nothing else to do, adding that this appalled me because given the minuscule odds of any of us even being born at all, surely it was a waste of this one life to be spending time deliberately making plaits look more bad in order to justify doing them again?

Jon laughed uncomfortably and said, 'Whoa. Quite deep for eleven a.m.'

I said that my other skill, in addition to plaiting my own hair, was my ability to be deep before midday, actually at any time of day. *Arguably more of a flaw than a skill*, chirped the snide voice inside my head.

'So, how are you?' Beth asked. She had evidently decided to face the question head-on, and I admired her for this.

'Well, I've been better,' I told her. 'And I don't think I've ever been worse.' I said this objectively, without emotion, which was rare for me, and went on to explain that it wasn't just the time I'd spent with Barney up until now that I was grieving for, it was also the time that hadn't happened yet that I had banked on sharing with him. How could you factor someone so entirely into your life and then be OK with the fact that they were no longer in it – present or future? This was surely such a hard and unreasonable demand that we made for ourselves by falling in love. Beth chewed the side of her mouth as she presumably tried to think of a suitable reply. Jon nodded and said, 'Yeah, tricky one.'

'Anyway, what's new with you guys?'

I hoped this would take us into more stabilizing territory, as somehow their lives always remained steady while everyone else's around them went in and out of flux, but Beth looked excited and said, 'We've actually got some news.' She paused and I braced myself for whatever was coming. 'We're pregnant.'

'Congratulations,' I said, hearing a strange break in my voice which I really didn't want to be there.

'Thanks. We're twenty-four weeks already but I was waiting to tell you in person.'

I said congratulations again but this time the break in my voice sounded even more broken.

'I didn't even know you were trying.'

'We weren't really. It just kind of happened.'

I imagined Erica rolling her eyes once again and saying, 'Sure, you just happened to accidentally not be using contraception during your six-day ovulation window, did you?'

It wasn't that I even wanted a baby. I just didn't want Beth to be having one, which I knew was petty and made me dislike myself, but this still didn't eradicate the feeling.

Watching them both, how sorted and settled their lives were, I felt so unbearably lost. But I didn't just feel lost, I *was* lost. I had no idea what my future looked like. I had never known in terms of my work, but now I also had no flat and no Barney to go back to in London, and this was terrifying.

'I need to go to the loo,' I said, getting up from the sofa and hopping towards the door on my crutches. 'I'll leave you to discuss my sad little life while I'm gone.' I'd meant it to sound like a joke but it came out wrong; I think because there was too much truth in it.

'Oh, Misty, please don't say that,' said Beth, looking pained and embarrassed. 'You're just going through a rough patch right now.'

This made me even more ashamed – the implication that I was making things worse than they had to be or actually were. For a moment I wished I was going through a death or a divorce and not just a break-up and an injury, because it often wasn't appropriate to add the parenthesis (but I was planning to spend my life with him and I've started to doubt if I'll ever walk again without apparatus).

I made a mental note to make a jovial remark when I came back from the loo in order to make things less uncomfortable for everyone. I don't remember exactly what I said now but it was in reference to the latest health advice concerning antioxidants that my mother had ripped out of the newspaper and stuck on the wall so we could all be informed about the benefits of blueberries while we urinated.

Shortly after Beth and Jon left my mother came into the living room carrying my lunch on a tray – a plate of carrot batons and a ramekin of peanut butter.

'Beth's pregnant,' I said.

My mother winced. 'You know—'

'I know. My suffering is not unique.'

'I was actually going to say, I think this is all rather shitty for you.'

She placed her hands, which were always cool, on the back of my neck and held them there.

'The thing is . . .' I said. And I told her how it wasn't just Barney and my home that I'd lost, but it was something more abstract too – where I thought I'd be at this point in my life. 'And if that wasn't enough,' I added, 'I don't even have a career.'

'Well, that's hardly new; you've never had one of those,' my mother accurately pointed out as she frowned at her spider plant, drooping under the weight of its offspring. 'I'll have to cut off those plantlets. They're sapping the mother's energy.' Her metaphor was not lost on me.

The day Barney and I moved in to our flat, I was working part time in telesales and trying to write a publishable book. The day I moved out of our flat and back in with my mother, I was working part time in telesales and still trying to write a publishable book.

When my first manuscript got rejected, my mother sent me an email with the subject heading, *Of interest to you?* The body of the email was empty aside from a link to an article titled, *What Can I Do with an English Degree Other Than Become a Writer?* I replied, *I'm struggling to see the link!* She resent it and I replied again, *I mean the link between me and this article.* This time she did not reply.

'*Some* people have to succeed at writing. I mean, look around you,' I said to her the following Christmas, gesturing to the bookshelf in the kitchen. 'Published books are definitely a thing.'

'They are a thing,' said my mother, reaching in her rubber glove to unclog the sink. 'But so are unpublished books, and there's a hell of a lot more of those you can't see.' But this I knew and had no time for as an argument. In the end I stopped talking to her about writing and she stopped sending me job links. It seemed we had reached a truce, or at least an impasse.

When my second manuscript got rejected on the grounds that it wasn't very thrilling (a judgement I agreed with and thought to be a reasonable requirement of a thriller), I told Erica that my taste and ambition continued to outweigh my skill. 'But that's just imposter syndrome,' she said. I asked how

I was meant to tell the difference between imposter syndrome and genuinely being unqualified.

'Fail again, fail better,' she replied, swerving the question. I pointed out that there was a paradox to this line because surely to fail better meant to get even further away from succeeding. Erica told me I needed to stop pulling apart established sayings that were designed to offer encouragement, and then added, 'But lol if you're right. I know a theatre director with that Beckett quote tattooed up his arm.'

Erica and I had met during our first week at Leeds University, where I had gone to study English, and Erica, Drama. We had been put on the same corridor of our halls, at opposite ends, bracketing a row of Millies and Lotties and Indias who wore pearls and pashminas and had turned their bedrooms into shrines to their gap years with drapes of batik fabric hanging from the walls, tie-dye cushions and poufs. During Freshers' Week, Erica had walked past the open door of my room, which was sparse aside from two framed photographs – one of my mother and grandfather, and another of me and Beth on our last day of primary school.

'Have you finished unpacking already?' Erica asked, not yet bothering to introduce herself. 'I mean, including decorating.'

'Yes.' I nodded.

'Based solely on the fact that your room doesn't look like a shisha lounge, do you want to come with me to the SU bar?'

We were already halfway there by the time we asked each other our names. Erica said it was a good job she hadn't found out any sooner that I was called Misty, or else she would have immediately rescinded the invitation.

She told me as we watched a group of hockey boys downing snakebites that it hadn't ever occurred to her to be attracted to men, that women were so clearly the superior species she felt fortunate to have never had the affliction of desiring the male anatomy. I told her that with lines like this she could become a modern-day Jane Austen, to which she replied, 'I probably could, if I had even the remotest interest in being anyone other than myself.'

After my third failed attempt to write a book, I stopped telling people I was writing, and would say if anyone asked, 'Oh, just bits and bobs, the odd line, nothing in particular,' but quietly and doggedly I was going at it again. 'Like Bertha up in her attic,' said Erica, who was big into Gothic literature.

Each time the novel I was working on got rejected and I would open it back up and try to diagnose the problem, I would hear myself asking: Misty, is there no end to your resolve? The snide voice inside my head would counter, *Is there no end to your delusion?* I didn't really resent the voice for this. I thought it sounded reasonable and offered objectivity – which I wanted because I shuddered at the thought of becoming one of those really confident pumped-up people who had either forgotten how to doubt themselves or chose not to in order to manifest success – but I did think it was a shame the snide voice always got the last word.

Aside from Barney, Erica was the only person who I told about my writing in any granular detail. I think partly it was because she was so unshockable. I could have revealed I had half a dozen unwanted manuscripts in my drawer, and she would have reacted in the same manner as if I'd referred to half a dozen unwanted moths.

On days my writing went well, I felt completely sustained by it, as though I didn't need anything else. But on days it went badly, I was so grateful for other things: trees, buildings, light, but mostly other humans. When I said this to Erica her sole response was, 'Gross.'

'Jennifer's daughter met her fiancé on an app,' said my mother, apropos of nothing as she took her blood pressure at the kitchen table.

It was the end of August and the morning of my thirty-second birthday. We had been living together for almost three months. By now, the shock of my grief had been replaced by the daily grind of functioning without Barney, which in many ways I found more tedious than the raw pain of missing him.

'Isn't she a bit young to be getting married?' I asked, alarmed I'd once babysat her.

'She's twenty-seven. Hardly a child bride.'

I turned away from my mother's compressed bicep to admire the small row of birthday cards I had been sent. That four people cared enough to sit and write a card and find a stamp and post it in advance, that moved me. *In fairness, what doesn't move you?* said the voice.

'Apparently it's less hook-upy than Tinder,' my mother continued. 'This Hinge app. More self-respecting.' She spat those last words out, along with her evident judgement.

It was surprising to hear her talk about dating apps, or dating altogether. She had never fed me the narrative of needing a partner, or even allowed me to watch Disney films growing up, although a VHS of *Cinderella* had somehow evaded her ban which I had watched and rewound so many times that the tape had gone static until the ending had eventually cut out. When I'd asked as an adult, 'Why *Cinderella*, though? It's, like, the least feminist one,' she had simply said, 'I was too tired that day in Woolworths to fight you.' 'No greater relevance?' I'd asked. 'Nothing greater than my great exhaustion,' she'd said.

'It's weird you trying to matchmake me. It's very off-brand for you,' I said, picking up a raspberry and sucking on it.

'I'm not trying to matchmake you. I'm just saying you might as well get on with meeting someone if that's what you want.'

I stroked the orange-shaped pimpled candle Erica had sent me (along with the note, *Happy birthday, dear one. I'm obsessed with how ugly this is*) and said that what I presently wanted was not to talk about this.

'Look at me, I'm living proof you don't need a partner to have a fulfilling life, but if you do want one then you ought to crack on with it. Time waits for no woman.'

I knew my mother was right, but I didn't want to crack on. I wanted to stop time like the boy in the children's television show I used to watch. Except that I wanted his gold stopwatch so I wouldn't have to end up alone, rather than to score a goal or reposition a bucket of water to stop it falling on someone's head.

That afternoon I tested my newly mobile knee by venturing to Waterstones opposite the clock tower to spend the gift voucher my grandfather had given me. Inside the shop I noticed engagement and wedding rings everywhere, like a computer game full of sparkling little nuggets to collect. Some of their owners looked offensively young and so I left and went to the Amnesty bookshop in the Lanes where the woman who served me had a wooden ring on her wedding finger, which partially consoled me.

At least you aren't worth gold or diamond either, I thought.

You aren't even worth oak, I heard her silently reply.

As I walked home, I felt ashamed to admit that I didn't want my mother's life, that as much as I admired her integrity and independence, I didn't want these attributes myself. I wanted a partner to look after me and grow old with me and find me lovable enough not to leave; and I couldn't even really blame Disney for this. I was frightened of getting hurt again but more frightened of being left single and alone for ever. It was like laying an ace card on top of a king that ordinarily would have trumped the rest of the deck.

Fuelled by my overriding fear, I downloaded Hinge as soon as I got back, dismayed by the number of people who worked in tech and finance and were dressed in ski or snorkel gear. It wasn't that these weren't excellent people for other people, but I felt very strongly that these were not people for me.

After seven profiles that listed the words *bucket list* and *Japan*, I was extremely disillusioned and wanted to give up, but persuaded myself that if I persisted, the app would start to learn my preferences and find me someone who wasn't passionate about street food and powder snow. I didn't really understand technology, but was pretty sure this was how algorithms worked, and because I wasn't on social media, I reasoned my profile was having to start from scratch. Once I'd accepted this, it became easier to emotionally detach from the task, and for the next six minutes I simply scrolled left, flicking through photos of ramen and snowy peaks as though I was looking at Tripadvisor reviews.

In the evening, I went with my mother and grandfather to a Catalan restaurant on the outskirts of town. There was a young girl with thick dark hair on her arms dancing fervently next to the speaker which was playing lively guitar music. She was frowning with focus and making lots of strong and committed shapes with her small thin body. I looked at her with complete admiration and thought, My wish for you is that you keep dancing this way.

'I've been watching the way you chew,' said my mother, interrupting my private moment. 'It's quite bovine-like. I think you ought to be doing more of a vertical movement rather than a sideways one.'

'Thanks for the feedback,' I said. 'But in case you hadn't noticed I've been prioritizing fixing my broken heart and knee.' After that, I tried to deliberately eat as much like a cow as possible, even inserting the occasional moo.

Shortly after we had finished our main courses, the waiter brought out a cake and started to sing 'Happy Birthday'. People joined in and I did too, even though I thought it was a bit weird to sing to myself. As the waiter walked towards us and placed the cake at the table next to us, I felt really pleased I'd made the decision to sing because at least it looked like I hadn't assumed the cake was for me, especially now it had been confirmed that it wasn't.

'I didn't think you'd want one,' my mother said, defensively.

'I don't,' I said, and I didn't, but I still wanted her to have got me one. *Such contradictory wants*, said the voice. Me and the rest of the human species, I silently replied.

My grandfather broke the awkwardness by telling us that the son of his friend Kevin had just left his wife and two children as well as his job as a Chief Marketing Officer, all on his forty-fifth birthday, and moved to a new city to start all over again.

'But why?' I asked, incredulous.

'That's what Kevin asked. And all his son kept saying was, "I did it to slow down time."' This was wild to me, that this man had actively chosen to erupt his life, to go through the process I was currently embarking on out of *choice*. Or was that the crucial difference – that because he had chosen it he felt empowered by its eruption rather than exhausted and broken by it?

'Couldn't he have just had an affair or bought a sports car?'

asked my mother, disapprovingly. My grandfather disregarded her remark and looked admiringly at his glass.

'Kevin can take a sip of Guinness and land just below the harp and above the G of the pint lettering every time. I've never once seen him even a millimetre off.'

'And we're meant to be impressed by that, are we?' Here she went again, quashing my grandfather at every opportunity.

I smiled encouragingly at him but he ignored her provocation and said calmly, 'You're not meant to be anything. But I'm allowed to be, yes.'

Along with my mother, I didn't find this particularly impressive but thought it was interesting how much it interested my grandfather. It was curious, the things that made some people tick and left others cold, or tepid at best.

After we had dropped my grandfather home and got back to the house, my mother went straight into the kitchen to fix her pot of chamomile tea – her routine refreshment for our nightly episode of branch lines. I slumped down onto the sofa inside the living room, rearranging the cushions to prop up my leg, which still benefited from elevation if I'd been vertical for several hours. When she entered the room minutes later, she was pursing her lips and holding a cupcake with a lighted candle in it. 'I thought you might find a whole cake a bit overwhelming,' she said gruffly. And she was right, but what she'd underestimated was how overwhelming I would find this cupcake. But I didn't cry. I thought, Nope. Let's have a day without tears, Misty. We split the cupcake in half and shared it like two annoying skinny women I had once seen inside a café trying to push the bigger half of a brownie onto each other.

I kept up my Hinge activity for the next few days, viewing it in the same way as I did my physio – an annoying but necessary chore – hopeful that if I sucked it up now, I wouldn't still be doing it two years down the line. And so, it was gratifying when on the third morning of swiping I came across Christopher.

His profile stood out immediately, not just because his job title said Neuroscientist, which I found deeply intriguing, or because his photos contained no hot dogs or mountainous sunsets, but because – and this is kind of a kooky thing to say – I felt this weirdly strong connection to him, as though we were meeting in real life, even though I was only looking at him through a screen. There was something so un-static about his face, even in the shots where he wasn't caught in motion, he looked completely alive. I think his hair had something to do with this because it was shaggy and quite wild. I could see from the four photos he had uploaded that his beard ranged from stubble to full-on unkempt. There was a dishevelled and almost brutish look to him that I found very enticing.

He was forty, which seemed old, but not in an unattractive or eye-raising way. I read the answers to his prompts, which I thought were witty and clever without being pretentious, although I didn't get the reference to the last one. I scrolled back up to the top of his profile and studied the words *Have Children*. I had initially brushed over this detail because it hadn't concerned me, and looking at it again now, it still didn't concern me. I had no present or even particular future desire to have a child myself but also had nothing against them, and therefore saw no problem dating someone who already had one.

I felt disproportionally nervous as I swiped right, as though a huge amount was riding on this moment. Please match with me, I thought. And so when nothing happened and I was presented with yet another Sales Manager standing next to an elephant, I threw my phone onto the bed and had a small cry.

Later that morning, I logged onto my work email and saw my inbox contained eleven new messages, six of which were junk. I had done an array of jobs since graduating eleven years ago – the last three of which I'd worked exclusively for a man called Richard who ran a sourcing supply service and was passionate about the world of industrial supplies. He wore paisley shirts that looked like William Morris wallpaper, and was married to a woman who did weekly triathlons.

Richard had said I could take as much time off as I needed, but a month into living with my mother I had decided I was in need of both the income and the distraction and so had been working remotely for the last six weeks. As I began deleting them, one of the subject lines caught my eye. *Why aren't you married? You're pretty enough.* Well, that's nice, I thought. Someone else thinks so even if my ex-fiancé doesn't.

I opened the email, which turned out to be a newsletter sent by a trade publication, and saw the subject line had been taken from an article titled *Tackling Misogyny in the Workplace* and that it went on to give a detailed account of sexual harassment. Alarmed I'd been flattered by it, I deleted it and then emptied it from my bin folder in an attempt to further minimize my shame.

Around lunchtime my grandfather called in on his way back from the golf club. He was ninety-five and still played weekly. During lockdown when the course had closed he had become mentally and physically weaker and despondent, the way old people often get when their partner dies, but since the club's reopening he had returned to his prior state of health, which my mother said was basically equivalent to receiving private medical care. But because my grandfather had grown up in poverty and slept six to a bed as a boy, she couldn't fully judge him for playing a capitalist sport, or at least not in the way she could judge people who were born into families that played golf and owned a Land Rover which they referred to as 'the Landy'.

Since his early twenties my grandfather had memorized a new piece of poetry every day while he shaved. He knew more lines of poetry than anyone I knew, even Barney and his friends who were actual poets. His favourite was William Blake's 'Ah! Sun-flower'. Every time he recited it, I saw the ball in his throat choke up a bit.

I hadn't spoken to my grandfather about Barney since my arrival back in Brighton but now he came into the living room where I was sitting in the dark watching an old Attenborough series. A strand of sunlight was coming through a slit in the closed curtains, lighting up a cone of dust in the corner of the room by the television. On the screen, female Emperor penguins were returning to the colony after a winter away from the males who had stayed behind to guard the eggs.

Unprecipitated, although I suppose the trigger was the penguins, my grandfather announced, 'Love is not an end to loneliness, you know.' I carried on looking at the penguins but tuned in sharply to what he'd just said. 'At the end of the day, you only ever have yourself to come back to.' How could this be true, though? I would either have just myself or have a partner to take care of me. These were categorically not the same thing. But before I had a chance to point this out, he excused himself to go to the loo. He had a habit of doing this – throwing out a pithy aphorism and then making a swift exit before it could be countered.

I stayed watching the screen and ignored a call from my friend Antoine, whose classiness I was not ready for. He would expect me to comport myself with charm and grace and, presently, I had neither of these things at my disposal.

He sent a message following his unanswered call,

If you wish to postpone this season's meeting then we will reconvene at Dukes in the autumn.

I sent back a heart emoji which I knew he would find crass but would usefully end the conversation. I was right. He did not reply.

That evening I made a list titled 'Reasons to get a cat', and read it aloud to my mother as she chopped onions in her sunglasses – the only time since *The Railway Children* her eyes ever watered in my presence.

Something to hold
Something to sit on you
Something to cry on
Something to need you

'Those are all variations on the same point,' she said. 'You're just lonely.'

'Go figure,' I replied, and started calling her Sherlock until she told me to stop that.

'You're having to clear up dead birds anyway,' I said to her the following morning, watching her wrap a mauled pigeon inside sheets of newspaper that the neighbour's cat had dragged across our lawn.

'You need to drop the cat thing. And I don't need anything

else to look after,' she said as she stuffed the packaged bird into a bin liner and then went back outside to inspect her courgettes to check she hadn't accidentally planted the poisonous kind.

When I was around eight or nine I got into the habit of asking my mother and grandfather on a daily basis, 'If I murdered someone would you still love me?' I wanted assurance from them that I was safe in their love, that even if I became a serial killer they would still take care of me. My mother said, 'It's impossible for us to answer that question without context.' My grandfather just said, 'Always. Whatever you'd done, we would still love you.' I wanted to test him to check this was true but there was no way of doing this without murdering someone and I was emphatically not going to do that. But I did believe him, because of the very matter-of-fact way he said it, and how blunt he was about all the other stuff I asked.

For the last few years that Barney and I were together I had been having this recurring dream that he was cutting off parts of me he didn't like until in the end there wasn't anything left of me.

'Why are you acting like a victim?' he said, the third time I'd woken crying and told him this.

'I'm not acting like one, I'm just dreaming like one.'

'Well, can you not?'

'Don't you think if I could control my dreams then I'd wake myself up laughing every day, rather than just approximately twice a year?' This was something I did on a roughly biannual basis, triggering Barney's friends to refer to me as *happy*. They said the word as though they were putting inverted commas around it, as if it was an insult. When I'd asked Barney about this, he'd said, 'Put it this way, would you want to be called *nice*?' 'Oh, so it's like saying I'm boring?' 'Exactly. Only you're not boring, you're just happy.' But I'd detected an edge of cynicism to his voice.

By the time I moved back in with my mother I counted that it had been almost two years since I had woken up laughing. I thought this was a shame but probably something most people only got to experience once or twice in their entire lifetime, and maybe not even at all, and so to complain about it would have been spectacularly unrelatable.

At seven o'clock the following evening, I was doing my actual physio while listening to a radio programme about overlooked wives of great men when my phone pinged on the floor next to me and Hinge told me I had a new match.

I tried to keep my expectations low as I opened the app but I knew that Christopher was the only person I had swiped right on, and, well, hope is such a clingy thing. Surely it must be him, *surely*. When I saw that it was, I smiled in such a big way that it felt like my mouth was unfurling after being curled up for lots of months.

He had sent a message. It said,

Is it fun being named after the weather?

I waited four minutes while I finished my physio and thought of a good reply and then wrote,

Yes-ish!
Misty is probably the least fun one though
(Out of the weather names)

He replied almost immediately,

Ah, true.
I had Christopher as my starting point.
As opposed to Stormy, Sunny, etc.

I watched the three dots move as he typed,

Are you named after a particular Misty?

This time I replied straight away,

*Apparently after the Ella Fitzgerald song
Which is weird cause I've never heard my mother listen to it*

What was even weirder was I had never heard my mother listen to any form of music. The nearest thing that could classify as notes were the pips before the Radio 4 headlines. Beth's mother listened to Motown as she cooked and sometimes Beth and I would catch her dancing while she boiled broccoli or whatever, and she'd say, 'Come on in, girls, let's have a disco,' and so, giggling, we'd all shake our hips and slide along the kitchen floor. When I'd told my mother about these kitchen discos, suggesting we ought to have one too, she'd looked revolted and said that in case I hadn't noticed she had a full-time job and no husband, which left her with no time or interest in prancing around.

*It's a good song!
Also, she hates the name Ella?*

Ha! She said Ella was too girly

Unrelated to girliness but did you know Ella Fitzgerald had her legs amputated?

*How come!?
I've recently come off crutches so this is very topical*

Diabetes?
Re her legs, I think.
Not yours, I'm assuming.

Nope
Mine was an egg-hunt gone wrong

Sounds treacherous, like a Jumanji sequel.

I don't know films but I'm pretty sure this is a reference to one?

It is! How come you don't know films?

I began typing my reply – how, thanks to my mother, I had grown up largely in a pop-culture vacuum, but then he went offline or just didn't reply. When he messaged two hours later, he'd written,

Sorry to disappear.
My son required urgent assistance with his science project.
Which I've now helped make worse.

Such modesty . . .
What's the project?

A cardboard replica of his skeleton.
A tall order for a Tuesday night.
Or rather a 4 ft 5 order.

Sweet! How old is he?

9 but going on 90.

Explain??

He's really into old musicals.
Loves Cole Porter and Irving Berlin.
To mine and his mother's bemusement.

Oh! I'm really enjoying this

Try watching Top Hat seventeen times.
You might enjoy it less.

Ha, I'm guessing this is an old musical?

Correct.

Buy him his own separate TV?

I don't think my son would object to this.
Although perhaps my partner would.

I thought it was odd the way he phrased this, that he hadn't added the word *ex* before partner, but thought this either was a typo or had to do with his son – that they referred to themselves as parenting partners instead of co-parents. I wanted to know more about Christopher's set-up but didn't want to ask this in writing and think maybe he felt the same way because he changed topic entirely and said,

I'm intrigued to know which other films
you don't know.
But I suppose you can't make a list of
things you don't yet know.

> *I like this!*
> *It sounds like a riddle even though it's a fact*

Do you know Wittgenstein's *Tractatus*?

> *Is this another film?*

Ha!
It would lack substantial narrative if so.

> *It's a shame I can't share in the*
> *joke I just apparently made*

Ha! (Again.)
There's something noble about this though.
The *Tractatus* is a philosophy book that uses
logic to pick at the limits of language.
You might enjoy it if you like riddlely facts.

> *I'll look it up*
> *Thanks!*

We carried on chatting for another five minutes until Christopher said he had a paper he needed to review before tomorrow, and I said I urgently needed to plait my hair.

He said *ha!* to my plait comment (which was now the third *ha* he had given me) and added,

Very Brontë-esque.

I was a bit intimidated that Christopher clearly knew films and literature as well as science, as I've always been impressed by people with all-rounder brains.

Assuming the conversation was over, I put my phone on charge and picked up the jar of coconut oil beside my bed which I was using to massage my surgical scar. The oil had melted from having been left in direct sunlight and had since reset so that it now looked like an untouched ice rink. I scraped my fingers across the top in a circular motion, breaking the surface, and had begun rubbing it over my knee, when my phone buzzed again.

07764 276 809 (My number, if you'd like to switch to WhatsApp.)

I felt my heart swoop, and wondered if it was my actual heart, or if I just had the Brontë sisters in my head who were encouraging Victorian sentiments. Either way, the swooping felt outstanding.

Christopher and I messaged on WhatsApp over the next twenty-four hours, during which time I found myself thinking about him constantly. It was like having a new picture to look at on the wall inside my head, where Barney had been hanging for the last couple of months (and eight years before that).

I had sent Erica a series of screenshots of Christopher's Hinge profile which she had read and not yet replied to, but there was nothing unusual in this as she often did her WhatsApping in sudden bursts followed by bouts of silence, due to the demands of parenting twin three-year-olds and living in a fourteenth-century chateau that required hourly upkeep.

Erica had spent most of her twenties in an on-off relationship with a Scottish experimental artist called Suze whose work had become increasingly obscure so that by the time they had broken up for good, Suze's main medium had been dust. Erica's life had bifurcated when she met Adrienne – a French derivatives trader for an international bank who had been temporarily transferred from the company's Paris office to the London office where Erica was temping as a receptionist between acting jobs. Adrienne came from a distant line of Parisian aristocracy and had been engaged to a base-metals trader named François who came from equally good French stock and who (according to Erica) Adrienne was 'probably-but-not-affirmatively related to'.

Apparently Adrienne had always had an inkling she might be

bisexual but had only confirmed this when Erica had seduced her inside the prayer room – a setting Erica was thrilled to discover made her feel both 'pious and sleazy'. (Erica and Suze's sex life had been so varied and exhaustive that by this point Erica was looking for sexual experiences that evoked contrasting adjectives.)

She and Adrienne had begun a physical, and subsequently emotional, three-month affair following which Adrienne had returned to François in Paris – and Erica briefly back into Suze's bed until she realized she 'simply couldn't get on board with the dust thing'.

Adrienne had belatedly waited until the night of her wedding to call it off when everyone had already gathered inside her family's chateau on the outskirts of Paris, admitting she was in love with a tall skinny English woman with long orange hair who looked 'un peu comme la Reine Elisabeth I'. The reference to royalty had been intended to soften the blow for Adrienne's mother, who had apparently shrieked so hard the candles had gone out. Erica relished the drama she had caused and her only regret was that she had not been there in person to witness it.

Twelve months later, despite fraught resistance from Adrienne's family, the two of them had got engaged and Erica had subsequently retired from acting and moved to Paris, hopeful this next chapter of her life would involve more stimulation than the previous half a decade, which she referred to as glorified reception work.

Although disapproving of her daughter's choice of partner, Adrienne's mother had insisted on announcing the engagement in *Le Figaro* where the *a* of Erica's name had been missed off – an omission Erica was convinced was not accidental. 'Your mother's institutionally homophobic. It's de rigueur for her class and generation and – no offence – your nationality. You just have to not take it personally,' she had reasoned to

Adrienne, who had been fuming and threatening to axe her mother from the guest list. 'Plus, who do you think's going to pay for the wedding? I'm madly in love with you but I madly want a massive spectacle.' Erica was the most pragmatic romanticist I knew. But I digress . . .

Charmed by its Gothic grandeur and under pressure from Adrienne's parents – who were keen to hand over the running of the chateau to their only offspring in order to permanently relocate to their Parisian apartment – Erica had keenly agreed to the move, but now found herself essentially trapped looking after two under-fives in a decaying mansion that provided a constant source of hazards and haemorrhaged money by the minute. The novelty of stone floors and vast fireplaces had given way to mental fatigue and acceptance of permanently cold extremities. 'I've just stopped even expecting to feel my fingers between the months of November to February,' Erica had told me last winter. The twins currently believed the house was haunted because they reportedly saw tiny ghosts moving around in front of their faces at night. Erica had explained to them that these moving wisps were 'just their breath', following which she had made the executive decision to install central heating in the property, to the objection and distaste of her mother-in-law. Adrienne commuted into Paris every day for work, which left Erica to do the bulk of the childcare and maintenance on the house, prompting her to declare that the closest she came to wearing jewellery these days was as buckets around her wrists.

Sure enough, she replied to me with a flurry of messages the following evening while I was in the bath.

YES to you dating!!
Give me the juice
He looks rugged and delicious

Such a shame he has a penis . . .
Although not for you I guess

I watched it say 'Erica is typing' and then another message pinged through.

Also interesting re ENM!

This last comment was in reference to the final prompt on Christopher's profile which read, *You shouldn't match with me unless: You're open to ENM*, reminding me I had meant to google this.

What's ENM?

Seriously??
Ethical non-monogamy
All the rage right now!

My chest felt as though it was being crushed by one of those iron claws that presses and squashes metal to use for scrap.

Wait, are you joking?

Wait, I don't get it
What did you think it was?

I just assumed it was a band??

She sent a trio of laughing emojis followed by,

HOWLING!
You're thinking of NME??
Also not a band fyi

I felt so disappointed, I couldn't even share in the fun of my mistake. Not only was his partner his co-parent but by the sound of things, also very much his present partner. It was so unfair. I splashed the bath water with my fist and got my phone and hair unintentionally wet.

This is actually gutting
I really like him already

Have you met yet?

Next Friday
But I'm going to cancel

Don't cancel!

What's the point?
I don't want what he's offering

You don't know what he's offering
And you might not know what you want

I want a guarantee
and this is the opposite of that!

Guarantee?!
You haven't even gone on a first date yet lol
Either way you should go!
If nothing else it'll be a low-stakes scenario
to get yourself back out there

I took Erica's point, albeit reluctantly. If I knew already that I wasn't wired for non-monogamy (which I did), then she was right that I could use the date as a zero-pressure situation to re-enter the world of dating, which I had now been absent from for close to a decade. There was something less intimidating about going on a date that couldn't go anywhere, like a practice run before the real thing. Not to mention, I was bored of living at my mother's and craving some excitement, and the offer of spending an evening with Christopher was too appealing to turn down and far preferable to another night in my mother's company watching that railway show. But as I typed back *FINE* I heard the voice's warning, *Walking blind out of the pan and into the fire* . . . Although I thought it might be conflating two expressions.

Because of Christopher's work and childcare schedule, there were still six more days of waiting to get through until our date. During this time we continued to message daily and he confirmed that the mother of his son was, yes, his current partner but worked away a lot and that they had an open relationship. I still had many more questions but decided these could wait until we met because WhatsApp didn't feel like the ideal platform to ask them.

He messaged me on Wednesday morning:

What are your views on small plates?

I like them. Even more than regular plates

Good! Me too!

I liked how liberal he was with exclamation marks. Barney was always cautious of using them because he was wary of displaying any form of enthusiasm.

Christopher had chosen a restaurant in Highbury that I had walked past several times before but never been inside. I had told him that I was currently staying at my mother's but hadn't mentioned that I was presently homeless in London and so had arranged to spend the night on my friend Dan's sofa bed.

I arrived early on the evening of the date – pumping with nerves and excitement – and so went to read in a pub around the corner that sold Italian produce with colourful vintage packaging on a large table by the entrance. I didn't want to drink anything because I knew I would end up needing the loo as soon as I arrived at the restaurant, and so picked up a bright yellow tin of sardines and asked the woman at the counter if I could buy it instead of a drink. She asked me if I was planning to drink the sardines, which I found naturally amusing and unforced as a connection and so warmed to her instantly. I explained that I wasn't thirsty but would feel rude and weird sitting here without buying anything, adding that she also probably wouldn't let me. 'You're right,' she said. 'I can let you buy the sardines, though.' Thanking her, I took them over to a table in the corner, placing the tin in her sightline to remind her of our arrangement.

I took the *Tractatus* out of my bag, which I had got out of the library two days ago and was attempting to read but was struggling to make any sense of. Each time I opened it, it felt as though I was giving my brain a workout; I imagined the neurons inside my head sweating and panting like they were doing circuit training. But it turned out I couldn't focus on it inside the pub even a tiny bit because there was a child squawking at a nearby table and because I was too hyped up about finally meeting Christopher. And so I went on WhatsApp and read back through all our messages, considering if the term 'moderately obsessed' made any technical sense as a phrase.

When I got to the restaurant Christopher was already there, sitting at the bar on a chrome stool, reading. I wondered if he was also struggling to concentrate because of us being about to meet but he looked genuinely engrossed, unless he was just a good actor, which I decided would be quite random for a neuroscientist. He glanced at me as I approached, and then when he realized who I was, smiled in a big way and stood up. I was shocked by how broad and tall and handsome he was in real life, and as he leant down to kiss my cheek it all felt very grown-up.

'It's good and, well, a bit strange to finally be meeting.' He looked directly in my eyes as he said this, and I saw how his irises were lots of different colours up close so that I wasn't sure if they were mainly blue or green or yellow or brown. 'Slight meeting-your-pen-pal vibes.'

I laughed at this but didn't say anything.

'You found the restaurant OK?' he asked.

I nodded and smiled but, again, didn't speak. I felt strangely shy and decided I needed to make a bold move to assert myself or else would be in danger of being mute the entire evening, and so I held out the tin of sardines and said, 'These are for you.'

He looked surprised and as he took them from me, I saw how thick and hairy his hands were.

'You brought me a present?'

'Yes, but not intentionally.' And I told him about being early and not wanting a drink, etc.

He looked briefly unsure how to respond before thanking me and asking what I'd like to drink, now the date had officially begun.

I looked at his cocktail and said, 'What's that?'

'It's a negroni.'

Negronis weren't even in my top three cocktails because I found them too bitter and the jumbo ice cube always knocked my nose, but I didn't want to ruin the vibe and so I said, 'I'll have one too, please.'

He got the barman's attention, I think just because of his size as he didn't appear to make any discernible gesture or noise, and then he turned to me and said, 'The table's not booked until eight thirty but my thinking was we could sit at the bar for a bit. Get two locations in one.'

'You mean in case we get bored of each other's company then at least we'll have a new view to look at.'

He smiled and suddenly looked slightly unsure of himself. I thought because of how supremely unbored I was that it was obvious my comment had been a joke but then remembered that he couldn't feel inside my body, all that adrenalin jangling around.

I pointed to the book that was lying on the bar and asked what he was reading, which didn't really make sense as a question because I could see the cover right in front of me.

'It's a book on cognitive processing by a contemporary of mine. It's annoyingly good.'

'Are you going to leave it a bad Amazon review?'

He laughed, which relaxed me, and said, 'I don't think that would be very sporting. Tempting, though.'

'Is it as interesting as it sounds? Your job, I mean.'

'I suppose that depends on how interesting it sounds.'

'Very.'

'I always think it would be quite strange not to find the brain interesting but I'm also aware I come at this with a substantial amount of bias.'

'Like the opposite of unconscious bias.'

He looked confused for a second and then said, 'Also known as conscious bias.'

'Oh yeah.' I felt embarrassed to have phrased this wrong and insecure about not knowing as much stuff as him in general and so decided to announce this aloud so that it didn't fester and become bigger than me. 'By the way, I can't really understand that book you recommended, and I've had to google quite a few of the references you've made, which I'm not going to be able to do now you're right here in front of me, so anyway, yeah, I think you might have a wonky impression of my knowledge.'

He smiled again, which was something he seemed to do a lot, and it had a way of making me feel relaxed and good about myself.

'I haven't made any prior assessment of your knowledge, but I did just enjoy your use of wonky.'

I smiled too then, and told him about the time I had worked for an events company the first summer after I'd graduated and had been hired along with fourteen others to stand in Leicester Square and spell out the words WILL YOU MARRY ME? with alphabet helium balloons for a live proposal, and that because it was windy and I have poor upper-body strength, my letter had been wonky so that it read as WILL YOC MARRY ME?

Christopher laughed and asked if the person had said yes to the proposal. I confirmed they had and that if they hadn't, I'd have felt a lot mortified instead of just a bit mortified.

'It's often struck me as odd that people choose to deliver such an intensely personal question in a public space. But perhaps I'm strangely private or just cowardly.'

I told him I agreed and said that along with skateboarding it ran the risk of being a very public form of failure.

He laughed and added, 'Without the cushioning of kneepads.' I noticed he had almost finished his negroni, which surprised me because I hadn't been aware of him drinking it.

I wanted to ask about his set-up with his partner but thought this needed some preamble.

'Is your partner a neuroscientist too?'

'She's an interpreter for the ICRC.'

'I don't know what that is.' He looked concerned and so I clarified, 'I mean, I know what an interpreter is but the ICRC bit.'

'Ah. It's the International Committee of the Red Cross.'

'OK, phew, I do know what that is.' There was a pause, a

not unawkward one, which I broke by asking, 'So, does she, like, go into war zones and stuff?'

'She does, yes.'

'Wow. We're basically complete opposites.'

'Is an ICRC interpreter the opposite of an aspiring novelist? I could think of more opposing jobs.'

'How about an ICRC interpreter and someone who works in B2B telesales?' He looked amused, as if I'd said something self-deprecating rather than factual. 'I guess I just mean you've got to be really brave to do that job and I'm very unbrave.'

He tilted his head and said, 'You don't seem unbrave.'

'Oh, I definitely am.'

'You're honest, though, and that's a form of bravery.'

'How?'

'Well, in that it's quite an exposing and committed thing to be.'

Even though I felt this was a real stretch of the definition, I felt bolstered by it and told him that in this case he might as well know that along with not knowing films and the acronym ICRC, I'd thought ENM was an indie band until my friend Erica had told me otherwise.

He looked briefly shocked and then laughed, a different laugh to before, this one was fuller and louder but it wasn't unkind. It was the way you'd laugh along with a child who had made a funny mistake so as not to give them a complex or make them self-conscious.

'That's incredibly endearing,' he said. 'Also, I'm sorry, because in that case you probably matched with me under false pretences. Unintentionally false, but still.'

I said that was OK, that it wasn't his fault because he'd been clear. And then I added, 'Also, I'm glad I didn't know what it meant because otherwise I wouldn't have matched with you and I'm glad I did match with you.'

'I'm also glad you did.' We held eye contact again and it was so intense, like the sun scorching the top of my head in a pleasurable burny way, that after a couple of seconds I had to look away.

'So how does it work?' I asked. 'Does—'

But then a waiter came over to tell us that our table was ready, which was disappointing because I had no interest in moving to sit across from Christopher with a square of wood between us when here at the bar our legs were almost touching.

As we got up, Christopher folded his jacket over one arm and gestured with his other arm for me to pass in front of him, which seemed kind of old-fashioned but mainly just kind.

We followed the waiter, who led us to a table right at the back of the restaurant underneath a neon sign that said, *This is the place*.

I waited until the waiter had left and then said, 'Does she know you're on a date tonight? Your partner.'

'Not specifically this evening. Sometimes the signal's quite bad in the area she's in and so we don't speak for several days, and when we do, the priority tends to be discussing our son. But, well, our arrangement is that we date and have sex with other people so in that sense, yes, she's not unaware.'

My spine tingled hearing him say the word, sex. 'I want to ask why you're in an open relationship,' I said. 'But I think it might be too big a question for a first date.'

'I think you just asked it anyway,' he said, smiling. He looked around the room and adjusted his legs before looking back at me and saying, 'Something to do with authenticity. Wanting to lead an authentic life.'

I was intrigued by this and wanted to know more. 'But why is being with lots of people more authentic than only being with one person?'

'Well, I'm not saying it is in a binary sense. I'm sure monogamy works well for lots of people but it seems there are also lots of people doing it because it's the default rather than an active choice.'

I paused while I thought about this in relation to myself.

'It sounds quite boring and obvious to want monogamy and to get married but I want those things anyway. Even if they're a bit lame.'

'I don't think there's anything boring or obvious or lame about wanting them.'

'But now I'm not sure whether I want them authentically or just because they're the default.'

He shrugged and said, 'I guess asking that question's not a bad place to start.'

We looked at each other intensely again, and this time, stayed looking at each other. Even though I felt there was still so much to say, suddenly I wasn't capable of saying any of it. It was impossible to make conversation with this level of wanting in the way. My forearms were resting on the table and so were his. I inched my hands towards him so that the tips of our fingers were almost touching, hoping he'd take hold of them, but instead he moved his hands onto the tops of my wrists and slowly rotated my arms outwards so that the pale white skin of the underside was facing up. Still holding my wrists, he released his thumbs and very lightly stroked the soft bit of skin where I could see the blue of my veins. I felt paralysed with longing, unable to move but desperately wanting him to know that I wanted him to kiss me. I channelled all my energy into my eyes, hoping I was broadcasting this message, and after what felt like for ever but was probably more accurately around seven seconds, he leant in towards me. The table was too wide for our lips to reach and so he stood up and leant over it and the kiss was, well, it was ridiculously good. We stayed kissing like this for such a long time that at one point I thought it must be getting painful for Christopher's back muscles. When he eventually withdrew his lips and sat down again he gave a quick little smile, and said, 'We should probably look at the menu.'

'We could do that. Or we could go somewhere where it's easier to do more kissing.'

He looked surprised by this but said, 'I'm on board with that. The kissing option. I know a bar around the corner, unless you have a place in mind.'

'I was thinking maybe your house.' Now he looked very surprised. 'But we don't have to, if that's too . . .' I tailed off, unsure how I wanted to end the sentence.

'It's not too anything. It just wasn't what I was expecting.'

'I'm quite embarrassed now.'

'Don't be.'

'Where even is it?'

'My house?' I nodded. 'Now it's my turn to be embarrassed. I un-magnanimously chose a venue very near to it.'

'How near?'

'Eleven minutes away near.'

I laughed and then remembered about his child, and said, 'What about your son? I mean, will he be there?'

'He's at a Marvel-themed sleepover.'

'That's fun for him. What's he gone as?'

'Hawkeye, from *The Avengers*.'

'I haven't seen it, but I do know of it, so at least that's something.'

'Without knowledge there can be no progress.' He left a beat and then added, 'You could also watch it, though.'

'If it's better than that book you recommended, sure.'

He laughed, and said, '*That* book happens to be widely regarded as one of the most influential philosophical works of the twentieth century. Now what do you think we say to the restaurant staff? It's a bit strange to just get up and leave, isn't it?'

'We could stage a row but that feels like a lot of effort.'

'I agree,' said Christopher, signalling to the nearest waiter, this time with a slight raise of his hand. The waiter had corkscrew curls piled in a clip and one of the curls dropped and landed next to their mouth while Christopher was speaking.

'I'm sorry about this but I'm not feeling very well so we've decided to leave. If I could just settle the drinks bill?'

I admired their gold nail varnish as they placed the curl behind their ear, and said, 'I'm sorry about that. No problem.'

While they were gone, I asked Christopher if he liked the blue neon sign on the wall and he said, 'Not much. You?'

I said, 'Me neither,' and told him I mostly didn't like neon signs, with the exception of Tracey Emin's one at St Pancras.

'I don't think I know that. What's it of?'

'It's just pink letters, below the big clock. It says, *I want my time with you*.'

He nodded and said, 'That is good,' putting the stress on 'is'.

The waiter came back then with the bill and the card machine. I asked Christopher if I could pay and when he said no, I thanked him and watched him pay. I thought his fingers looked too large for the card machine buttons but they functioned perfectly fine. The waiter said, 'I hope you feel better' and then walked off with their mound of curls bouncing slightly as they walked.

'Do you think they know we're about to—' I cut myself off, realizing what I was about to say.

'I don't think I mind what they think.'

'Me neither.'

As we left I took hold of his hand without having consciously decided to. It felt completely instinctive, like a reflex rather than a decision.

'Yikes. Big palms.'

He smiled and said, 'I think you'll find they're proportional to my size.'

'Can anything be big without context? Or is the size of stuff only ever in relation to something else?'

'Erm.' He paused, seeming confused by the question. 'I'd say the world's pretty huge.'

'But not in comparison to, say, the solar system.'

'True.'

'Yey. A point to me.'

'I hadn't realized we were keeping score.'

'It's basically just a series of tallies to you, so we'll only bother noting if I get one.'

He looked bemused and slightly uncomfortable. 'A game in which you've predetermined I'm the winner. You cut a tough deal.'

Then it started to rain and he let go of my hand and put his arm around me, I think to shelter me from the rain even though it was September and still pretty warm.

Christopher lived in a two-storey maisonette on a road full of Victorian terraced houses lined with evenly spaced trees. There was a concrete stoop leading up to the entrance, which made me feel briefly like we were in Brooklyn and not just Highbury.

As we walked up the carpeted staircase, which had bike tyre marks on the wall, he explained that there was a ground-floor flat which somebody else lived in and that his bit was the first and second floor. I told him I thought he'd got the best section, and he agreed and said the trade-off was not having a garden, but that the upshot of this was not having to look after a garden.

He unlocked his front door and flicked the light switch on the wall. Inside the hallway we removed our jackets and he hung them on a row of hooks on the back of the door. I noticed several small-sized jackets which I assumed were his son's, and realized I still didn't know his name, and that this now felt like private information.

I watched to see if Christopher would take his shoes off but he didn't, and so I kept mine on too and followed him into the open-plan kitchen-living room. It had wooden floorboards and other period features like a real fireplace and sash windows, which were all immediately to my liking. One of the walls had exposed brick and there was a painting hanging on it of what I think was a nude man and woman intertwined, but it was too abstract to say for sure. Other than that, the walls were bare but there was lots of stuff on the floor and the table – a big indoor fig plant, a record player with lots of records, and piles and piles of books, as well as a trumpet and a guitar and some sort of pipe instrument I didn't recognize.

Next to the sink was a small stack of unwashed plates and bowls, and I spotted various glasses dotted around the room. Barney had been very particular about where we put things back down after we used them and just generally concerned with maintaining a minimalist aesthetic which made me a bit on edge whenever I used a mug, but Christopher's place felt like a relaxing free-for-all.

I noticed a multi-pack of mini raisin boxes on the counter and, pointing at them, said, 'I eat those too,' feeling pleased we shared this.

'I don't eat them, but my son does.' I felt less pleased I shared this with his nine-year-old.

'Music,' said Christopher, scratching his ear. I wondered if he would maybe play one of the instruments and felt concerned it might be the pipe thing, but he moved to the record player and put on something that was hard to classify as a sound, but I didn't not like it.

'What kind of music is this?'

'Lebanese math rock.' I hadn't even known this existed as a genre. 'I saw them play live in Beirut several years ago,' he said, turning up the volume.

It didn't really seem like the kind of music we could dance to but it was also quite loud to talk over. Christopher asked if I wanted some wine and I said yes, even though what I really wanted was more kissing.

While he was in the kitchen getting the wine I sat on his sofa and thought about how fourteen weeks ago I was sitting inside mine and Barney's living room in a leg brace still engaged to him, and now I was on a date inside a stranger's living room – with two working legs – and basically, well, how insane like that life is. Time just kept moving, with or without anyone's consent, and that was kind of alarming but mostly comforting.

Christopher came back then holding the wine in two thin glass tumblers and placed them on the wooden stool next to the sofa. He looked unsure whether to sit down and so after a couple of seconds I stood up again and positioned myself in front of him so that we were very close but not touching. I stroked the fabric of his grey flannel shirt, which was soft but also fibrous, and felt his hands spreading over the back of my top. We stayed like this, stroking and holding each other in a strange kind of hug, until I stepped back and arched my neck to look up at him.

The tempo changed quite suddenly when I did this. He lifted me up so that my legs were dangling above the ground, but my face was still too far away to reach his. He hoisted me up higher and this time I wrapped my legs around his waist so that our eyes were level.

The kissing was different to before. There was still a tenderness to it but now there was also an urgency. I stayed hooked around him like this, our tongues and hands doing lots of roaming, until he pulled his head back and asked if I'd like to go into the bedroom. I nodded and he released his hands from the base of my thighs where he was holding me so that I slowly slid down him, back to the floor. We were both breathing heavily.

The master bedroom was upstairs in the attic and Christopher could only just stand up straight inside it but said he had got used to it, and that most of the time he spent up there he was horizontal anyway. The low ceiling made him look extra tall. The mattress, which was large and directly on the floor rather than on a bed frame, had smoky blue linen sheets that looked tasteful and expensive. There was an antique tasselled lamp in the corner next to an armchair piled with clothes, and when he turned it on, it gave the room a very inviting glow.

'I like your room.'

'Thank you. I like it too.'

I took my shoes off and lay down on the bed and he did the same and lay down next to me. I rolled onto my side so that I was facing him and he rolled to face me too but still didn't make a move to undress me. I wondered whether in this post-MeToo era men like Christopher, who seemed to be so clearly privileged in all the ways, might feel they needed direct instruction, and so to avoid any ambiguity I said, 'Can we please have sex now?'

He laughed and said, 'Yes, all right,' scooping one of his arms underneath me to lift me on top of his chest. I put my legs on either side of him and felt him becoming hard and pushing against my pubic bone. I couldn't remember ever wanting to have sex this badly. We lay rubbing and kissing like this until I couldn't wait any longer and stood up to take my clothes off. He pulled himself up to sitting so that his back was resting against the wall, and watched me, smiling.

'Are you not going to take yours off too?' I asked.

'I am. I was just enjoying this bit.'

I smiled and felt self-conscious. Barney had never looked at me naked in the way Christopher was doing.

He held out his hand and I got back on to the bed and lay down. He leant over me, kissing my neck and collarbone, and then I felt his fingers go very gently inside me and heard myself do a sharp gasp.

'You're wet already,' he said.

He moved his fingers around some more and I winced with pleasure and felt myself opening.

When my thighs started to shake I asked if he had a condom and he said, 'I do, but I quite want to make you come first. If that's OK.'

I said, 'That's definitely OK.'

I felt his fingers go deeper inside me and then his tongue joined in, making flickering circles, and I knew I was very close to coming already. I reached my hand out to find his, wanting to hold on to it, and gripped his knuckles hard as I came. I thought he would reach for a condom then, but he kept his fingers and tongue inside me, making tiny movements which I found so unbearably good that it made me twitch and judder and at one point I pulled his hand away and said, 'I don't think I can come again. It's too much.' He placed his palm on top of my pelvis to steady me and went deeper inside me with his tongue. I felt something in my core release as I let out a low guttural sound I didn't know I could make.

He brought his head up and leant over me again, kissing my forehead. 'I like the way you come,' he said.

I waited a couple of seconds until my breathing had settled and asked, 'Is it different to other women?'

'It's quicker than most women,' he said, smiling. 'But it's good in other ways too.'

I undid the top button of his trousers and pulled down the zip and he stood to take them off. He took his underwear off too and I saw how hard and big he was.

'I'm a bit intimidated by your size.'

He smiled in a way that looked apologetic and said, 'How about we go very slowly and if it's painful then we'll stop. Does that sound all right?'

I nodded and said, 'Yes.'

'I think it might be more comfortable for you if you go on top.'

And so I climbed across him while he put a condom on. As I eased him inside me there was a moment of pain and then it was . . . it was just the best.

Afterwards I tucked myself into him and he stroked the side of my arm. My body was pressed against his as close as was physically possible, but still I wanted it to be closer. Such a failure of our anatomy!

He moved his hand up to brush my hair and we lay in silence for a minute or so until he said, 'I think I ought to cook you something.' I had zero interest in eating but did like the idea of him cooking for me, and so I said, 'OK.'

When we got up from the bed there was a thick white substance on my thigh. I looked at it, and asked, 'Did that come from me?'

Christopher knelt down and peered between my legs. 'It did.'

'Oh. I don't think I've come like that before.'

'How gratifying for me.'

I laughed and said, 'I think I need to use the bathroom.' He handed me a maroon-coloured towel robe from the back of the door and asked if I'd like to wear it.

'Is it hers?' I asked.

'No. This one's hers,' he said, pointing to a green one next to it.

'OK, then yes please.' It came down to my ankles and the sleeves were cavernous but Christopher rolled them up and said, 'It's a good look on you.'

When I came out of the bathroom and into the kitchen Christopher was still naked, and frying oil in a wok. Barney had always put his underwear back on as soon as we finished sex as though he was embarrassed, which made me feel a bit ashamed, even though I don't think this was ever his intention.

'I'm due a food shop so I'm afraid it's looking like vegetable stir-fry with the added option of your sardines,' said Christopher, scraping garlic off a chopping board.

I told him I'd eaten a protein-heavy lunch so just the vegetables and noodles would be fine and good.

'Inadvertently strategic. I like it.'

'Should I help you cook?'

'I don't think that's necessary but kind of you to offer.'

'Good, because I'm more of a watcher and conversationalist.'

'A reciprocal exchange.' *Only because you're still vaguely cute*, said the voice. *Just wait until you get old.*

There was a photo on the fridge I hadn't spotted before, of Christopher with a woman and a young boy. The boy had fairer hair than Christopher but it was wavy and wild like his, and his eyes had the same intensity.

'Is that them?' I said, pointing to the photo.

'It is, yes.'

'I still don't know their names but maybe that's because you don't want me to know them.'

'It's not.' He paused and then said, 'Sara, that's my partner's name, and our son's called Rowan.'

'They're nice names.'

Sara was tall and slender and had silvery blonde cropped hair cut close into the back of her neck – the kind of style I could never have pulled off with my full cheeks. She looked, not cold, but not warm. When I stared at her the word that came to mind was *formidable*.

'Where did you meet?'

'At university.'

'You mean Oxford? I've already googled you, so you don't have to be modest.'

'I don't think I was being modest, I think I was being nondescript.'

'That's also quite a modest thing to say.' He smiled at this and added chopped vegetables to the wok. 'It doesn't seem like an obvious subject for a neuroscientist to study. Philosophy.'

He raised his eyebrows and said, 'You have done your research,' as he opened a cupboard and took out a bottle of soy and jar of chilli oil. 'It's not a traditional pathway, no. But the two are more linked than you might think, and my Masters and PhD were in more science-based stuff. But I guess you might already know that from your googling.'

I smiled, deciding not to answer this either way, and asked, 'Did she study philosophy as well?'

'She read Arabic and Persian, but we were at the same college.'

I hoped Christopher wouldn't ask where Barney and I had met, because the answer – at a workshop titled 'Blending Poetry and Prose' – was inescapably wanky.

As Christopher boiled noodles, I sat down at the table, tucking my feet up on the chair in front of me.

'Do you mind talking about her?'

'I don't mind if you don't.'

In one sense I didn't want to keep bringing her into the room with us but in a stronger sense I felt compelled to know more about this woman who worked in war zones and who left her partner and child for chunks and months of time.

'I guess I'm wondering if it was a joint decision to have an open relationship.'

'Not entirely, no.'

'She didn't want it?'

'The other way around. She had to remind me that we'd promised to keep exploring and, at some point, had stopped doing that.' I liked how honest this was as a response.

'Aren't you ever worried one of you will fall in love with someone else, though?'

'That's happened before.'

I was shocked by this; I didn't know it was even possible to love more than one person at one time. 'But weren't you scared she'd leave or that you would?' I asked.

'That's just part of loving someone, isn't it? People leave each other in marriages too.'

I knew this was true, but still felt there was something safer about a legally binding contract, and said this to Christopher.

'But in one sense, it undermines it, doesn't it? If you're locked in, rather than choosing to stay. I guess the deal you're making is in the daily decision to be together.'

I wasn't convinced by this. A love that didn't ask or expect anything, that just turned up and left whenever it chose? I so wanted to be as cool as Christopher and Sara, but it just seemed entirely infeasible, more like an ideal rather than an actual possible way to live.

'I'm pretty convinced I don't have the right constitution for polyamory,' I said. 'But I take your point about the flaws in monogamy. Is there maybe a third option instead?'

Christopher tilted his head and said, 'I'm not sure. What would that look like?'

I tilted my head in the opposite direction to his and said I didn't know but that I would continue to think about it. Then he brought two ceramic bowls over to the table and said it was time to eat his extraordinarily average stir-fry.

After we had eaten, I followed Christopher upstairs and we got back into bed and had sex again, two more times. I didn't know this was physiologically possible and asked if it was normal, telling him that Barney and I had only ever had sex one time each time we'd had it – and that this had not been very often, especially by the end, but also for quite a few years before that.

'Barney's your ex, right?'

'Yes.' I'd mentioned him a couple of times in conversation, but this was the first time Christopher had really registered him.

'You said he had bad mental health, didn't you? That might have had something to do with it.'

Then I told Christopher that because Barney was on

antidepressants he had sometimes told me he didn't know whether his lack of attraction towards me was because of the pills he was taking or because of me as a person and that I'd tried to help him work this out by saying things like, 'Did you feel more or less attracted to me before you started taking Sertraline?' and, 'Do you look at other women while you're on Sertraline and find them more attractive than me?' But his answers were vague and inconclusive, and after a while this became a demoralizing Q&A for me until eventually I told him, 'OK I think we have to stop trying to figure this out. It's not good for *my* mental health.'

I thought Christopher might laugh because I'd tried to deliver the last line like a punchline, but he held me tighter and said, 'That sounds painful for both of you. Also, you're extremely attractive.'

I felt my whole ribcage expand with air when he said this.

'So, what's the deal? If I wanted to see you again, then could I? Or are you only allowed to sleep with different people every time?' I tried to ask this casually even though my heart was thumping like heavy bass.

'We don't have that rule, no.' I felt hope then, as though a match had been struck inside my chest producing a tiny flame.

'What rules do you have?'

He paused while I assumed he was thinking and then said, 'We don't introduce people to Rowan. Or at least we haven't ever yet.'

'Do you think he knows?'

'I don't think so, no. It's not that he's not perceptive; it's just, well, we're quite discreet.'

'But as he gets older, he's going to find out, isn't he?'

'We haven't crossed that idiomatic bridge yet.' Christopher raised his eyebrows and sort of grimaced as he said this, as though wanting me to know he was mocking the expression.

'I was going to cancel when I found out you were in an open relationship.'

'That makes sense. You don't seem to want to be in one yourself.'

'That's not completely true. I mean, I definitely don't want to be in one but I also wish I did want to be in one, or at least that I was capable of being in one.'

'Why's that?'

'Because then I wouldn't get as attached to people and so badly hurt.'

Christopher frowned and said, 'Being open, in its ideal form, isn't about not getting attached to people. It's about sharing attachments with multiple people.'

'Sure, but I'm guessing it's not like a "I'm going to die if you leave me" feeling you have for everyone you end up seeing?'

He looked perplexed, as though he didn't know this level of feeling was even possible to have for anyone. 'No. That's true.'

'When does she get back?'

'Sara?' I nodded. 'The middle of next month.'

'Shall I tell you what I'm thinking?'

'I think you're going to anyway. You seem like a very open kind of person.' It was true that I found it a lot of effort to hold stuff in and couldn't remember ever not being this way.

'Barney always said I never suited my name. That I was too clear to be called Misty and that my mother must have been making a joke, even though she doesn't really do jokes.'

He smiled, or was he holding back a laugh? 'Based on first impressions, I agree.'

'OK, well. I'm thinking for the next six weeks I could carry on seeing you while she's away, to learn to be less attached – or fine, sorry, more healthily attached – to better prepare me for next time I get into a proper relationship.' Christopher pursed his lips; this time I was sure he was trying not to laugh. 'What? You think it's a stupid idea?'

'I think it's a . . . very sweet proposal. I suppose I'm just slightly reticent to take on a mentor role.'

'You wouldn't be actively mentoring me. It would just be me experimenting with casually dating someone knowing it wasn't going to go anywhere.'

He did a full smile then and said, 'Famous last words spoken by protagonists throughout literature who make pacts to keep their feelings out of it and then end up falling deeply and irrevocably in love.'

'Oh, don't get me wrong. I'll probably-definitely end up falling for you but having the six-week cut-off date will safeguard me from falling too hard. Plus, the fact I know upfront it can't go anywhere.'

He paused and then asked, 'Why couldn't it go anywhere?'

'Because, no offence, but you absolutely can't give me what I want.'

He continued looking at me while he removed his watch and placed it on the bedside table. 'It's a tempting proposition.'

'So, what do you think?'

I badly wanted him to say yes to it. Not only did I very much want to see him again, but thought my plan had mileage in terms of helping me long term so that I didn't ever end up as broken as I'd been when Barney had broken up with me.

He smiled again and narrowed his eyes so that they became almost just slits. Then he opened them back to normal, shrugged and said, 'Six weeks it is, then.'

I thought I ought to try to hide my excitement and so said very coolly, 'Let's not bother shaking on it,' as I shimmied down under the duvet and Christopher reached to turn off the bedside lamp. But as soon as we were lying there in the dark – dark has a way of doing this, doesn't it? Opening up conversation that couldn't be had in the light – I blew my coolness and said, 'I don't really want to go to sleep. It seems like a waste of our time together; like I'd rather just stay up all night doing more talking and sex.'

'I'd definitely also like to sleep,' he said, rolling us over onto our sides, so that he was holding me from behind. He moved his hand, resting his palm between my thighs, and kept it there while he fell asleep. I didn't fall asleep for quite a bit more time and just lay there enjoying the feel of his hand between my legs. At some point in the night, I woke and squeezed my thighs together to see if it was still there (sadly it wasn't) and decided that what I wanted was some kind of hand trap, although ideally one that also involved Christopher's free will.

I assumed that because of our pact and the obvious success of our date Christopher would be big on comms during the week, but he was . . . not ghosty, but aloof. We had exchanged a few messages since I'd left his flat on Saturday morning but there had been no mention of a second date yet, and I was beginning to get agitated about this. I told myself I wanted to plan my weekend and to know whether I should ask Dan if I could hypothetically stay on his sofa bed again, but really I just wanted to know whether Christopher still wanted to see me.

On Wednesday morning I was due to return to London for a check-up MRI and ECG test at the hospital. I toyed with messaging Christopher but then remembered he'd mentioned a mid-week conference in Cambridge and so held off contacting him, deciding that if he hadn't reached out to me by the following morning, I would message him. I felt encouraged, knowing I had a plan, in spite of the voice's repetitive refrain, *It doesn't bode well . . . you having to initiate.*

Although my mother was retired, she still worked a Wednesday-afternoon clinic fitting coils. She asked if I needed accompanying to my appointment more than her patients needed her, given the fact that I could now walk without assistance and they were at risk of unwanted pregnancies in her absence. I felt the answer was contained within her question and so set off to London alone. I was quietly grateful for the space and time apart, but also consumed with love and gratitude for her, of knowing that something had passed between us that I couldn't retract just because I could now shower again without my blue waterproof sock and eat solid food without wanting to throw up.

When I arrived at the hospital reception I was made to wait in a hard plastic chair for fifty-five minutes because the technicians were all running behind. I knew this wasn't even that long a wait given the crisis state of the NHS but how time-consuming it all was, nonetheless. The hours I had spent in this building just to attempt to reset me to the same level of health I'd previously enjoyed were so wasteful and unproductive. I felt panicked at how behind I was compared to Erica and Dan and Beth with their marriages and babies and successful careers, wondering if I would ever catch up.

During the ECG test the nurse hooked me up with wires and stuck small sticky pads on my chest as she told me to relax. She wouldn't tell me the results while we watched the line of my heart rate go up and down making a scribble line on the screen, she just told me the cardiologist would be in touch if anything abnormal was detected, which made me the opposite of relaxed. My skin stung as she ripped the sticky pads off me and I felt cross she wasn't being more gentle but then I saw a tuna sandwich with only a single bite taken out of it in the corner of the room and it occurred to me she might not have eaten lunch yet even though it was three o'clock, and I felt her roughness was understandable, although still not desirable.

Inside the MRI waiting room I was given a big gown to put on and told to remove my shoes and place them in a grey tray. When I entered the room with the scanner in it went cold, as though I had suddenly stepped inside a walk-in refrigerator. The assistant radiographer gave me soft large headphones to try to blot out the noise of the machine but I could still hear it, an electronic thump in my chest. There were six backlit squares on the ceiling above my head showing the image of a bright sky and rugged mountaintop. It made me think of the trip Barney and I had taken to Slovenia and how inside a restaurant he'd accidentally bitten into a candle thinking it was a cheese dumpling and we had laughed so hard that we'd cried actual tears and an older American tourist had stopped by our table on her way back from the loo and said, 'I just want to say, watching the two of you laugh like that, well it's quite something. You should hold on to it, whatever it is you have.' But I made myself stop thinking of that because it hurt to remember the happiness.

On the way out, as I passed the receptionist on the front desk, she said, 'You'll be running again in no time,' which briefly confused me because I hadn't mentioned to her that I used to run prior to my injury, but thought that this information was probably included in my notes or else it was just a generic line of encouragement she gave to everyone.

By the time I got back to Brighton my mother was home from her surgery and listening to the end of a News item on declining crop yields.

'How was the hospital?' she asked.

'Hospitally,' I said.

She grimaced and not for the first time I could tell she felt vindicated by her decision to do general practice.

'How was your surgery?'

'Fine.'

I took a cheese string out of the fridge and had begun peeling off the strands, dropping them into my mouth like a bird feeding its chick, when she said, 'Actually, something a bit odd happened. A young woman came in for a third attempt to get a coil fitted. She'd been referred to me because the other doctor who'd previously tried twice to do it was less experienced, and, well . . . I couldn't get it to go in either. I've inserted thousands of coils by now but this one just wouldn't go in.'

I paused peeling my cheese string and said, 'Why not?'

'The size and shape of her cervix weren't having it, or maybe she wasn't relaxed enough, I don't know. It's just strange; it's never happened to me before.'

I thought my mother looked oddly young as she said this, young and slightly less sure of herself, as though she had been momentarily disarmed. I was pleased to glimpse some vulnerability but also unsettled by it.

The next morning, at my own word to myself, I messaged Christopher,

> *What are you doing this weekend?*

I found it less awkward to ask him this outright than to find a segue into the question which felt so clearly see-through. Now this was done I wished I could put my phone in a separate room, but needed it to make my work calls and so turned off my WhatsApp notifications and opened the spreadsheet Richard had sent me with the file name *Cold Leads*. I mentally added the word *War* after cold and found the list fractionally more compelling.

Christopher's reply came through that afternoon when I was walking along the pier during my late-taken lunch hour. It said,

> *Tomorrow I'm taking Rowan to the Barbican to see Anything Goes (another musical).*
> *Saturday I've been invited to a colleague's Indefinite Leave to Remain party.*

It said, 'Christopher is typing' and then it didn't say this any more, and so I wrote,

Good luck with Anything Goes!

Thanks; I'll need it. There's a 12 minute tap dancing number.

Yikes!

I waited to see if he would type a response to this but he didn't and so I replied to the second part of his message,

Will you have to dress in a Union Jack for the party?

*I hope not! I can't think of worse attire . . .
Other than a St George's flag.*

I started thinking of other 'British' fancy dress options but Christopher's next message arrived before I'd typed anything.

Thankfully the host is a Europhile but wants to celebrate her newly acquired status in a civilized setting (rather than drinking wine out of mugs inside our faculty basement).

And so she's hired out the Ivy?

Not quite! A pub function room in Wapping.

Ha, good for her

I've never been to the Ivy. Is it all it's hyped up to be?

*I've never been either
It just felt like a swanky go-to reference but it's probably a dated one*

He started typing again but then stopped and I worried he was about to go offline and so wrote,

> *I'm guessing I'd crush your vibe? At the party I mean*

Oh! Not at all, but I think it might crush yours.
I imagine there'll be lots of academics . . .

> *This sounds like a polite way of not inviting me*

You'd be very welcome! Some of them can be quite fun.
Just a few dry ones to avoid.

> *You can steer me towards the wet ones?!*

Deal. Kira, the host, will be pleased to have you there.

> *Only if you're sure?*

Resolutely. 8pm at The Prospect of Whitby x

It was altogether a confusing exchange and I felt no clearer about his feelings towards me as I overheard three schoolgirls in green tartan skirts complaining about how their loft conversions were taking ages and conclude that building work always overran, though. Could it be that even twelve-year-olds had more grown-up concerns than me?

I took a deliberately long route back to my mother's house so that I could justify it being the end of my working day when I got home, but then felt bad about this when I thought of how good Richard had been to me and so chased my two warmest leads, one of which I converted into a meeting to discuss joining their preferred supplier list, and the other of which cut me off abruptly and said, 'Don't call me again, OK.' I was not unhappy with either outcome.

It was only four o'clock and there still seemed a lot of hours left to fill before I went to bed. I wasn't currently writing anything, or at least I was writing down lines and thoughts when they came to me without actively seeking them out, which was problematic in moments like this, as it relied on inspiration rather than hashing out a daily word count (I had previously tried this method too).

I googled *how to fill time* but Google misunderstood my search and showed me an article titled *How to Find Twenty Minutes to Yourself Each Day*. Twenty minutes! Was this a joke? I had so many sets of twenty minutes to myself, it didn't seem right or fair that some people didn't even have one set, and clearly enough people that it was the top search result. Surely something was way out of whack, that the people who had demanding jobs also probably had demanding children and a demanding partner and the demands of a house to look after, while nothing and nobody was demanding anything of me. I felt sad and lucky, as well as happy and unlucky about this all at the same time, as though an arrow was wavering inside me that couldn't decide where to settle.

That evening I reported my findings to my mother who said, 'If you're fed up of freedom then have a child. You'll never be free again.'

But I had been ambivalent about parenthood even with a partner, let alone without one, and told her this, adding, 'Also, Barney took me off your hands for a good eight years.'

'Who's got you next?' said my mother wryly as she removed a supermarket quiche from the oven which had burnt considerably around one side of the crust. I watched as she automatically put the burnt section onto her own plate and served me the good bit.

When I met Christopher outside the pub on Saturday evening, he was wearing a dark green jacket, black jeans and lace-up boots. His outfit looked trendier than last time, and I decided this must be his party look. I was carrying a small succulent inside a speckled pot, which I told him was a present for Kira.

'You're very good at bringing presents,' he said, prompting me to ask after the sardines and whether he had eaten them yet.

'I have. They were deliciously salty.'

This sounded flirtatious but also just like an accurate description, which I was learning was very much Christopher's go-to phrasing.

We hadn't kissed on the cheek or the lips and now the window for any kind of kissing seemed to have passed, as Christopher held open the door for us to go inside.

The pub was right on the riverside and claimed to be the oldest pub on the Thames but Christopher said a pub in Rotherhithe also laid claim to this title. The floor was made of big stone paving slabs which I later heard one of the people at the party refer to as flagstone, and added this to my word-bank.

On the way upstairs I asked Christopher, 'What does Kira lecture in?'

'Artificial intelligence.'

'Oh,' I said, trying not to sound intimidated. I still carried actual money around and printed out tickets and documents rather than having them on my phone, which Barney said was one of the few cool things about me, as if I had deliberately gone and got myself left behind, rather than accidentally finding myself confused and flustered in a world that had moved on without me.

'Specifically, the ethics around technology,' said Christopher, holding the door open as we reached the top of the stairs. 'She's on a council that advises governments on regulations involving AI.'

I was relieved to hear that at least someone was keeping these machines in check. *It's not the machines who need keeping in check, you dummy. It's the people who are making them.*

That's what I meant, I told the voice crossly. You just stole my second thought and passed it off as your own.

I thought Kira's job sounded very senior and asked Christopher how old she was. He shrugged and said, 'About my age?'

I didn't understand how Christopher and Kira could only be eight or nine years older than me and so much more accomplished, but then thought of my four unpublished manuscripts and concluded that being unaccomplished had also taken a lot of time and effort.

The function room upstairs had panelled walls, red velvet curtains and old-fashioned windows made up of small separate squares of glass. It felt as though we were inside a captain's cabin, probably because there were also lots of nautical-themed things, like framed oil paintings of ships, hanging chain lanterns and gold-medallion plates that reminded me of treasure.

Christopher said, 'Let's get a drink,' but on the way to the bar we got accosted by some people who knew him. He introduced me by saying, 'This is Misty,' and they shook my hand and said it was nice to meet me but then started talking about someone they all knew called Rosalie who had a predilection for the macabre. They said a word I didn't know but that I decided from the context meant either deformed or decapitated. Then they said two more words I didn't know and also didn't have the context for to even get me going, and so I said to Christopher, 'I'll get the drinks,' and left him while I went to the bar.

I was still wearing my coat, which made me feel protected, as though I hadn't committed to staying. I desperately wanted to leave and be there at the same time. *You and your impossible wants*, said the voice. Tell me something I don't know, I said back to it.

I ordered two red wines because this was the colour of wine we had drunk at Christopher's, but couldn't carry them at the same time as the succulent and so had to leave it on the bar and go back for it. When I re-entered the circle, there was a new woman standing next to me who hadn't been there before and who was wearing a badge in the colours of the EU flag saying *Citizen of Europe*. I decided there was a high chance that she was Kira, which was confirmed seconds later when a man across from her asked what she would like to drink and she replied saying she would have another half pint of pale ale, to which he replied, 'Kira the carouser.'

I waited until the man had gone to the bar and then turned to her and said, 'Congratulations on your Indefinite Leave to Remain, if that's a thing to say. Also, I'm crashing your party, so I brought you this plant.'

'Thank you. I should have invited more strangers, then maybe I would have received more presents,' she said, taking it from me. I laughed and tried to work out if she was Austrian, German, Icelandic, or none of these. 'Are you actually crashing my party, or do you know somebody here?'

'I came with Christopher.'

She looked at him and then back at me and I felt her wanting to ask in what capacity I had come with him, but she didn't.

I checked the others weren't listening but they were deep in a discussion about Elizabethan pets, and then said, 'Christopher said you work in AI.'

'I do.'

'Well, I was wondering what you think about this.' And I told her how last year I'd read a poem that was written by an AI but hadn't realized this because it sounded like lots of the poetry that Barney and his friends wrote, and that when I'd found out about the AI having written it I'd felt cheated and alarmed because if machines could now write poetry then what was left for humans?

'Here's the thing. People assume that the more intelligent AI gets the more human it becomes but really that's as random as saying the larger my ears grow the more like an elephant I become.' I smiled, intrigued, and nodded for her to continue. 'What's happening increasingly is that AIs are exhibiting *in-human* levels of intelligence and we should be concerned about that for other reasons, but poetry should be safe, or at least good poetry should be safe, because isn't the whole point of poetry to describe what it means and feels to be human? And this is exactly what AIs can't be.'

I wanted to thank her so much for this, for explaining it so clearly and reassuringly, but then a new group of people entered the room, singing in a language I didn't recognize, and she excused herself.

When I turned back to the group I caught Christopher looking at me from across the circle. I smiled to signal that I was having a nice time and then tuned into the conversation, which appeared to be about the canals of Britain, which one of them had written a book about. It turned out that most of them had written published books on quite niche subjects, like rare shrubs and the history of gunpowder. They all had a very particular way of speaking and it was the same way

Christopher spoke. There was a depth to the content which they offset with a slight flippancy in their delivery. Listening to them talk felt like watching a professional game of tennis. I couldn't partake in the discussion, but it was stimulating just to be a spectator. At one point Christopher moved to stand next to me and said quietly, 'Are you OK? You're not saying very much.'

At this moment the group happened to go quiet so that I was aware of everyone listening for my response. I felt incredibly nervous as I said, 'I don't really have anything to contribute but I'm getting lots out of just listening. It's like a really good and informative podcast.' I said this audibly so they could all hear, and they laughed collectively, which made me pleased, even though I hadn't said it to be funny, I'd just said it because it was what I actually thought.

Another hour passed like this, with me listening in on the fringes of different conversations, and occasionally adding something, but mainly not.

'Is this grim for you?' asked Christopher with a playful wince as we stood at the bar waiting to be served.

'No, it's fun, it's just . . .' And then I said the thing that had been weighing on me all evening. 'It's just that everyone here has actual knowledge and they've managed to publish it in a book, whereas I can't even get made-up stuff published in a book.' I think I must have looked and sounded quite sad and embarrassed – no more than I felt but more than I meant to let on – because Christopher's face changed so that now he was looking thoughtful.

He tilted his head and then tilted it back to straight again and said, 'Have you ever considered that writing down real stuff might be easier than making made-up stuff sound real?' I thought this was pretty implausible as a theory but sweet of him to try to make me feel better. 'Also, you may not know stuff per se, but you've got takes on things,' he said, and then he turned back to the bar to add wasabi peas to our order.

In the taxi home I asked Christopher, 'Does Kira know Sara?'

'They've met a few times, but we have quite separate friends.'

I wanted to know if Christopher did this a lot, brought other women who weren't his partner to parties, but this felt too possessive and so instead I asked, 'By the way, my friend Erica wants to know why you're on Hinge and not that Feeld app, considering you're non-monogamous.'

'I am on Feeld too.' He said this sort of sheepishly.

'Oh.'

'It's not that I'm going on lots of dates all the time. It's just not all that appealing to a lot of women to date a man who's already in a relationship, hence why I'm on a few of them.'

'So you matched with me out of necessity?'

He looked surprised and a bit awkward and then said, 'I matched with you because I was attracted to you.' Then he paused, and said, 'Not was. Am.'

'You mean you're physically attracted to me?'

I kind of expected him to deny this but he said, 'That's definitely a big part of it, yes. It's not the only thing, though. You're also funny.'

I thought about this for a second and then asked, 'Intentionally funny or inadvertently funny?'

He smiled and looked amused. 'Only you can answer that.'

I was dissatisfied by his response and looked out of the window, where I could see half of my reflection as I worked out how to ask my question again.

'I guess it's just that I get quite a lot out of our conversations and it feels as though you might get quite a lot less than me.'

Christopher laughed and said, 'I get lines like that out of

it, as a starting point.' But then the taxi pulled up outside his house so this turned out to also be an ending point.

As we walked up the stoop, I remembered again that Christopher had a child and wondered if we might be about to encounter a babysitter or if Rowan was at another sleepover. When I asked Christopher this, he said, 'He's staying with his cousins at my sister's house.'

'Where does your sister live?'

'Balham.' He injected a lot of derision into this one word so that I knew immediately he judged Balham as a place and possibly also judged his sister for living there.

'What does she do?'

'She was a very brilliant historian but then she married a hedge-fund manager and now they have three children, which seems to be the required number of offspring to prevent, or legitimize, her not working.'

There seemed to be a different energy to Christopher this evening, a less protective and more provocative, sparring one. I decided I needed to up my conversational game and meet him on his level.

'I once temped at an agency with a receptionist who lived in Balham. She called Secret Cinema *edgy*.'

He enjoyed this and did his full laugh. 'That's the first snide thing I've heard you say.'

'Is it? I often have snide thoughts.'

'Do you? You seem very virtuous.'

'I don't feel virtuous. A lot of the time I feel quite jealous and intolerant of people and sometimes I have pretty appalling instincts.'

'Do you ever act on them, these appalling instincts?' he asked, looking at me curiously.

'Sometimes, yeah.'

'Tell me more.'

And so I told him the first thing that came into my head, which was that a few years ago I had been on a long-haul flight and there had been a toddler who wouldn't stop toddling up and down the aisle and making a particular gleeful sound, the frequency of which felt like an electric jolt going down my spine, and that after a while of this continuing I had become so desperate to make the noise stop that I had stuck my foot out and deliberately tripped up the toddler so that it fell on its face and started to cry, and even then I didn't regret it because the crying was preferable to the jolting electrical sound that made me squirm and judder in my seat. I said I felt that this officially made me quite an awful person, maybe even a very awful person, but perhaps we were back to the point of things needing a comparison to provide scale.

Christopher had been looking at me like he wanted to have sex with me, but now wasn't sure how to go about this, and I realized that he'd probably meant for me to tell him something sexual instinct-wise, and instead I'd talked about tripping up a toddler.

'It feels like a strange moment to kiss you, but I think I'm going to anyway,' he said.

'I think you should too.'

We had sex on the sofa with me sitting on top of him. Halfway through I got up and turned to face the wall, leaning forwards with my hands on the edge of the sofa, and motioned for him to enter me from behind. After a minute or so, I said, 'I thought you'd like this position.' He paused and said, 'I do, but do you like it too?'

'It hurts a tiny bit,' I said casually. 'But I like it when you're turned-on.'

He pulled out of me slowly and turned me around so that I was looking up at him. He touched his finger to my face and drew it lightly across my forehead and then behind my ear as if tucking in a strand of loose hair.

'I don't think we're short of positions that turn us both on,' he said. And then he sat me back on top of him and pulsed so gently inside me, I thought, Surely I won't be able to come like this, from such tiny incremental movements, but oh was I wrong, and happy to be so.

'Who knew she was so into pelvises?' mused Erica aloud, as we wandered the third floor of the Tate Modern that Sunday. Erica was back in the UK for her brother's wedding and had managed to wangle an afternoon and evening with me in London. Under pressure to capitalize on her brief window without family obligations, she had booked us tickets to see the Georgia O'Keeffe retrospective on the recommendation of Suze, her ex.

'I didn't even know you and Suze were still in touch,' I said as we passed a painting of a ram's skull next to what looked like a cocktail umbrella.

'We've just been messaging a bit on Instagram.'

She said this very casually, which I thought was odd because Erica and Suze's relationship had been supremely far from casual. Her blasé tone didn't match the high stakes and drama of their history. I was about to ask who had initiated their Instagram contact when Erica pointed to a painting of a close-up purple and red flower and declared, 'Full disclaimer: I'm seeing vulvas everywhere.'

'You must be due some sex.'

'Well, yeah, who isn't?'

I thought of Christopher and wondered what he was doing right now at this moment, and whether he would be having sex with anyone before I next saw him. Picturing him in bed with another woman was not an enjoyable image, and I had only known him a fortnight. How did Sara, who had been with him for twenty years, handle these images? Presumably she had one of those enviably obedient brains that fell asleep on cue and avoided dwelling on unpleasant topics.

Now Erica was squinting at a placard next to a painting of a limewashed building with a blue front door. '*I bought this house because I just had to have that door,*' she read aloud. 'Imagine buying a house purely for its front door. I mean, most of the time you're on the other side of it.' She moved on and lingered by a painting of a green leaf and a brown bulb titled *Skunk Cabbage 1922*.

'This one's the best.' She announced this loudly and with certainty so that a gallery attendant looked over and frowned. Erica, along with my mother, liked literal forms of art, which, awkwardly for me, had excluded Barney's poetry – which was hard to make any sense of but, I was sure, contained underlying brilliance. When I'd said this to Erica she'd replied, 'Yeah, see, my taste leans towards overt brilliance.'

I left her looking at the cabbage and wandered into an airless dark room where people were sitting on the floor watching a video playing on a loop. I was grateful to have escaped the echoing noise of the gallery and the sudden quiet warmth made my limbs go soft and floppy. I stood against the wall and slid down it until I reached the floor, slumping over myself. My cheeks felt heavy like small hot weights pulling down the side of my face. I hugged my knees as the mountains of New Mexico appeared on the screen, creased and red. I need a place, I thought. *You can't afford a house*, said the voice. I'm not talking about a house, I said back to it, although I did need one of those too. But no, somewhere to hang my longing, more than actual walls.

Georgia O'Keeffe had now appeared on the screen in black-and-white footage talking directly to the camera. 'It just happens that I've been in touch with my time,' she said. 'But I could have been a much better painter and no one even would have noticed me.' I think she'd intended this line to be humbling and comforting but it panicked me hearing it because for all my doubts, I had this quiet deep-rooted confidence that if I kept going with my writing it would eventually find its audience, that it was essentially a battle of perseverance, but I had forgotten all about luck and timing. These were mammoth factors; how had I just ignored them? But wait, even being aware of them didn't change anything, because they were outside of my control. I wanted to be liberated by this but instead I felt very flat and uneasy so that I was glad it was dark and that Erica couldn't see my face when she slid down the wall next to me.

We sat in silence together for a couple of minutes until the video began to play from the beginning again and Erica turned to me and said, 'Are you into this?'

'Not massively. You?'

'Not even marginally. Let's go.'

I followed her long strides out of the room and back into the bright white light of the exhibition hall. At one point I had to do a little run to keep up with her.

On the way out she paused next to the final painting on display titled *My Last Door*, which she read aloud and then added, 'Yeah right. I bet she drew it again. I bet she couldn't help herself.'

'Do you blame her?' I replied. Who could resist that kind of stirring desire?

We ate an early dinner in an Asian restaurant on the South Bank that Erica had selected because she was sick to death of European food and I had no real preference about any food, which I largely considered to be sustenance rather than something to construct my day around or get hyped up about; Erica had told me that this was an unusual stance for an adult and made me a very amenable dining companion.

Her meal had arrived inside an upright pineapple, which didn't seem to faze her even though she had to sit up very straight and tall to peer into it.

'You'd need a highchair for this,' she said, rummaging around inside it with her chopsticks like a lucky dip.

I twirled the noodles around on my plate and watched a young girl on a carousel through the window tip back her head looking crazed with pleasure.

'You know how people say the key to a good life is being satisfied with what you have, but how do you feel that at the same time as striving towards getting the things you want?' I asked her. 'Because at the moment I'd say I'm definitely tipping more towards hunger than satisfaction.'

'I think that's normal,' said Erica, pausing from her pineapple. 'I think you're just in the prime of your wanting right now.'

'But where does it end? Or do we just go on wanting stuff until we die?'

'Probably yes but also probably not as much. I'd say these are undoubtedly our hungriest years.' She pointed with her chopstick at a pigeon on the paving slab that was flapping its wings and looked like it was trying and failing to take off. 'Wow, that pigeon is really bad at flying.'

'In fairness, you don't fly at all.'

'Much is my pity.'

'Ideally, and don't judge me for this, I'd like to be trapped by now with a child or at the very least have a divorce behind me.'

'You're being glib, right?'

'A bit but also not. Nobody wants or needs or expects anything of me. I'm kind of offended by my freedom. And yes, I know that's an offensive and privileged thing to say.'

Erica shrugged and said, 'If we're doing *offensive don't judge me* confessions then sometimes I fantasize about Adrienne and the twins being dead.' I must have not been able to hide my shock because she added, 'Obviously they die in a very beautiful and painless way, and I get to grieve all alone and answer to no one and not have to worry about letting anyone down.'

'I worry I have no one to let down.'

'How blissful and sad.'

I valued Erica for not just saying, 'how blissful,' but for adding the sadness bit too.

I looked again at the pigeon outside the window. Weren't safety and freedom kind of in opposition? We were led to believe that freedom was what we should all be aspiring to but too much of it felt dangerous. Didn't everything need some form of parameter to push against?

'Maybe the pigeon wants to stay grounded, maybe it finds all that open air relentless.'

'By "the pigeon" we mean you, right?' said Erica, as she went back to her pineapple while I reflected on this. In one sense I was excited by the miles of sky that had appeared since I'd begun seeing Christopher, but in another I was unnerved by them. So much possibility. Who would I end up with after him? And would I always be this appallingly free?

'Maybe I don't actually want to be long-term trapped, maybe it's more that I want the taste of a trapping, just to experience it.'

'Ah, but it's not a true trapping if you know it's only for a bit.'

She glanced at her phone, which had just pinged on the table next to us, and rolled her eyes comically wide.

'Mon *dieu*. Now she's asking if I can take a photo of where I'm going to position it inside the courtyard.'

Erica was in the process of bidding for a gargoyle on eBay. The woman who was selling it wanted to make sure it was going to go to a good home and so was asking lots of questions like, *How much shade and ivy are you planning on giving it?*

'Why don't you message her back with a reminder it's not alive,' I said.

'That will just aggravate her. If I want it, I need to play the game.' I watched Erica smile mischievously as she googled images of shaded courtyards and then screenshotted one which she sent to the woman with the caption, *I was thinking here, but open to your suggestions and flexible to its needs.*

'Do you think our problems are relatable?' I asked, once Erica's focus had returned to the pineapple.

'Quite obviously not. I mean, look at me, I'm in a bidding war for a gargoyle.'

'True,' I said. 'But you're also a tired parent whose partner goes out to work and leaves you to do the majority of the childcare.'

'Well, yeah, but one of us has to work and it's not like I want to sit at a desk in the city and crunch numbers every day, or whatever it is Adrienne does.'

'How come she even has to work?' I asked. 'I thought her family were super rich.'

'They're old-money rich, as in it's all tied up in the manor house and the Paris apartment,' she said offhandedly. Erica hadn't grown up with family wealth but was entirely unintimidated by Adrienne's, which dated back from so many generations that Erica said she was loath to walk around in reverence to some old merchant dude who was probably racist and homophobic and a ton of other offensive adjectives. 'And anyway,' she added, 'I'd go equally mad if we were both there with the twins all day.'

'But still, it must be isolating being all alone in that big house.'

'Oh please. No less isolating than being all alone in a tiny house. Let's face it, money's such a salve.' She threw down her chopsticks and sat back victorious. 'Et voila! I declare that an empty pineapple.'

The momentum of mine and Christopher's messaging remained the same the following week, with him leaving chunks of hours before replying to me, and always being the first to go offline if we were speaking in real-time. My feelings for him had developed considerably by this point to the extent that I found myself shamefully hooked to my phone as I waited for his replies. Outwardly I was reassured that Christopher didn't know how much I'd fallen for him but inwardly I knew I was doing a shoddy job of battling against my attachment; it was annoyingly tricky to trick oneself.

Because I felt such a strong connection to him it was strange to consider that this connection could be a one-way feeling, and actually, if it was one-way then was it really a connection at all, because didn't a connection imply a joining of two things? I wondered if perhaps he did really like me and his distancing was intentional for my benefit – whether it was part of my six-week 'training' – and on Wednesday morning I messaged him exactly this.

Is your sporadic messaging part of my attachment training?

Eleven hours later he replied,

Hm. This message has strong pet-owner vibes.
I should probably mention I'm averse to dogs
for their dependency.

> *Ah you're more of a cat-guy?*

I'm not sure I'm an anything kind of 'guy'.

> *A nothing-man?*

Ha. Rowan wants a pet rat.

> *Will you get him one?*

Undecided but likely not.

> *I don't like their tails*

I don't mind their tails.

> *Alas. It appears we've reached an impasse . . .*

I watched the words 'Christopher is typing' appear and then disappear before appearing again.

It's been a busy week!

> *All good!*
> *I know you're a father/partner/head of an academic research department so won't take it personally*

A glamorous trinity.

> *Are you religious?*

I am not.
I am free this Friday though if you'd like to see me?

> *One sec. Just checking if I can squeeze you
> into my single/childless/freelancer schedule . . . (I can)*

It's a date. x

This was the thing, it wasn't as though Christopher was opposed to seeing me. He had even initiated it this time around, but I suspected he might as easily not, had I not caught him at that exact moment in time in that particular mood. I wanted to feel this way about seeing him too; why did I have to form such strong attachments to people? It was extremely annoying. *You know why*, said the voice. I shushed it and told it off for being almost as annoying as my needy attachment.

That Friday we went to a restaurant in Drayton Park with an industrial-looking interior and large faded lettering above the door in the style of an old shop front. Christopher stooped to kiss me on the cheek on arrival, which felt unnecessarily formal and no more intimate than his initial greeting on our first date, despite it now being our third, as though he had deliberately reset himself. Was this how he maintained his independence, by not allowing himself to get close to people? But he had told me himself that being open didn't mean not allowing himself to be intimate with people, and yet I sensed a definite block between us, put there by him, that I was convinced I wasn't imagining.

I had become concerned about him being bored in my company and so for the last week had been storing up things to tell him, thoughts and questions and observations, to make sure we had enough stuff to talk about when we met, but also just because there was so much stuff I wanted to talk about with him and if I'd responded to these impulses as they arrived I would have been permanently bombarding him with WhatsApps, and I had no intention of presenting like a crazy person – even if privately at points I was feeling like one.

I waited until our drinks had arrived and then began telling him about an article I had read that had concluded by saying that in the future we might evolve as a species into something that isn't human, and I badly wanted his opinion on this.

'Well, I haven't read the article, but if you go back long enough our ancestors weren't human so I guess there's every chance we may evolve again and become post-human.'

'But that's so wild. What would we look like?'

'I have no idea why you think I'd know the answer to that.' He sounded minorly annoyed by this assumption, or at least uncomfortable with the status I was giving him, so that it felt like a cold rush of air had just entered the restaurant.

'I just feel even your guess would be more accurate than mine. Like, I'm genuinely picturing E.T.'

He smiled then and said, 'I'm not sure there's any reason not to picture E.T.'

'But what are you picturing?'

He looked a bit embarrassed and said, 'Erm, well, I'm currently picturing you naked.'

I felt my thighs tingle and tried to keep my face neutral to conceal how happy this made me. 'Because you think I look post-human?'

'No. Quite off topic. My mind's wandered.'

'I like where it's wandered to.'

He took hold of my ankle and ran his hand up inside the leg of my flared trousers. He stopped halfway up my calf and stroked me so gently I thought it would tickle but I felt too serious and turned-on to laugh.

'If anything you have pre-human features, like Lucy.'

'Who's Lucy?'

'As in the hominid.'

I continued to look blankly at him and he added, 'She's a fossilized ape. One of our earliest ancestors.'

'You mean I look like a monkey?'

'No, but you do have large eyes.'

I took a sip of water, rolling a piece of ice around inside my mouth, and said, 'You know how babies have evolved to have big eyes so people want to protect them? I think I have that a bit. Like, it doesn't help my self-sufficiency.'

'You could always do a Gloucester and gouge them out.' I knew this was in reference to a Shakespeare play but wasn't sure which one. In any case, I told Christopher this was an awful idea a) because I'd be blind and b) because then I'd depend on people even more.

He laughed and said, 'You're right. I didn't think that through.'

I leant in towards him then and we began kissing. Having instigated the kiss, I promised myself I would break away first but couldn't bring myself to. I heard the voice say, *You are failing miserably at this.* And I counter-replied, Yes but for every second I fail miserably I am getting his lips that bit longer . . . Reasoning this, in and of itself, was a mini victory.

I thought about Christopher relentlessly, even when he was in the same room as me, which seemed weird and unnecessary. He'd be making us coffee in the kitchen while I'd be lying in bed reading one of the books by his nightstand, but instead I'd be thinking about him plunging the cafetière or imagining a conversation we might have when he returned. The only time my mind got any respite from him was when we were having an actual conversation, and I couldn't really classify this as a break since it involved a real-life interaction.

I told him this on the morning after our fourth date. We were sitting at his kitchen table eating muesli with chopped nectarine.

'Sometimes I have conversations with you in my head even when you're right here.'

He laughed, and asked, 'Am I good in them?'

'Less good than you are in real life because I can't make up lines for you I don't understand. It's like trying to write a character who knows more and is cleverer than me.'

He didn't respond to this and looked awkward, so I decided to wrap it up. 'So anyway, yeah, sometimes I just end up leaving a dash line, like _____ *insert fact or funny clever joke here.*'

He smiled but also frowned and bit the top row of his teeth into his bottom lip so that it made a kind of sucking sound.

'Do you think you feel awkward when I say things like that because you're older than me and a man?' I asked. 'Like if it was the other way around it would be OK, but this way around it seems a bit sexist and generic.'

'I think that probably adds to my discomfort, yes.'

I felt bad at his feeling bad and said, 'I'm going to give you a fact, OK? To balance it out a bit.' His shoulders dropped and his face relaxed when I said this.

'OK. Good, I'd like that.'

'Great. What don't you know about?'

'Tons of stuff. Federal architecture, futurism, town planning, Bitcoin—'

'OK, I'll rephrase that. What don't you know about that I do know about?'

He paused and asked not unkindly, 'What do you know about?'

I found the answer to this (nothing in any real detail) quite depressing but wanted to keep the mood light and so said, 'Gymnastics?'

He looked relieved and sat up straighter, as if I was about to perform a mini recital for him. 'I safely know nothing about gymnastics.'

'Great. Well, my old gymnastics coach Shaun spent seven months learning to do the splits. He practised every day while he watched *Countdown*, and even though he was quite overweight and in his late forties he did it. He got all the way down to the floor and when he showed us it was this giant deal. And then when he came back after Christmas, which was only a two-week break, he'd already lost them. He wasn't even close to that floor any more.'

'Is that . . . that's the fact, is it?'

'Well, I didn't want to give you something you could just google; I think you might have felt a bit short-changed.'

'Thank you. I liked it was empirical,' he said, leaning forward to kiss me. His mouth tasted sweet and oaty. I didn't want the kiss to end, but listen, there was nothing new in that.

Christopher asked if I still did gymnastics, and I told him I had stopped when I was eleven under pressure from my mother, who hated me doing it.

'Hated? That's a strong stance to take against gymnastics.'

'She couldn't stand the sequinned leotards and tightly scraped-back hair and perfection of the whole thing. She said she wanted me to be outside and getting messy and muddy, but I loved all the things she loathed about it. Anyway, I took up running instead and that's been one of my three main occupations ever since.'

'Three?'

'Running, writing and loving. Although, since messing up my knee and breaking up with Barney, I haven't been doing any of them.'

Christopher looked confused and said, 'I've never thought to classify loving as an occupation.'

'I think it is, if you do it a certain way.'

'What way is that?' he asked, scratching his fingernail at one of his bottom incisors to remove a strand of nectarine.

'I guess quite actively and with perseverance even on days you're tired and don't really feel like showing up.'

'Go on.' He leant in towards me and I felt the full force of his attention.

'OK, well, I guess everyone does it in their own style, but I'd imagine I was an oven pumping warm air out into him, sending him lots of good thoughts and energy.'

'Him being your ex?'

'Barney, yes.'

'That must have been nice for him.'

'That's what I hoped. It still wasn't enough, though.' Christopher looked a bit sad for me then, which I didn't want and so I said flippantly, 'You know, it was technically two facts.'

'Was it?' he asked, sitting back in his chair.

'Yep. That even with a body like Shaun's you can teach it to do the splits, and that flexibility takes daily effort to maintain and only a very quick time to destroy.' I paused, thinking about this, and then added, 'A bit like love.'

He looked up to the left-hand side and asked, 'Is love like that? I think love can be quite persistent.'

I breathed in very sharply when he said this and found it hard to breathe out again. When I did, I looked down at my bowl, at the bits of muesli stuck to the bottom, and said, 'I can barely bare to do it again.'

When I looked up at him he was looking at me cautiously, and I felt the need to protect myself and clarify what I meant at the same time.

'I don't mean with you, I just mean, in general. Like, it's weird we haven't evolved to protect ourselves. Why do we keep doing it as a species even though it hurts so much to fall out of it?'

'Good question. I think it's probably because the alternative is equally awful.'

'What's the alternative? Not loving?'

'I guess just nothing happening.'

We looked at each other very intensely and I felt no doubt in this second that something noteworthy was passing between us which emboldened me to say what I said next – and would later supremely regret.

'I know I said not with you but what if it was with you, just hypothetically?'

He paused, looking irrefutably uncomfortable, and said, 'I feel we'd have failed quite spectacularly in terms of our arrangement.'

'And is that . . . is that all you'd feel?'

He softened a bit then and said, 'No. But I think it would be my overriding feeling.'

'Noted,' I said, breezily, but inside I felt winded.

The October sky was bright and sharp when I left Christopher's house that morning. I had my sunglasses with me but didn't put them on because I wanted the light on my face even though it stung my eyes considerably.

I had arranged to meet Dan at a coffee shop in Canonbury that was full of mid-century modern furniture and borrowed nostalgia. I had started purposefully planning lunch or coffee with Dan directly after I left Christopher because I found the idea of walking out into the day without him and having nothing to distract me mildly intolerable. Dan was enjoying my weekly instalments of hearing about Christopher, and said it was like the old days when you used to have to wait all week to watch just one episode of a show. I was pleased to have him as an attentive audience but also conflicted that my feelings and experiences were functioning as entertainment, as though it somehow made them less valid.

As I waited at the bus stop, I felt myself hollowing, which was how I repeatedly felt when I said goodbye to Christopher, only this time the sensation was even worse. Each goodbye had begun to feel like a countdown until our last meeting and I had started to do obsessive things like memorize the magnets on his fridge and make a mental list of the products in his bathroom so that at least I could access the smell of him once our time together was up.

When I got to the café, I saw Dan had secured the comfiest armchairs, which were also window seats. I felt he'd done well to achieve this on a Sunday morning and told him so as

I sat down. His glasses were slightly steamed from the heat of the café or maybe from his coffee, and as he took them off to wipe them I thought he looked a bit down, which was very unlike him because he was always such an upbeat energy.

I asked if he was OK and he said, 'Yeah, good,' but I thought the way he said this sounded too forced and jovial. I went up to the counter to order and when I came back he wasn't on his phone or anything, he was just staring out of the window and looked quite lost. Dan's thoughts had always seemed to me to be relatively shallow, not in a superficial sense, but as though he was gliding along inside his head doing breaststroke rather than something faster or splashier or deeper.

'Are you sure you're OK?' I asked.

I decided that if he said 'yes' again I wouldn't probe but he sighed, giving into the weight of whatever was bothering him, which made him seem a tiny bit lighter.

'It's just been a bit of a tough week.'

'At work?' Dan was a medical researcher and was part of a team who were doing something to do with changing the protein of a gene. He'd explained that this involved trying lots of various combinations and had helpfully analogized it to 'like Wordle but with proteins'.

He scratched the side of his head, which was bald, and said, 'With Shiv.' Shiv was his wife and a human rights barrister who also happened to be a really good cellist and interior designer. I had only met her a handful of times and had found her very friendly and impressive, which wasn't always a natural combination, but she was firmly both of these things.

'I'm sorry to hear that.' While I waited for him to carry on speaking I overheard a girl with very glossy lips telling her father off for taking a bite of his panini before she'd had a chance to Instagram it.

'It's OK, it's . . . basically things have come to a head on the kids front and I can't really see a solution.' This oddly came as a shock to me. We had previously joked about Dan being broody and Shiv showing no signs of wanting children, but I hadn't known that this had become a real problem and that he was in actual pain.

'I'm really sorry,' I said, again. 'I didn't realize.'

He shrugged and said, 'She didn't want them when we met and she told me that but I just figured she'd change her mind. She keeps saying, "But you knew this when you married me." And she's right, I did.'

'People do change, though. I think that's normal, isn't it? To have hoped she'd change her mind.'

'That's the thing. I didn't realize I'd been holding on to any hope, not until this week.'

'Why, what happened this week?'

He did an embarrassed laugh and said, 'We went to see a guidance counsellor. It had always kind of been there in the back of my mind as a last resort, I guess. But she was, the counsellor, she was pretty pessimistic. She said she'd do her best to help us but that in her experience when couples found themselves in this lock, taking binary positions over whether or not to have children, it was hard to resolve because each person had already backed themselves into a corner.' He laughed again, and I saw how much pain he was in. 'It was stupid really, to have assumed she'd have some kind of miracle solution. But yeah, now I feel pretty rubbish because I think I must have been holding on to the hope of a professional being able to solve it for us and now I feel like we don't even have that any more.'

'But she shouldn't be giving up before she's even started. The guidance counsellor, I mean.'

'I don't think she was giving up, I think she was just being realistic and, I don't know, managing our expectations.'

It was so hard to give someone the right amount of hope

and to meter that hope so that it didn't either grow too large or totally disappear. It felt a bit like one of those games where you had to keep your hand very steady as you guided the loop along the wire and it buzzed if you accidentally touched it. Too much hope! Not enough hope!

I wasn't sure if it was right to ask this next question, but asked it anyway. 'How come Shiv doesn't want them?'

'She just never has and said that asking someone to interrogate their wanting or not wanting children is as random as asking someone why they preferred doing woodwork or working-out at the gym, that it's just the way different people are programmed. I pointed out that wasn't really a good comparison because we'd die out if nobody wanted children whereas there's no biological imperative to CrossFit or carpentry.'

This seemed a fair and reasonable response, although perhaps a slightly riling one for Shiv. 'That's technically true,' I said.

'Right? Well, it didn't help because then she started saying that we're at no risk of dying out as a species, that the world has no shortage of people in it, and then she said – actually this annoyed me, because then she threw the climate thing into it and said it was a contradiction that I went on marches and protests and didn't eat meat when the biggest thing I could do to lower my carbon footprint would be not to bring another person into the world.'

This is probably a relevant point to mention that Dan and I had met at an Extinction Rebellion branch meeting several years ago and bonded when I'd confided in him that I'd been running late and so had got an Uber to the meeting, at which point Dan said, 'That's small fry. I just flew back from my honeymoon in the Seychelles.' I'd confessed to Dan after our third meeting that I wasn't into the hippy chanting or eco-aesthetic and that I didn't even really believe that protesting would change anything, but I just couldn't not do something; so here I was, the reluctant disillusioned campaigner.

'And I agree, it is a contradiction,' Dan carried on. 'But I can't help it if I want to stop the planet burning up and simultaneously be a father. I mean, why should one cancel the other one out or stop me from trying to be a decent person just because I'm also a flawed one?'

'Well, exactly.' I said this so emphatically that he looked hopeful for a second, but then went back to looking defeated, as though remembering it wasn't me he needed to convince.

'There's not really anything I can do, though,' he said despondently. 'It's her body.'

It felt like an impossibly difficult situation and one I so wanted to solve for him but couldn't, so instead I said, 'I don't think it will stay this hard. I think either she'll change her mind about wanting them or you'll make peace with not having them. But it won't just stay like this.'

'Yeah. You're probably right.'

I watched the effort it took him to smile and thought again of how I hadn't known what he'd been going through even though I also had known because he hadn't kept it secret, not really, and how this was a thing that people sometimes did: said a problem jokingly or glibly to lay the foundation to prepare you, or maybe to prepare themselves, for if and when this problem became a bigger problem, almost like they were trying out saying it aloud. And I felt naive for not realizing this and for not acknowledging sooner what Dan had been going through, and wondered if I had become too wrapped up in my own saga of Barney and now Christopher to notice other people's pain, and thought probably yes to this.

The next time I saw Christopher would be the final time, or at least the final time for quite some while, but I didn't know this yet. We had messaged even less during the week than previously, and as I made my way to meet him that Saturday, I felt weakly optimistic that our lack of communication would have made him miss me and draw him in closer when he saw me. What exactly was I hoping for from this penultimate date? I couldn't answer entirely. I still knew that he was ultimately unavailable but was managing to short-circuit my thoughts so that any time I got close to imagining further than our six-week endpoint, my brain cut out and refused to visualize beyond this. I was hopeful that some unknown solution would present itself; perhaps Sara would be stuck out in whichever war zone she was in for lots more months so that Christopher and I could continue seeing each other. It seemed feasible, or at least contained enough plausibility, to make it just about an attainable desire.

When I entered the pub I went to kiss him on the lips, and he looked taken aback and quite awkward. *Not off to a great start, are you?* I tried not to be disheartened and told him how nice it was to see him. Again, he looked uncomfortable and said, 'It's nice to see you too,' very quickly and quietly and not fully looking at me, as though he was professing to an illicit kink. He was already drinking an ale and asked what I'd like to drink. I said I didn't know yet but would go to the bar and decide on the spur of the moment once I was up there.

I ordered a gin and tonic and told the barmaid who was serving me that I liked her jade earrings, a) because I did, and

b) because she looked quite demoralized and I thought she could do with a boost to get her through her shift. As I sat down at the table Christopher raised his glass, without clinking mine, and we took a sip of our drinks. I waited to see if he would ask me a question and when he didn't, I asked, 'How was your week?'

'Good. Busy.'

I looked across at the barmaid with the jade earrings, who I thought looked fractionally but discernibly more perky, and said, 'Busy with work?'

'Partly, yes. There's a study we're doing that's quite all-consuming.'

'A study on what?'

'In a nutshell, the relationship between psychedelics and consciousness.' His eyes were shining as he said this, and I realized he looked excited and that I hadn't seen this emotion in him until now. I felt threatened by this study with its exciting psychedelics but also deeply curious.

'In what way?'

'Well, the common conception of drugs that alter your mood and perception is that they give you a sort of otherworldly experience, but might it actually be that what you're seeing and feeling when you take them is just as real or unreal as your everyday version of reality?'

I think he could sense I wasn't convinced, because I wasn't. 'I don't think I get it,' I said.

'You look at this glass,' he said, pointing to his pint, 'and you think you're seeing an accurate image of it, but you can only ever see your interpretation of it. There's always a gap between how things actually are and your subjective experience of them. Our brains are constantly making tons of predictions in order to make sense of external stimuli, so arguably in one sense, all perception is a controlled hallucination.'

'Huh.' I paused and then asked, 'Do you take the drugs as part of the study?'

'We have participants who do that.' I paused again while I found another way to ask the question I wanted answering.

'Do you take drugs outside of the study?'

'Sometimes, yes.'

There were always lots of drugs at the parties I went to with Barney and his friends but I never wanted them. One time, someone suggested we went around in a circle and said our biggest trauma and the winner would get the rest of the MDMA. When it got to my turn I said, 'I have a dead dad but it's not really a trauma because I never knew him.' An emotionally abusive stepmother turned out to be the winner, and the last dab was aptly awarded to a girl named Molly.

'I don't,' I said after a beat. 'Take drugs.' I thought this made me sound boring and tame and that Christopher must be thinking this about me too and so I called myself out, which felt less exposing than sitting with the silent acknowledgement of it. 'I feel intimidated by them and so I don't take them, and because I don't take them, I feel intimidated by them.'

'Vicious cycle,' he said, smiling. 'You could always break the loop and take some.'

'I could do. I just have this hunch I won't like them.'

'Based on what?'

'Mainly how my body responds to turbulence and theme park rides.'

'Ah. You're the one in the group who holds the bags.' I felt his smile contained pity but perhaps I was just projecting this.

'It's fine,' I said brightly. 'I don't really need them. Most of the time I find life way too sharp and vivid anyway.' This was true and not just to make us both feel better. I was thinking of how the brick wall on my road the other night had looked like bars of solid chocolate and the purple cones of buddleia were bright and yet somehow vague and undefinable.

'Drugs aren't really about need, unless you're an addict. But for me and most people I know who take them they're enhancers.' I tilted my head, indicating I wanted him to continue. 'Put it this way, you wouldn't say you needed sex or wine or music, but they add to your life, in a good way, right?'

While I considered this I noticed he had folded the crisp packet into one of those small triangles that I've never known how to make.

'No,' I said. 'I mean yes, they do, but that doesn't work as a comparison.'

'Why doesn't it?' He looked happy to be challenged and leant in closer.

'Because I already know what sex and wine and music add to my life and so to go without them would be a subtraction. But I haven't had mushrooms or acid yet so as long as I don't take them I don't know what I'm missing.'

He smiled and, raising his eyebrows, said, 'Quite a lot, in my opinion.'

I left a beat and then asked, 'Does Sara take them?'

'Occasionally.'

'Are you looking forward to having her home again?'

'There's always a period of adjustment but, yes, it'll be nice.'

I wanted to ask more but sensed this part of the conversation was closed and that we would move on to discussing something tangible and inconsequential. Right on cue, Christopher pointed at the velvet curtains and told me he had a cousin who had a phobia of velvet but could still wear suede so it wasn't as debilitating as it sounded, but still quite restrictive, especially in gastropubs and rich people's sitting rooms.

The pub was only serving burgers, which neither of us wanted to eat, and so we walked to a nearby Georgian restaurant. During the dinner I had this sense that Christopher was withdrawing from me and that he didn't particularly want to be there any more but because he was a decent person he wasn't just going to get up and leave. I felt sad and envious that he had a prosperous career to validate him and wished I had chosen to do something with my life that wouldn't make me feel, on some days, entirely worthless as a human being.

'What do you think makes a book a book?' I asked.

'What do you mean?'

I'm sure he was bored of hearing about my writing woes by this point, but I felt so low about the way the evening was going that I didn't have the energy to even try to be resilient.

'I mean, what makes something work or not work as a work of fiction and why can't I work out what that thing is?'

He paused and said, 'I don't think there are any rules, are there? Didn't Henry James say the only requirement of fiction is that it be interesting? Or something to that effect.'

'But why would what's interesting to me automatically be interesting to someone else?'

'It might not be. And it certainly won't be interesting to everybody. But I suppose you can only really start from the place of what interests you.'

'Yeah, see, that's the problem. I've done that already, multiple times, and nobody wanted it.' This was partly true, while being partly untrue. Each time I'd attempted to write a book I'd also tried to guess what would be interesting and topical to other people so that it was now hard to work out whether the things I had written about were originally my own interest or an interest I had imposed on myself because I felt I had a higher chance of getting published.

'Well, then I guess you try again. Or you don't. Depending on how much you want it.'

'Enormously,' I said, embarrassed to want something so much more than it wanted me.

'I don't really know, to be honest; I don't read much fiction these days.'

'How come?'

'I guess I prefer to read stuff that's real, or at least feels real.'

I paused and silently agreed with him on this last point before admitting, 'I haven't read any Henry James apart from *The Turn of the Screw* at university and I didn't really get the hype.'

'Fair enough. I do like that one, but I prefer later Henry James like *The Ambassadors* and *The Golden Bowl*.'

'Should I read those, do you think?'

'I think they're two of the finest books ever written. But I think you should read what you want to read.' It was funny, I often heard women complaining about men telling them what to do or how to think and here I was actively seeking this telling from Christopher and here he was refusing to give it to me. But maybe he knew this and knew it added to his appeal because it marked him out from other men.

'What makes them so good?'

'Lots of things. But I suppose, chiefly for me, their opaqueness.'

I felt very disheartened by this and said, 'I'm not a very opaque person so I don't think you'd like the way I write.' As I said this, I accidentally dropped my fork and it clattered onto the floor. I leant down to pick it up but the waiter got there first and said, 'Do not worry. I will bring you another one.' I said sorry and thank you to the waiter and when I looked back at Christopher, I was sure he looked embarrassed and I felt such shame, as though I was a child out for dinner with him. It was excruciating.

'I might like it if it was honest, though.' I could tell he was now trying to make me feel better (I repeat – excruciating).

'And anyway, like I said, I mainly read non-fiction. I'm definitely not an authority on this.'

'But you do tend to know what you're talking about.'

'I'm not going to agree with you on that. I am wondering whether you're going to eat any more of your food, though,' he said, pointing to my plate, which looked alarmingly full. But I couldn't eat another mouthful. I was so churned up by how much I had fallen for him and how little he had fallen for me, and the imbalance of this was terrifying. This should not be allowed to happen, I thought. How is this possible after less than half a dozen dates?

After Christopher had finished his meal and eaten part of mine, he asked for the bill. I tried to split it with him, because this was something we had done the other times we had been out to eat together, but on this occasion he wouldn't let me and said firmly, 'This one's on me.'

As we exited the restaurant, I wanted Christopher to put his arm around me like he'd done on our first date, but he didn't. We kept walking side by side in silence until we stopped at a nearby bus stop.

'I'm afraid I couldn't get Rowan a sleepover tonight and my sister's away so . . . I'm going to have to leave you here.'

'That's OK.' But inside I was crushed.

We looked at each other for another few seconds and then suddenly at the same moment, moved to kiss. The kiss was long and hard and confirmed that there was definitely still a very physical attraction between us, even though Christopher was acting weirdly. A middle-aged couple walked past as we broke apart and I saw them smile approvingly at our public display of affection, hoping Christopher would be encouraged by their endorsement.

'It feels very teenage, doesn't it? Not having anywhere to be private,' he said, smiling.

I nodded, trying to imagine him as a teenager, but struggled to picture this because he was so intensely grown-up to me.

'What will you do? Will you go back to Brighton tonight?'

'Probably. It's not that late.'

'Most of these buses will take you to King's Cross, if that's useful.'

I nodded and Christopher said, 'I'll wait with you.'

'You don't have to.'

'No, but I want to.'

I smiled and moved to kiss him again but this time I felt his lips were not giving me as much back as I would have liked, or as much as they had done on previous evenings. When we broke apart, I saw a bus approaching in the distance and felt panicked.

'So, I'll see you next week then. Friday or Saturday?'

'I don't know yet. I need to look in my diary.'

I felt very needy then, and made no, or at least little, attempt to hide it.

'It will be our final date so maybe we could do both nights?'

'I think that's unlikely what with Rowan.'

As the bus pulled into the kerb I got on and when I looked back at him he smiled at me through the window, but he felt very distant, even though there was only a layer of glass between us.

I didn't hear from Christopher for an entire five days after that night. On the third day of no contact I scrolled back through our WhatsApps to check if this was the longest we hadn't ever spoken and confirmed, yes it was. I wanted to message him, asking whether he'd had a chance to look in his diary, but refused to. Go me! But my willpower wasn't really empowering because my ultimate goal was to obtain his affection by not contacting him, which cancelled out its integrity.

On the fifth day of no contact, I went for a walk down to the seafront and along into Kemptown, where I passed a row of women with pink and black sashes saying *Bride Squad* trudging down St James's Street. The woman who was wearing a white and pink sash (who I assumed was the bride) looked harried, and kept glancing behind and in front of her, presumably wanting to check that everyone was having a good time. Not for the first time I wondered who hen parties and weddings were for. The bride and groom were often so stressed leading up to the day that they seemed to think they were doing everyone *else* a favour by throwing this big party in honour of themselves, while the guests often resented the time and money they were required to part with in order to attend yet *another* wedding. It seemed to be quite a mad and ineffective exchange for both parties that nobody was convinced they benefited from. Or was I just jaded because I was currently as far away from having a wedding as I had ever been?

When I got back to the house my mother was out and had left a note saying, *Gone to Grandfather's to fix boiler – unsure of return eta.* My mother's note-writing style took the form of a telegram, as though she was paying for every letter. But I was glad she was out and not in the kitchen at that moment, because then it came: Christopher's message. I don't know what I was expecting at this point; it was Thursday and so perhaps I was still clinging to the hope of a last-minute plan for the weekend, but this felt optimistic even by my standards. Anyway, it said,

> *Apologies for not messaging sooner. I'm afraid I don't feel comfortable with us meeting again.*

The message actually went on for more lines, but I failed to take in the rest until I leant against the door of the fridge and went back and read the whole message several more times. I read it very quickly the first time, like ripping off a plaster, and then went back and read each line very slowly as if peeling off the same plaster I'd reapplied.

> *Apologies for not messaging sooner. I'm afraid I don't feel comfortable with us meeting again. You're incredibly wonderful but I've started to feel responsible for you and I don't want that for either of us. I'm happy to discuss things further on a call if you'd like. Otherwise, I'll sign off by reiterating how much I've enjoyed our dates and spending time with you. x*

I wrote below my mother's note, adopting her perfunctory style, *Not feeling well, gone to sleep*, and then went upstairs to my room and got into bed and didn't leave it for multiple days. This is an exaggeration. I left it for no more than three-minute intervals, solely to go to the kitchen and loo.

I couldn't understand how a message could read as so considerate yet brutal, studying it repeatedly over the following days. It was the contrast between the care and formality of his words that was the real kicker. Lying there inside my childhood bedroom I felt heavy in my grooves, as though someone had snuck into my body and poured cement mix inside.

On the fourth morning after Christopher's break-off message, I panicked because I couldn't remember the name of his sister who lived in Balham and had no way of now acquiring this information. Of course, it didn't matter what his sister was called but the fact of not being able to ask him made me rage with helplessness. It felt like the time they had brought that doom clock forwards, and I had turned off the radio and stormed into the bedroom, shouting, 'How dare they! How dare they just do that!' And Barney had to calm me down by making assurances about tipping points and North Korea he had no authority to make. I felt touched remembering this, how he had done that for me. But he was not here now to console me about the fact that I would not see Christopher again.

That afternoon, I left my bedroom and migrated to the living room, where my mother was sitting with the newspaper and a biro. I hadn't told her about Christopher because I knew she would have judged his open set-up and disapproved of my seeing him. Thankfully she assumed I was having a relapse and grieving for Barney again, which was at least a useful decoy. 'I suppose a blip was going to be inevitable,' she'd remarked as we crossed paths on the landing a couple of days prior. 'Just make sure it stays a blip.'

As I lingered by the door deliberating whether to fully enter, she looked me up and down in my pyjamas and said acceptingly, 'It's a Wallack day,' before returning to her sudoku. Back when she had been a medical student, one of her consultants – a man named Geoff Wallack – had invited my mother and the rest of her cohort over for dinner on the day he was due to fly back from Dallas with the explanation, 'I won't be up to doing much that day anyway,' and it had since become our shorthand for a write-off.

Aside from Dan, who I didn't feel I could burden with my petty yearning in light of his concrete marital problems, Erica was the only other person who knew about Christopher and she only ever had five-to-seven minutes to speak on the phone, three of which were used up telling her boy twin (who was particularly hoardy with her time) that she was busy speaking on the phone.

'I think you'd do best to assume he's not thinking about you at literally any moment,' she said during a videocall in which she was bathing the twins. 'And if you do cross his mind at some fleeting point, it's best to assume he's probably thinking about you thinking about him.'

'These are valid objective thoughts,' I said, as I watched her intervene to separate the twins, who had begun pushing each other's heads under the water. *Yeah*, said the voice. *But 'Is he thinking of me?' is also a valid subjective thought.*

Beth visited me again while she was staying with her parents, this time without Jon, who was on a row of night shifts, and brought their month-old daughter, who was perfectly healthy but had been born three weeks early and as a result was tiny! As she draped a muslin over my shoulder and placed her into my arms, I told her that I wasn't sure who was more incredible – her for birthing her daughter or her daughter for simply existing – but that they were both right up there, neck and neck.

She smiled a beatific smile and said, 'So, do you think you'll ever go back to living in London?'

'I'm sure I will,' I replied, stroking her daughter's teeny fingers. But what if I didn't want to? Would somebody make me?

As she was leaving she lingered by the door and said, 'They say break-ups are like getting stitches without painkillers. Each stitch is excruciating, but necessary to closing up the wound.' She said this with surprising authority given she herself had never been through a break-up, but then I guessed she was coming at it more from a stitches angle. I just nodded and went back to staring at those tiny perfect fingers.

It was strange because even though I had proof from my break-up with Barney that things ending with Christopher would become less raw, I still didn't believe it. It was like being shown evidence and going, 'Yeah but nope.'

I was embarrassed to be grieving for a month-and-a-half-long fling rather than an eight-year relationship and was glad to have Barney as my cover, but felt deceitful about the fact that I was privately mourning the loss of someone I barely knew. It was scary and unnatural how someone could come into your life like that for all of five weeks and then just disappear: owe you nothing, have no ties to you, just a weeny slither of time with them and then bam. Gone.

The problem, I decided, was that I hadn't had a chance to see Christopher's flaws, or rather I'd seen them but hadn't felt them. I hadn't lived through them until they exhausted me or bored me or caused me sufficient pain that I could see the advantages of not getting to see him again, even though I knew he couldn't give me what I wanted long term.

Early in the evening I put on my mother's coat, which came down to my ankles like a wizard's cape, and walked out into the garden where the autumn sun had just finished setting. The sky was a rich pale blue and the moon was fully out and I was thinking (of course) about Christopher. Maybe it was just the light and the air but I was suddenly overwhelmed with longing; could love be boiled down to these elements? At least the first part of love: the part that was pure wanting, void of any commitment. Or was that just infatuation? How was one meant to know the difference?

I recalled how I had loved Barney from pretty much the get-go. 'But you can't have loved me right from the beginning,' he'd said when I told him this after we'd started going out properly. 'OK maybe not the promise part of love,' I'd said, 'but the other bit – the I'd do anything to see you at any moment of the day and pretty much exclusively think of you – that bit I did.'

The following morning I left the house for the first time in over a week and walked to the beach, where I sat on the sun-lit shingles and began reading *The Golden Bowl*, which I had ordered online on Christopher's recommendation of late Henry James novels. But it was too dense and made me cross to have to keep untangling the sentences – as well as it being too reminiscent of Christopher – so I put it back in my bag and listened to a group of girls nearby talk about how their gap years were going so far. It was mostly very dull but not quite uninteresting enough for me not to tune into at points. They were dressed in thin jackets and ripped jeans that exposed their knees and ankles and didn't seem to be even slightly shivering, whereas I looked like I belonged in an alpine resort, even though it was only mid-October.

I googled, *Why do I get so cold?* and then scrolled though my search history.

Did frank o'hara write novels?
Aukus deal what is it
Christopher Hamlin sister historian balham

I hadn't previously thought of myself as an obsessive person but was struggling to come up with a more suitable term. I didn't feel obsessed in a stalker way because I had too much self-restraint to message him and because (not being on social media) I lacked the technical nous to follow him online, but privately, in terms of my thoughts, I felt I might be. I typed *obsession synonym* into Google but none of the other options – *unhinged, devoted, manic* – were in any way preferable.

I still hadn't replied to Christopher's message even though a week had now passed since he'd sent it. It was unusual for me to leave things unsaid but in this instance I couldn't see the point in sharing anything I had to say. 'It's annoying and painful that I fell for you so hard.' 'I guess I grossly misjudged my ability to get attached.' Etc., etc. And any attempt to convince him otherwise by trying to claim that I wasn't attached would be a) laughable and b) redundant. It was abundantly clear my plan had failed.

I spent the next few days doing lots of staring at the sea and making stilted conversation with my mother and grandfather. I also did a lot of thinking about Christopher but I think that's a given at this point and doesn't need further noting.

After a further fortnight of languishing in Brighton, it was time to face Antoine. Having graciously accepted my absence at our last quarterly drink, he had sent a message saying that we were at risk of missing our second quarter, which would give our meeting the unacceptable ring of a biannual board meeting.

Antoine was a Martinican antiquarian bookseller who owned a shop in St James's around the corner from the Asset Management firm where I had been temping several summers ago as an Executive Assistant. The regular EA had gone on holiday to Thailand for two weeks and had told me before she left that she hadn't had a proper holiday for five and a half years so I was only to contact her if something hugely bad like a cyber-attack or fraud investigation suddenly took place.

I had wandered into Antoine's shop on my lunch break and spent my entire day's earnings in one whack, purchasing a beautiful bound copy of *I Capture the Castle*, which was my comfort read whenever I was ill or sad or just wanted perking up a bit. When I told Antoine this he looked at me solemnly and said, 'You strike me as someone with soul.' I returned each day on my lunch break to chat to him and browse the store's collection and at the end of the week he had taken me for a martini at Dukes in Mayfair.

Antoine and I only ever drank martinis together and would meet quarterly at Dukes, which had its own martini trolley. He was very grand and did his weekly shop at Fortnum's. He was also a big-time Oscar Wilde fan and threw a party every year downstairs at The Savoy in his honour. I always met good and interesting people at these parties and would google them afterwards and often discover they were quite famous, but there was nothing new in my not knowing this at the time.

He had once been married to a Finnish woman, but this was before he and I had met. He almost always had a girlfriend, and rarely the same one, but he threw himself so fully into each relationship, like a weathered boat going back out into the storm.

We had never slept together because he was old enough to be my father and because he knew I was in a long-term relationship even though for the purposes of our meetings we pretended Barney didn't exist.

Nobody in my life had ever met him. He existed as an entirely separate entity. The first and only time I ever referenced him to Erica was to say, 'My friend Antoine has given up canapés for Lent.' She held her hand up in front of my face like a stop sign and said, 'Tell me nothing more. I have the most perfectly complete image of his character.'

Going back to London, where I hadn't been since that last time I saw Christopher, I knew would require a level of confidence I currently didn't have but told myself that if I could make my voice and gestures appear confident this might, in turn, generate the actual feeling. And so, I dolled myself up and trotted off to Dukes with a false spring in my step even though inside I felt boulderous.

At the station it said there were delays due to a shortage of drivers and I asked a guard what platform the train was expected to arrive on so I could be first in line when it came. Antoine didn't tolerate lateness, or at least only in extreme cases of force majeure, and even then it was hard to imagine him not being punctual for Dukes' martini trolley. The guard shouted to one of his colleagues across the platform, 'This girl wants to know what platform for the next Victoria train.' I liked the fact he had referred to me as a girl and not a woman, and felt encouraged that the afternoon might yet be salvaged.

I had never wanted to be seen as a woman, not even as an adolescent. I'd wanted to stay young and cute for ever and thought other teenagers were stupid and mad for wanting to grow up, for favouring independence over protection. Even as a child, I could see how good we had it compared to the adults. Unlike the girls in my class who wanted to grow breasts and get their periods, I had cried when I got mine. 'But I don't want it!' I had said to my mother when she found my knickers stained with blood that I had put in the laundry basket without comment, hoping I might deny its existence by not acknowledging it. 'I'm afraid it doesn't operate a returns policy,' she had said, soaking them in a bowl of Biotex. 'And by the time it does, you'll want it back.' I later worked out my mother was going through the menopause at the time.

I was nineteen minutes late to meet Antoine but he must have seen my inner fragility because he decided not to comment as he rose to kiss me on either cheek. 'I'm not going to insult your pain by not referencing it, but neither do I intend to dwell on it. From thirty onwards there will always be someone announcing a marriage, a birth, a divorce or a death. We cannot stop life's quarterly rituals for such things. Not even heartbreak.'

He gestured to the martini trolley, which arrived on cue, and we watched in silent appreciation as we always did, as the barman fixed my drink and wheeled off to the other side of the lounge. 'To your presence,' said Antoine, raising his glass. He took a sip and swiftly announced that he had begun weekly life-drawing classes since we'd last met and was keen to show me his latest piece, which he now took out of a poster-tube and unscrolled in front of me.

It was surprisingly bad and looked as though it had been drawn by a child. He had shaded very heavily around the pubic area, which I thought was uncharacteristically prudish for him, until he offered up, 'I did my best to depict her voluminous bush but consider it such a waste when a pudendum bears more resemblance to a beard than genitalia.' He paused and then sighed and said, 'But I suppose my sex aren't meant to hold or voice an opinion on the female anatomy any more.'

'I think you're allowed to still have preferences just so long as you mainly keep them to yourself,' I offered up.

'This is why one must have friends, to bridge the gap between one's thoughts and the public sphere.'

I felt Antoine's eloquence often made his points sound more profound than they actually were. He was someone who said not that much exceptionally well. Rhetoric, that was what this was called, wasn't it? Speaking for the art of speaking. Hadn't Socrates been executed for this? Or had that been for calling other people out for having too much of it? I made a mental note to google which way around this was.

We were nearing the end of our martinis and on to the subject of Antoine's latest partner – a woman called Heather who shared his penchant for Shibari and his distaste of condiments – when I took myself by surprise and proposed that maybe he and I ought to have sex, considering we liked each other's company and clearly liked looking at each other enough to drink together four times a year, so, yes, why not? I was hurting and wanted to be held by someone who I trusted not to further hurt me.

He took hold of the stem of his frosted glass and stroked it between his thumb and forefinger before taking my hand across the table. His palm felt papery and warm.

'My concern is that sleeping with you would be distressingly nice. And for that reason I'm going to decline your offer because I don't know where I'd personally, or indeed where we'd jointly, go from there.'

He had rejected me so graciously and kindly that I didn't even feel embarrassed, or at least not as much as I felt other things, like gratitude and fondness. I smiled and, trying not to cry, said, 'Thank you. For saying no and for the way you said it.'

He squeezed my hand before letting go of it and gestured to the waiter to return with the trolley.

Out on the street as we said goodbye, he took his silk pocket square and placed it into my hand. 'Courage and appetite, my friend. Courage and appetite. Those are the only two requirements for a good life.'

He started to walk away and I called after him, 'But I feel so weak.'

'All the more reason to be hungry and brave.' He said this still walking, with his head turned over his shoulder as he raised his hand to hail a taxi and narrowly missed being hit by an electric scooter as he stepped off the kerb.

As I wandered down Piccadilly, which looked impressively festive with its stringed lights and window displays, I thought about Antoine's parting advice. Presumably this was an instruction to get back out there dating-wise, but Antoine was too classy and couth to phrase it so directly.

Outside Fortnum & Mason, the doorman smiled, doffing his top hat and wishing me a good evening; it gave me an unexpected surge of hope. I thought, Misty, get a hold of yourself. This city is so full of kind and decent strangers.

He's being paid to be kind and decent, you fool.

So what? Not all the kind and decent people are being paid to be that way.

He's even older than Antoine.

I'm not going to date the *actual* doorman.

You're so desperate, I wouldn't put it past you.

He's an emblem of possibility, of what's out there, OK?

It was a depressingly petty exchange but at least the voice was in agreement that I needed to get over Christopher and get back on track with finding a long-term partner. Christopher couldn't offer me what I ultimately wanted. He had been a useful, albeit painful, decoy highlighting my need for change. I would implement his feedback and turn myself into someone who another person wouldn't feel 'responsible' for and want to end things with, so that next time I met someone I liked (and who I could feasibly have a future with) I wouldn't get caught in the same trap as I did with Christopher of coming on too strongly and making them pull away. I felt galvanized by my plan of action and returned home to Brighton in much zestier spirits than when I had left, soon quashed by my mother's insistence that we begin another documentary – this time about abandoned coal mines.

Having deleted Hinge, I didn't want to return to it because it made me think of Christopher, and so on Remembrance Sunday I downloaded two other dating apps and over the course of the next couple of months, went on several dates with several different men. Here is a brief snapshot of highlights – and by highlights, I mean things that happened that were not necessarily good or bad, but noteworthy.

The first date was with a man whose name is irrelevant but perhaps his job is worth stating because I think he expected me to be more impressed by it than I was. He was a film producer who had recently been nominated for a BAFTA for a documentary about BASE jumping, and he looked quite surprised by how nonplussed I was when he told me this. But I barely watched films or television whereas I chomped through a couple of novels a week so it didn't hold the same allure for me as if he'd been an author, shortlisted for the Booker. Anyway, the date wasn't awful or excellent, or rather some bits of it were verging on excellent because he was funny and clever – although he was also too performative and full of 'bits' (and wit without sincerity has always left me cold) – but the thing that really made me certain I didn't want to see him again was the sex, specifically the things he said to me during it. 'You have sensational eyes. I absolutely insist you look at me with them.' The reason I wasn't looking at him was because I was crying a bit that he wasn't Christopher whereas if I closed them I could a) hide my tears and b) think of Christopher.

Afterwards we lay there and he said, 'Your personality's a bit like your cunt. It's quite closed and dry and makes me work quite hard to get let in.' And even though this made me shudder as a line, I was so thrilled I wanted to immediately call Christopher and say, 'I did it! I shut myself off! I'm now officially less open and needy!' But saying this would have opened me up again, and also we'd never spoken on the phone so that would have been a lot weird to launch straight in with this declaration on our very first call. But it made me wish I could start over with Christopher – meet him for the first time having mastered this skill – but then again, had I really mastered anything or was I simply being myself? And the difference was that I didn't feel a connection to this BAFTA man, whereas with Christopher I'd felt this mad connection right from the start. It's got to be one of life's greatest tragedies, hasn't it? All right, fine, inconveniences: that we unfurl so readily – are blooming bursting sprawling hearts (ugh too much!) – for the people we want to love us, and remain tight enigmatic buds for those we have zero interest in ever seeing again. But I kept this thought to myself – at risk of sounding like a poor imitation of Oscar Wilde (no doubt inspired by my recent drink with Antoine).

The next notable date was with a barrister who lived and worked near the Barbican and who requested we meet at a bar very near his chambers because he was working on a highly important case for a highly important trial that was highly confidential. I said that was highly fine because I was highly available and had no time constraints or commitments whatsoever. I think he could tell during the date that I was a bit lost but didn't want to acknowledge this even though I kept bringing it up – how lost I was – because he was hoping we might sleep together, and I didn't not want this either.

I'll cut to the morning after because the date itself was

unremarkable in that it was good enough for me to want to go home with him but not so good that I cared particularly about whether I saw him again. The only context needed from the night is that during the evening part of the date I must have told him that I could technically drive and that I had a licence (both of which are true) but that I couldn't remember how to drive and hadn't driven since I was seventeen (also true), because the next morning he asked if I'd like to go for a quick breakfast and when I said sure, he said, 'Good, in that case you can drive us.'

I assumed he was joking, and still assumed he was joking when out on the street he handed me his car keys. I handed them back to him and said, 'You'd definitely regret that.' But he handed them back to me again and said, 'I'm serious.' I said I was also serious about not remembering how to drive and that this was a seriously bad idea, but he was so insistent that in the end I said, 'OK fine, but I'm warning you now, I'll probably crash.' And that's exactly what I did. It wasn't a bad crash – I just rammed his car into the side of the kerb and up onto the pavement because I couldn't remember which pedal the brake was. Luckily we rolled back onto the road and nobody was on the pavement and so nobody got hurt but he looked quite shocked, which I thought was understandable but also a bit obvious as I'd literally just told him that this is what would happen. I said that to him, I said, 'I'm really sorry but I did warn you.' And he was very good about it and said, 'You did, you absolutely did, I just didn't believe that anyone could forget how to drive.' When I told Erica what had happened, her only response was, 'That's ridiculous. Who *drives* to breakfast?' which I hadn't intended to be the main point of the anecdote, but was nonetheless a reasonable takeaway.

I didn't end up seeing the barrister again because he said his next available window was in three weeks' time after another highly urgent deadline, and despite my abundance of free time, I told him I didn't have time to wait that long because it gave us a status imbalance that wasn't healthy or good for my self-esteem.

The third and final date of note was with a biology teacher called Andy. He gets a name because I ended up seeing him for a whole month, during which time we went on five dates – the same number of dates I'd ever gone on with Christopher, even though I only felt a fraction of feeling towards Andy by comparison. But he was kind as well as clever, and he often made me feel clever, which was something Christopher made me feel only a bit of the time. He was big into paddleboarding, which I didn't mind, but he talked about it a lot, which I did mind; I was into people getting their kicks in whatever way suited them, but unless it was a shared hobby it was tiring to hear it banged on about all the time.

I liked the idea of seeing Andy and of him being there in the background of my thoughts, but the actual impetus to see him decreased with each day that I didn't see him.

'I'm not crazy about him but I'm not sure if that's a sign of my growing self-sufficiency or just that he's the wrong person and I'm not that into him?' I said to Erica as she turned our videocall to audio so she could extract Sellotape from her girl twin's hair.

'I think if you have any doubt then you owe it to yourself to keep seeing him,' she said.

I agreed and then proudly told her that as of last week I had progressed in my physio programme to impact training so that I could now hop and jump across the floor as though playing an imaginary game of hopscotch, and that I attributed this milestone to my newly acquired state of independence, free from pining after Christopher or Barney.

'Not to undermine your sense of empowerment, but do you think you might be attributing things to your independence that you could equally have accomplished in a state of pining?'

'Quite possibly. But at the same time I don't think the two things are unrelated.' Could this level of growth be reached when the mind was fixated on somebody else? And even if it could – was it?

The following Saturday afternoon I went on another date with Andy.

During the date we bumped into my mother on the seafront and ended up walking with her up through town, following which she invited Andy back to the house for a cup of tea – a herbal one because it was after four o'clock, which was her cut-off window for caffeinated drinks, and she automatically applied this rule to everybody.

He was very good with her and asked lots of questions about her life and her work, which Barney had never done, and I could tell she liked him even though she was keen not to show this. I couldn't imagine Christopher inside my family living room. The image of him sitting on my grandmother's old chaise longue was completely incongruous to me. I wasn't infatuated with Andy the way I'd been with Christopher, nor was I dependent on him the way I'd been with Barney. But could this just be what healthy relationships felt like?

As I said goodbye to him by the front door, I told him, 'The fact that even my mother likes you speaks parsecs' (a word I had learnt last Tuesday and had been looking for an opportunity to use, although I wasn't sure if I'd pronounced it correctly).

During dinner that evening my mother let it be known that she approved of the fact that Andy was a teacher and that he seemed straightforward. I scrunched my face up when she said this, making it clear I was enticed by neither of these things.

'You don't have an obligation to complicated men,' she said.

'I know I don't have an obligation to them, I just happen to be attracted to them.'

'Perhaps you could try being unattracted to them,' she said, but I could tell that even she knew this was like asking someone not to sneeze or think an inappropriate thought. It was out of my control – not who I dated, but who I wanted to date. That bit wasn't up to me, was it?

The next day she left a *Guardian* article torn out of the paper on the kitchen table with the subheading, *Chemistry v. Compatibility: The Two Are Not Always Aligned*. She had circled in red pen, *Try to focus on how you want to feel, rather than fixed attributes or characteristics that you think will make you happy*. How did Andy make me feel? Mostly lovely. How had Christopher made me feel? Excited and anxious and, increasingly by the end, not lovely. But oh the longing! There was a kind of loveliness to that too.

As it turned out, it was thanks to a single line that things ended with Andy. He told me he wanted to take me to his *favourite* Pizza Express. 'But they're all the same!' cried Erica, when I told her. 'Well, exactly!' I said. When I told this to my mother she looked exasperated and said, 'At least tell me there were other factors and that the line just clinched it.' But Erica agreed that the line alone was enough to shatter even the strongest foundation, including a marriage. When I repeated this to my mother she said I was being picky and asked, 'What exactly do you want from a partner?'

'Quite a few things,' I replied. 'But crucially someone who doesn't have a favourite chain restaurant.'

After this, I deleted all the apps from my phone and turned my focus to writing. I didn't write anything of my own during this time but I read other people's books and made a list of the things they had in common:

Characters who don't say what they're really thinking
Characters who don't feel much
Characters who don't really like themselves and/or other people
Front covers of women with their heads in their hands

I tried writing to the above formula but it didn't sound like me and it wasn't very good; plus, I didn't really care about what I was saying. What was I even saying? I decided other people did those things much better than me. What was my USP? What was I an expert in, other than not knowing stuff? I pictured my torso like one of those Velcro catch pads from the nineties. I so wanted to be more into current affairs and politics and science and things I thought were more worthy of my time and attention, but each time I walked into a library or bookshop or picked up a newspaper or had a conversation, I gravitated towards relationships. I couldn't help myself; I was obsessed with them. Love and sex and attachment styles . . . They occupied an endless loop inside my head to the extent it felt quite indecent.

I got old classic European novels and philosophy books out of the library, hoping they might answer my questions, such as: was it better to love vastly or specifically? To be selfish or sacrificial? In terms of what, though? Being a good person? Being a happier person? How could one fix on anything when there was a contingent question to every question? At this point my only fixed conclusion was that loving someone to the extent I couldn't breathe when I contemplated them not being there wasn't at all ideal. But I still wasn't sure what an alternative or happy medium would look like.

Some of the books I read were set in another time or country in which the characters were living through a war or blight or collective ordeal of some kind. These wars were only ever peripheral to the main storyline, which focused on the characters' interpersonal relationships, but it was still there, humming dangerously in the background. And even though I felt lucky in comparison not to have any first-hand experience of war, I also felt a bit jealous of these characters and their wars for giving meaningful backdrop to their lives, while I didn't have anything meaningful to fight for or against, to give weight and substance to mine.

When I mentioned this to Dan when we met up for an Extinction Rebellion swarm, which involved us walking out onto Old Street roundabout and blocking the traffic in a series of seven-minute intervals, he said, 'But we literally just stood in front of a bus. That's pretty full-on.' I paused while I adjusted the sticks of my banner and thought about this. Was it possible that I was actually living through history without even realizing it? On the way back to Brighton I considered how I had stood in front of that bus extremely casually in a way that had made it feel oddly unremarkable, but was this just an example of things never feeling as profound in the moment as they did either imagining them happening in the future or reflecting on them as past events? After this, I found I could read books that involved war a tiny bit more comfortably but still not fully at ease because my climate war did not currently extend any danger to me – only danger to my future-self and to my presently non-existent children I might never have.

That morning I thought of specific examples of progress, like the invention of the light bulb and the almost-eradication of polio, and then the fact I hadn't thought about Christopher until 11.04 a.m.

By now it was the middle of January and three months since I had last seen him, which meant I had spent more time getting over him than I had spent with him, which felt like an imbalanced equation. Nevertheless, when he entered my mind that morning it was with a curiosity and appreciation of the time we'd spent together as opposed to a painful burn that had filled the previous days and weeks. And so, ironically or fittingly or just coincidentally, it was later that day that I bumped into him, outside Brighton train station.

He looked surprised to see me even though I was the one out of the two of us who lived less than half an hour away.

'Hi,' I said, pleased by the calmness of my tone. I wasn't calm at all on the inside but also my heart wasn't thumping as much as I thought it might be when I'd imagined us meeting.

'Hello.' I thought he looked a bit ashamed but perhaps I was just projecting my own feelings onto him.

'You're in my city,' I said, hoping this would amuse him, pleased when he smiled and said, 'I was invited to give a presentation at the university's research institute.'

'How did it go?'

'Well, I think. Although there's not much audience feedback so it's hard to know.'

'You should put some jokes in next time, make it more like stand-up.'

'I think I'd rather live in ignorance,' he said, smiling again. 'How are you?'

I couldn't remember him ever asking such a generalized question as this, but perhaps even he thought that enquiring into the specifics of what I'd eaten or read or observed that day might be a bit intrusive after three months of silence.

'I'm beginning to be good again,' I said, hoping to convey an alluring level of enigma but also because this was just the truth.

He paused, looking at me quizzically, and then said, 'You seem good.' I smiled in agreement but didn't say anything as I waited to see what would happen next. He kept looking at me, his pupils flickering up and down and to the side as though he was trying to work something out.

'I was going to get on the next train but, would you . . . would you like to get a coffee?'

He sounded hesitant as he asked this, and I wondered if he was asking out of guilt, obligation, intrigue or even – dare I hope – desire. I didn't answer right away because I wasn't sure if this was an awful idea that would offset the time I had just spent trying to get over him, or whether this was a reasonable and appropriate suggestion given the abrupt ending of our last meeting, and would provide closure. Not only that but presumably it would allow me to see whether I had really changed at all in becoming less attached. So anyway, for all the above points (and because I was still insanely attracted to him, which is probably the stronger point), I said, 'OK, yes.'

I took him to a coffee shop on Trafalgar Street which had a hunter-green exterior and earthenware crockery that felt aspirational. He waited until we had ordered our drinks and then said, 'You never replied to my message.'

'No,' I said. 'I guess I didn't.'

I felt my energy was more contained than it had ever been in his company, and in an effort to keep it this way, I decided not to expound on my reason for not replying.

I asked after Rowan and Sara and he was concise and vague in his response, replying, 'They're both well.'

He asked if I was writing and I said, 'No, just doing lots of reading and word learning.'

'Word learning?'

And so I told him about the app I had downloaded that sent me a new word every day, only it was quite erratic and inconsistent with its choices so that often it was really basic and I already knew it like yesterday's 'lido' or it was so obscure that I couldn't see what occasion I'd ever have to use it.

'Like what?'

'Like I can't remember the actual word now but last week there was one that meant *a neighbour whose house is on fire.*'

'Ucalegon?'

I rolled my eyes and said, 'Only you would know that.'

He smiled and asked, 'What's today's?'

I said I hadn't checked yet but would check now. I brought it up on my phone and read aloud, '*Wantum.*'

'How are you spelling that?'

'W-a-n-t-u-m.'

'No, I don't know that.'

'Are you going to guess or shall I tell you?'

'Tell me.'

'A quantifiable deficiency or desire.'

Christopher nodded and looked pleased to have learnt something new.

'That makes sense. A cross between quantum and wanting.'

There was a pause, then, where we looked at each other for an intense amount of time, and I felt seized with yearning. *Uh oh, here you go again*, chimed the voice. *He's going to kiss you, just like your first date, and leave you wildly unable to get over him.* But what was my alternative? To not get his kiss? I wanted it!

Then I realized there was a third option, and chose this instead. I leant in and kissed him – and it was, yes, as extremely good as I'd remembered – but this time, it was me who broke away first and said, 'I should get going, I'm technically meant to be at work right now.'

He looked surprised but attracted to this new version of me who had places to go and ended kisses. As we stood up it seemed silently acknowledged that we would meet again – which he then verbally acknowledged by saying, 'If you'd like to see me some more, perhaps you could message me. Which I suppose is another way of saying, I'd like to see you, but don't want to make any assumptions.'

'Good, because I don't know about you but normally I reserve my kisses for people I have no interest in seeing again.'

He did one of his full laughs and said, 'I shall await your instruction.'

Even though there was a semblance of trying to make it appear that this time around I had more power, this wasn't actually true because I still only worked three days a week and had no child or partner, which meant despite our best efforts to alter the availability dynamic, our meetings remained dictated by Christopher's schedule.

Unsurprisingly, his next free evening wasn't until the following Thursday (eight days after our meeting in Brighton). It was ironic that open relationships gave off the outside impression of being heady and spontaneous when in actual fact they took a lot of advance planning and acute organizational skills.

Christopher had asked if I minded coming all the way to London and I'd said I didn't mind as I had other things to do there aside from see him (which was a half-truth that then became the full truth when I promptly booked to see an exhibition at the Hayward Gallery of an artist I had never heard of but thought I ought to know of given how much billboard publicity she was getting).

His faculty office was in Bloomsbury but he suggested we meet at a pub in Clerkenwell. On the bus on the way there from the gallery the driver suddenly diverted us without announcement and some people on the bus, myself included, got cross and started – not shouting – but saying quite loudly and semi-aggressively, 'Hey, driver, what are you doing? You're taking us completely in the wrong direction.' Etc. The driver didn't answer us but carried on driving the wrong route for two more roads until at last he stopped and as a bunch of us got off, someone said, 'That was a complete waste of time and money,' and we all agreed in rude tones. The driver just shrugged and said, 'I'm not allowed to talk when I'm driving and I got radioed there was a road closure.'

As I waited for the next bus I considered how all of us had laid into that driver as if he had purposefully gone the wrong way and maliciously contrived to keep us from getting to where we wanted to be, when all he'd done was drive down the wrong street for a couple of minutes.

Long term, I thought I wanted to move back to London because it made me hungry to achieve things, and because it sourced me with ideas and people who I felt were good for my writing and made me feel I was – not *not* alone, but – less alone than if I had lived in a different city. But there were other things about the place that I didn't like. I didn't think it made me the kindest version of myself. Just minutes earlier I had been listening to a podcast about a school of philosophy that teaches 'do unto others as you would do unto yourself', which lots of philosophers had decided was probably a good maxim to live by, and I agreed, I really did agree! And yet, there I was, so hardened to that bus driver, so live-wired. It alarmed me, how quickly I had forgotten to be decent.

When I got to the pub Christopher was standing by the bar with his massive-but-proportional palms placed on the counter. I had my rucksack with me and he looked as if he was going to comment on it but instead asked what I would like to drink and I surprised myself by saying whiskey. It was a punchy choice to kick off the evening with but I had never drunk whiskey with him before and I think it was a subconscious or even conscious attempt to make the evening different to any other evening we had spent together. I was determined to alter the pattern we had previously fallen into and feared that the slightest repetition had the potential to revert us to our former dynamic.

'Strong choice,' he said, nodding. 'Ice?'

'Yes please.'

I left him at the bar and went to sit at a table in the corner. While I was waiting, I thought about the fact that he hadn't used the expression 'on the rocks', as I had often heard people say, and reflected that, like me, Christopher didn't use expressions, which was something I hadn't registered until now. My reason for not using them was due to not knowing them – having not grown up with them as they were not in my mother's vocabulary or ethos – but Christopher knew almost everything so presumably his reason must be a different one.

He came back from the bar holding two tumblers with ice and whiskey, and I felt validated that he had copied my order. We raised our glasses and made eye contact before we drank. When he had finished sipping, I saw his lips were wet. It made me reach up and wipe my own lips even though they still felt dry.

'How was the exhibition?' he asked. I was surprised he had remembered I was going to this.

'Good,' I said. 'And even better when I looked at the captions for context.'

'Should the art speak for itself? The age-old question.'

'Ideally, yes, but if it doesn't then I'll take whatever steer I can get.'

Christopher smiled and told me about his friend Ahir who refused to read the plaques inside galleries or the jacket of books because he believed that it was the art's responsibility to deliver the requisite information and that if it didn't then that was the artist's problem. I said it sounded more like Ahir's problem, and Christopher laughed and said probably Ahir felt the same way but was trapped by the fact he had constructed his character around being a contrarian and now felt obliged to uphold this.

'Poor him,' I said, even though I felt a bit jealous of him for having a fixed point within himself to hold on to, where currently I felt I had lost mine, making me wonder if I had even ever had one in the first place.

It wasn't really that related but then I told Christopher that one of the girls in my tutor group had brought a peanut butter sandwich cut into quarters and a Granny Smith apple inside a lunch box into school every day, without variation, for five years, and that I thought about this a weirdly big amount and wondered whether she was still eating this for lunch now she was in her thirties and how come some people need so much more and less consistency than others.

'Where are you on the consistency scale?' he asked.

I considered his question and then said, 'I thought I was nearer the peanut butter end. But the way I've been living these past few months seems to suggest otherwise.'

He smiled and nodded his head, as if in approval, but didn't comment.

We spoke about lots of stuff: both big ideas and just tiny observations about events and objects and people – people each of us knew, as well as famous people Christopher knew and I didn't. Topics that were not inherently interesting in and of themselves (aka plants) fired me up when Christopher spoke about them; he even had an angle on soil!

When he turned to the side I noticed how similarly shaped his nose was to mine. Did I just want to sleep with my own profile? Alarmingly conceited if so.

Three hours had now apparently passed because the barmaid was ringing the bell for last orders.

'I didn't want to be presumptuous,' said Christopher, 'so I didn't book us anywhere to stay but I have provisionally checked at the bar and there are rooms available upstairs.'

'I think that could also be interpreted as presumptuous.'

He looked a bit naughty then, as though he had just been told off, and smiled out of the corner of his mouth, which was extremely sexy while being strangely childlike.

'I was hoping to label it as initiative, but you're right.'

'The problem is,' I said, trying to sound casual, 'I don't think I'm very good at the sex bit without the feelings bit, at least not with you. You'd leave in the morning and I'd feel quite bereft, which kind of offsets my wanting to sleep with you, even though I hugely do.'

'That's entirely fair and reasonable, and I hope you don't think less of me for asking.'

'I don't.'

We smiled at each other and he said, 'You seem different to how you were last time I saw you.'

'Including how I was in Brighton?'

'No. You were like this in Brighton too or else I wouldn't have suggested coffee.'

'You mean I was less clingy than before?'

'That's your word choice, not mine.'

'Your word was *responsible* for me. That's what you said in your message.' I left a beat and then asked, 'Do you still feel that now?'

'I don't. Otherwise I wouldn't have mentioned the room.'

'I do feel a bit different.' Neither of us said anything and the silence felt charged, like a build-up of static. 'Can I ask you something?'

He nodded and I said, 'I couldn't work out if I was imagining it or if it wasn't reciprocated but at moments I felt so connected to you and then I'd feel you pushing me away.'

'You weren't imagining it. I'd started to feel things I didn't particularly want to feel.'

'You mean towards me?'

'No. I mean, I had those too, but they were fine, they were good. It was other feelings that I wasn't so up for.'

'Like what?'

He breathed in deeply so that I saw his chest move up and down inside his shirt, and then said as he exhaled, 'Like perhaps why I'm able to have frank conversations like these with you and not with my partner and the mother of my child.' He paused for a moment, gritting his teeth. 'There's an intimacy you seem to access in me that I'm . . . not used to and, well, not all that comfortable with, despite wanting to be.'

There was something about knowing this, that I had got inside him and affected him too, that made me sit very upright, as though there was one of those invisible posture strings attached to the top of my head that someone was pulling.

'What would it look like, this time around, if we did sleep together? I mean, if we went upstairs now, what would happen after?'

'That would depend on what you want but I think ideally, if you were up for it, it could be the beginning of something.'

I cocked my head to the side, intrigued. 'How do you mean?'

'Well, it would be different to before, for one thing. I guess we'd be embarking on seeing each other without a fixed endpoint, for as long as it felt good for both of us.'

'What about Sara?'

'She's . . . understanding of the situation.'

'You mean she knows about me already?'

He nodded and then added, 'Yes.' I was shocked by this, and then felt naive for feeling shocked.

'What did you tell her?'

'I told her we'd started seeing each other while she was away and that I was seeing you again tonight and that I'd like to go on seeing you after tonight but that this would depend on your response.'

I turned and looked at the fireplace and then across at the thick stained-glass window to the side of it. This was not a situation I had expected to find myself in. If I said yes to Christopher's offering then I would be abandoning the things I thought I still wanted: marriage and monogamy, at least for the foreseeable future. But if I said yes then I would also get to go on seeing him, and even though he was tied to Sara and Rowan, he would still protect me from being alone.

I looked down at my glass, at the dregs of whiskey now diluted by the melted ice, and thought about how at the point of no return characters always choose to keep going with the adventure because otherwise it would kill the story, and how I felt the same about my own story; the desire to plough on and continue to see where I might end up was impossible to say no to.

'Yes,' I said, looking back up at him.

'You're sure?' he asked, smiling hesitantly.

I nodded and said 'yes' again, very affirmatively.

It still wasn't love, or was it? Not the promise part, but the feeling part. It felt as though it might be this for both of us as he followed me up the floorboarded staircase and onto the landing.

The room was furnished with a canopy bed and dark wooden dresser. There was an old-fashioned milk jug with stems of dried lavender on top of the dresser and hanging above it was an oil painting of a wheat field or some kind of crop.

'It's got the vibes of a country inn,' I said, taking off my shoes.

'Minus the view,' said Christopher, moving across to the window and peering down at the street below.

'*Tired of London, tired of life.*' This was a bit of a leap as a response but I wanted to segue into what I said next. 'Do you know, for years I went around thinking Oscar Wilde said that. It just sounded like something he'd say.'

'Did he not?' asked Christopher.

'Nope. Samuel Johnson.'

'That's the second fact you've told me this fortnight,' he said, looking impressed.

'Don't get used to it. My ignorance is still prodigious.'

He smiled and asked, 'Is that today's word of the day?'

'Yesterday's. I just thought it was a fun adjective for ignorance.'

'It's a good pairing.'

We stood smiling at each other until Christopher said, 'Come here,' which sounded strangely assertive for him.

I didn't move straight away. I knew I would go to him but

wanted to eke out this moment before I did. It was as though the less of myself I gave to him, the more of me he wanted, which I had heard existed as a phenomenon, but never yet experienced in person, as I had never yet succeeded in giving anyone less of me (except for BAFTA man, but I hadn't wanted him so that didn't count).

I took a bottle of water from the tray on the bedside table and poured some into a glass. I sipped from it before moving halfway towards him and sitting on the edge of the bed.

'Do you think if we hadn't bumped into each other you'd have messaged me?' I asked.

He moved to sit beside me and said, 'I thought about it a lot. I even got as far as typing out a message to you, several times in fact.'

'What stopped you sending it?'

'Partly the fact you hadn't replied to my message above it. To get back in touch with you out of the blue would have felt . . .'

'Irresponsible?' I raised my eyebrows and smiled as I said this.

He returned my smile but then looked serious. 'A bit, yes. But also. Also, I was being cowardly. It felt easier to just keep going and try to ignore how you made me feel rather than confront it. I did hope I'd see you by chance, though. I kept wanting that to happen.'

'Me too. Only I'm glad we didn't bump into each other any sooner than we did. I think if I'd still been the same version of me as when you ended things, it would have been easier for you to go on ignoring me.'

He leant in towards me then and took my whole face in his hands (ginormous cheeks and all) and it topped any prior tenderness that had come before it.

'It would have been hard to ignore any version of you, Misty.'

'I don't think you've ever said my name out loud before. Do you find it silly? My friend Erica does.'

'I find you lots of things but I don't find anything about you silly.'

'Lie down,' I said.

He lay back with his feet still slightly touching the floor while I unbuttoned his shirt and opened it out, kissing his chest without taking it off. As I unbuckled his trousers, tugging them down to the tops of his thighs, he immediately went hard. When I put him in my mouth, I felt myself becoming wet from the noises he was making; I'd never had that before when I'd gone down on Barney. It had only ever been for him but doing it to Christopher turned me on too. So many discoveries, so much excavation. Where and when would it end?

'I think I'll come if you keep doing that,' he said. I stopped and brought my mouth up to his; he kissed me deeply and gently. It was like being inside a cool dark canyon and hearing the trickle of water.

I took my trousers off and he started to lift me on top of him, but I said, 'No. You go on top.' Oddly, we had never had sex in this position. Even though he held himself up by his arms he still felt enormous lying on me like that, but I wanted his weight. I wanted the press of him, to be subsumed and engulfed by him. I thought of that line from *The Crucible*, 'More weight!' And how that was what I wanted too.

Very suddenly he pulled out of me and came across my stomach. He took off his shirt and wiped himself from me and then kissed the bit on either side of my chest where my rib bones were most pronounced.

'Did you come?' he asked.

'No, but it was still crazily good.'

He moved down the bed then and put his fingers and tongue inside me. It was ticklish for a minute and I thought

I'd have to ask him to stop but then his strokes got firmer or I just got used to their lightness, and I could hear myself starting to murmur and feel my pelvis tilting upwards.

When I came, my hips rose up as though they were on a hinge and stayed in the air for quite a few seconds before juddering back down again. I had pins and needles in my arms and couldn't feel my hands and had to bring them up to my face to check they were still there.

'What are you doing?' asked Christopher, amused.

'Checking all of me is still here.'

He laughed and then kissed me again; I could taste myself on his lips, which I didn't love but would tolerate a thousand times over in exchange for his kiss.

We lay there, half clothed, holding each other and I said, 'You know what I realized when we stopped seeing each other?'

'What's that?'

'That you don't really talk about yourself and that makes you very intriguing in that it makes people lean in and leaves them wanting more of you, but it's also a way of keeping people out.'

He frowned and asked, 'Do I not talk about myself?'

'You talk about actual things and people you know and your work but you don't really ever offer up how you're feeling. And I was trying to work out if you're deliberately this way because you want to be mysterious or because you're naturally just not that interested in talking about emotions.'

'Or the third option.'

'What's that?'

'That talking about them makes me deeply uncomfortable and so I try to avoid it.'

'What, you're saying you're just the archetypal intellectual? Charming and emotionally repressed?' I shook my head and said, 'No, that's too obvious.'

'Do you think it's possible you've constructed an idealized version of me? And by possible, I mean quite probable.'

Even though I thought this was quite likely to be true now he'd said it, I didn't want it to be true and so replied, 'Maybe but only maybe.' And then I said, 'In any case, it seems like an imbalanced trade.'

'That's a fair point. What would you like to know?'

'I can ask anything?'

'You have complete free rein.'

'OK, this is great. What are your parents like?'

He groaned and said, 'Does it have to take the form of therapy?'

'Yes, but I promise not to invoice you for it.'

'All right. Imagine the most conventional set-up and then increase it tenfold.'

'How do you mean?'

He groaned again but then explained so that I understood exactly what he meant. He said his father was a retired accountant and that his mother hadn't worked, although she had occasionally taught piano on the side. He referred to his childhood as 'entirely pleasant but drastically staid'. I interjected at this point to say that 'drastically staid' was another good word pairing.

'My mother made me wear special over-trousers when I played football outside in the garden. I never once heard her raise her voice or mention any form of bodily fluid. She kept her sanitary towels inside a locked cabinet in the bathroom.'

'That's weird. Also weird because you're so comfortable being naked.'

'That's because I've made a concerted effort to be. She was such a prude, I set out to be the opposite.'

'I get that. I mean, not in terms of the prude thing specifically,' I said, thinking of how my own mother had left the loo door open while she changed her tampon. 'But in terms of wanting to be the opposite to your parents.'

He smiled at this through gritted teeth and said, 'At some point, and I think I was probably quite young, I decided I was superior to them and that I didn't want their life, which seemed trite and parochial, and so I went hard in the other direction. But I think the other end of that spectrum has left me feeling just as detached and unconnected. My life looks entirely differently to theirs, but it's just as much a veneer. And that's probably the truest thing I've said in quite a long time.'

'That isn't a fact from a book,' I added, and he laughed weakly. 'Is that why you like drugs and sex?' I asked. 'Because they make you feel something primal?'

'They're when I feel the most connected and engaged, yes.' He paused and I took the moment to rearrange my head on his chest. 'My mother cared so much about what our house looked like and appearances and about what other people thought of us as a family that I decided I wouldn't care about any of these things, but I sometimes wonder . . . Aren't I just making the opposing statement? I'm still wanting people to think something about me, which is that I don't care, and I'm not sure why that's really all that different to her outwardly caring.'

I thought about this and then asked, 'How would you go about not caring at all?'

'Doing things instinctively rather than as a reaction to her, I guess.'

'Like what kind of stuff, though?'

He shrugged and said, 'I don't know. I've spent so long this way now, it's hard to figure out.'

Christopher and I continued to meet weekly after that night. I still felt obscenely into him but not with the same anxious attachment I'd felt before. There was a slight guardedness that centred me and gave me a sense of dependence, but I wasn't sure if this was actual growth or just because I was holding back part of myself in order to not get hurt again. How was I meant to work out the difference between secure attachment (good and healthy) and repressed emotions (bad)?

To help me figure this out I hired an imaginary therapist inside my head. For as long as she proved useful, I didn't think I could justify the cost of a real one. Another advantage to her was that I didn't have to waste time filling her in on my backstory, as she was already up to speed on my life.

'I don't look down on monogamy, but I don't look up to it any more either,' I told her.

'What about non-monogamy appeals to you?' she asked.

'I like the idea of a relationship being so secure that it could handle other people coming inside it. And it feels maybe more realistic than just relying on one person.'

'It sounds as though you're maybe scared of opening yourself up again,' she said.

'Quite obviously, yes.' I had no qualms about being blunt with her.

She was a psychodynamic therapist, which meant she was allowed to offer her opinion. I was hoping we could get through our time together without her drawing on my mother, as I felt this would be a real win. 'But I'm also worried if it turns out that I don't want monogamy, even though that way I could more easily keep seeing Christopher.'

'What about that is worrying to you?'

'Because the world's set up for people to have only one person, and what if I change my mind and regret not choosing someone to spend my life with and end up all alone?'

'Is fear of regret a good enough reason to do something?' she asked.

'I think so, definitely.'

'And what do you want right now? If regret didn't come into the equation?'

'That's easy. Christopher.'

The bottom line is this, said the voice (who liked to interrupt our sessions), *you're in an open relationship with someone you want to be exclusive with.*

This is not about you, I told the voice. This involves me and my imaginary therapist.

I decided to give my therapist a name and a face to help cement her in my mind. Inside my head I flicked through a selection of profiles, listing bios and credentials, landing on one called Anya who had scattered freckles and a very good smile.

'You seem to come back to this fear of being alone.'

Nodding, I held the silence. I didn't see why I should have to do all the work for both of us.

'Where do you think it comes from? This fear.'

'I don't think that needs dissecting, does it? It's just the human condition.'

'Possibly. But I think there's something deeper going on.'

She paused and I could sense it coming, feeling myself inwardly sigh.

'Talk to me about your mother.' This time I outwardly sighed. 'It sounds as though she's set you a strong example by choosing to raise you as a single parent.'

'Too strong.'
'What makes you say that?'
'I don't know. It was just my subconscious speaking.' I was squirming by now.
'Is it that you don't think you're strong enough to be alone like her?'
'Maybe,' I said, fast-forwarding the big hand on the clock on the wall inside my head to reach the twelve, whereupon the session would terminate.
'Misty, this is something I'd like us to discuss some more in our next session.'
I walked out and closed the door but not before acknowledging she had hit a nerve.

Let's be clear; it wasn't as though I had transformed my character overnight, rather that I had found a way to romanticize Christopher's absence. My attraction to him was still unrelenting but no longer in a way that felt tedious and something to be wrestled with. I still wanted more of him than was presently available but had convinced myself that it could actually be fun to be denied my wanting, as though my longing had been trapped inside all afternoon watching heavy rain before remembering it could just run outside and stomp in the puddles.

On Valentine's Day I paused my cold-calling and sent Christopher a partially nude photograph.

A Valentine's gift. Although you probably don't acknowledge this calendar event?

Not ordinarily.
But this photo makes a persuasive case!

> *I'm meant to be working
> but you're not great for my productivity . . .*

*Tell me more . . . Although I may have to disappear.
I'm in a funding pitch.*

> *Oh. Should I stop?*

*Not at all.
Just making you aware of my lack of availability.*

> *Nothing new on that front . . .*

He started to type a response and then went offline. When I came I pictured him hard under his desk, his cock pressing against his trousers, the tip of it wet, while someone presented a graph on a PowerPoint. I didn't actually know what happened in funding pitches but felt this wasn't too out of whack.

That evening Christopher messaged me a photo of Rowan reading inside their living room. I couldn't see the cover of the book clearly enough to read the title, but his forehead was scrunched up and he looked very engrossed. I noticed a woman's arm in the photo that I assumed was Sara's.

> *Cute! Also, most children watch tv
> or are glued to an iPad but of course yours reads
> ACTUAL BOOKS*

Christopher replied half an hour later with a photo of Rowan transfixed by an iPad, showing computerized ancient ruins and an active volcano. There were cartoon people dressed as archaeologists who were digging and a box in the bottom right corner of the screen with a scroll saying, *Pompeii Treasures.*

This still looks vaguely educational

Twenty minutes later he replied again – this time with a photo of Rowan playing a Pokémon game on an iPhone that I assumed must belong to Sara, since presumably Christopher was using his phone to take the photo and I couldn't imagine Rowan being allowed to own a mobile phone.

Did you contrive this shot especially?

Yes (to my shame).

I wondered how he had justified to Sara his reason for taking the photo, and whether she suspected or had been told that it was being sent to another woman he was currently sleeping with. Did they bother providing each other with answers or just leave these little questions floating in the air until they either evaporated or formed thick clouds? In any case, I thought it was sweet that he had messaged me the photos and brought me further into his world.

I lay on my bed and thought again about children and whether I wanted one, making a list inside my head with two columns, *Reasons to have/not have a child*, but quite a few of the pros also matched the cons so they mainly just cancelled each other out. *Less time to think* was top of both lists. It definitely gave a real purpose to people's existence – this upkeep of another thing. But was it a kind of false purpose? A mere distraction to avoid having to find a genuine one? I considered my mother, who claimed to have wanted me so much that she had contrived to have me in the knowledge she'd be raising me without a partner, while her own mother had been horrified by the accidental existence of her daughter. 'She never wanted me and she never missed an opportunity to let me know it,' was as much detail as my mother had ever provided, even when I probed. My grandmother had died before I was born and so I had no memory of this figure whom my mother referred to as 'the battleaxe'. I didn't believe my grandfather would have been married to such an unlikeable woman (although privately wondered if it went some way to account for my mother's tough character) and had pointed out this discrepancy to my mother on more than one occasion. Her response, 'His halo didn't shine so brightly back then', felt unsatisfactory but she would give no further explanation and so I was left to believe she was exaggerating, and went on loving my grandfather tremendously and unconditionally.

When Barney was in one of his up-moods, he would sometimes say to me, 'Oh, Misty, how come you're so easy to love?' I pointed out that he couldn't possibly be objective in this, as he was currently in love with me. 'Fine then. Subjectively you are a very lovable person. I don't get why or how, but you are.' When I asked what he meant by this last bit, he said that he was surprised, that's all, by my lovability, given I had no real template for it, considering my mother's hard demeanour and not having had a father. I pointed out that, in a way, our parents were doing us a favour with their flaws because they could make us decide to be different to them. Barney said, 'Like Larkin but with optimism,' and then quoted the first line of that poem. This was in the early years when we still talked about love.

We had been seeing each other again for five weeks when I asked Christopher if he was currently seeing anyone else in addition to me. He shook his head, smiling, and said, 'No,' adding that he didn't have the time or feel the need. I told him that this was the same response Erica had given when I asked her how come she didn't want to write a book (only she had said it in French while consuming an entire apple core).

'Is Sara seeing someone?' It was a Saturday afternoon, and we were inside their bed while Sara took Rowan swimming and then to a café for lunch.

'She tends not to when she's back in London. She wants to spend her time with Rowan when she's home.'

I rolled onto my side to face him and asked, 'How much does she know about me?'

'She knows you're . . .' He paused. 'Significant to me.'

'And she's OK with that?'

'She says she's happy for me.'

He laughed suddenly, prompting me to ask, 'What's funny?'

'She said you didn't match your name. I showed her a photograph of you and she said that you looked the opposite of a Misty, like someone who would wear a yellow hat.'

I smiled and said that was a nice thing to hear about myself but that my cheeks didn't suit hats. Christopher said that considering it was a metaphorical hat in this instance, presumably my cheeks could pull it off, and I replied that so long as it wasn't a metaphorical baseball cap, I felt this would probably be fine.

I wriggled a bit under the duvet and asked, 'Have you got to this point of significance with anyone else before me?'

'Yes and no,' he said, bobbing his head side to side. 'I've had what I suppose you could call relationships but they've always been with people in long-term partnerships, where . . . well, I suppose the parameters were more firmly established.'

'You mean, more firmly established than a six-week pact?'

He laughed and touched the top of my breast. 'Last time I checked we'd somewhat extended that.'

We began kissing and he started to put his fingers between my legs but I pulled back, using the moment of intimacy to ask, 'So, if we're exclusive, outside of what you have with Sara, then does that mean I'm . . . your girlfriend?'

He looked hesitant for a moment but then smiled. 'If you'd like that title, yes.'

'I'll get back to you,' I said with a faux coyness that fooled neither of us.

It started to rain as we had sex and I could hear it loudly hitting the skylight. We had moved to stand against the wall by this point but couldn't get the angle right because of our height difference and so moved to the armchair so I could sit on top of him, my legs wrapped around his hips. The skylight must have been slightly open because as the rain got heavier I felt droplets of it fall onto my back. When I came I felt a vibration in the central most part of my pelvis like a gong was going off inside me. I hung my head over his shoulder, gripping him hard.

He shifted me after a few seconds to take off the condom and then repositioned me on his lap, doing little taps up and down my spine. I drew myself closer into him, his arm wrapping around me like a giant warm tentacle.

'You told me on our first date that one of you, or both of you, had fallen in love before.'

He nodded and I waited expectantly. 'She did. It was someone she met on a job overseas.'

'What happened?'

'She came home and, well, she struggled to function. There wasn't really any question of her staying out there; she'd never have left Rowan, but she didn't really know how to exist with us again in our space, for, well, quite a while.' He rubbed his left eyelid forcefully for a few seconds as though recalling this was making him physically itch. 'I'd hear her late at night or in the very early hours of the morning crying and I couldn't remember the last time she'd done that, cried actual tears, and felt cross that her tears were for him.'

'Cross isn't a very strong word. I mean, that sounds really tough on you.'

'All right, angry.'

'Did you rage?'

'Did I rage?' he asked, confused.

'You know, throw a tantrum, kick your arms and legs about, that kind of thing.'

'I don't think I've ever done that kind of thing.'

'Not even as a child?' Now it was my turn to be confused.

'No,' he said. 'I take it you did?'

'Constantly. If I couldn't get my hair to look exactly the way I wanted, if we passed a homeless person looking cold and my mother refused to give them all the money in her purse. I was always raging. I felt there were so many massive and tiny injustices.'

'What did your mother do when you had these tantrums?' He was looking at me curiously, as though registering how little we really knew each other.

'She'd try and reason with me while I was still calm enough and when I really got going she'd hold me in this kind of lock hug with her arms. It was something she told me later she'd read about in a parenting book. It was meant to steady the child and make them feel safe and secure.'

'You must have felt pretty safe and secure to have had those tantrums in the first place.'

'How do you mean?'

'Well, there's an argument to say that children who are very well behaved are often slightly afraid of their parents or insecure in some aspect of their parents' love for them. But a completely secure attachment gives a child the security to kick off.'

'Huh.' I had never considered this take until now. 'Does Rowan have tantrums?'

'He doesn't, no. And yes I do find it slightly concerning.'

I could feel Christopher's shoulders stiffening and knew he was getting uncomfortable with the intensity of my questioning but I dared to risk this final one.

'Do you think you and Sara would ever have another child?'

He looked unsure how to respond and then said, 'Sara . . . She went through early menopause last year.'

'Oh. Sorry.'

'But I am, theoretically, open to having another one, yes.'

I clocked his use of the present tense, wondering if this meant we might have some form of a long-term future together, and held eye contact for as long as he would allow before he reached for his watch.

'Is it time for me to leave?'

'I think we ought to begin that process.' He said this softly, with tenderness, but I still felt abandoned.

As I dressed I felt panicked at how quickly our hours together had gone. Would I ever be satisfied with our snatches of time or permanently starved of him? Kissing him goodbye at the door, I gripped the front of his shirt with my fist, registering how in many ways the relationship felt like an affair. While there wasn't deception in terms of Sara's knowledge of me, the avoidance of my overlapping with her felt akin to secrecy, not to mention her hierarchal position as his primary partner.

But you knew all this, said the voice. *None of this is new information.*

Yes, but knowing something in concept is different to living it.

Then get on and answer the question: can you go on living it?

But this is exactly what I was in the process of trying to work out, and told the voice calmly but firmly that its pushy attitude wouldn't fast-track the end result.

I barely looked at my phone when I was with Christopher – too keen to savour our time together – but as I left his flat I saw a series of voicenotes from Erica. I listened to them as I walked up to Highbury Corner trying to make out her words above the background noise of the traffic and her twins shouting, *Allez, maman, allez!*

The gist of her messages was that she had persuaded her mother-in-law to look after the twins next week while Adrienne was in Geneva on a last-minute work trip, and proposed that I join her in Paris for twenty-four hours of 'childless chateau-free fun'.

Her last voicenote cut off abruptly after a thud, followed swiftly by a wail that I assumed had come from one of the twins. I paused outside the entrance to the Tube while I considered Erica's proposal, not that there was much to consider. Christopher was never available to meet mid-week anyway and Richard was flexible with which days I worked. I could afford to go due to my mother not charging me rent, plus it was Erica in Paris – two fun and brilliant things.

I messaged her,

I'm in! Looking/booking my Eurostar when I get home!

She replied immediately,

ESCAPE FROM THE CHATEAU officially in motion.

That evening as my mother and I ate cereal for dinner because neither one of us could be bothered to even assemble a salad, I asked, 'Why didn't you date while I was growing up?'

She looked aghast and said, 'I was too busy with my surgery hours and raising you.'

'But I left home fifteen years ago. Why haven't you dated anyone since?'

'Last time I checked you were still here, and anyway, this is a hideous topic of conversation for a parent and child.'

'I'm not a child, though, am I.'

'You're *my* child, in the parental rather than under-age sense.' She shuddered and added, 'And I can't stand it when parents and children start acting like friends or siblings.'

This was the same thing she had told me as a teenager when Beth had started having a weekly pizza night with her mum which her younger brother wasn't invited to. Beth told me it was called *girls' night* and that she and her mother would eat the pizza straight from the box and then do their nails, while her brother and father were at her brother's diving practice. When I'd asked my mother if we could have a *girls' night* she'd done that same shudder and said, 'I hate it when mothers do that.'

'Do what?'

'Go around acting like their child is their sister or best friend.' She did start buying frozen pizzas, though, which partially appeased me.

I changed the topic and told her I had booked to visit Erica in Paris next week. She pressed down on her bran flakes with the back of her spoon and said, 'Life seems to be looking up for you again.'

'It is.'

'Good,' she said, a smile seeping through her ordinarily pursed lips. 'You enjoy it while it lasts.'

I told her I intended to, and she repeated the word 'good', but I thought there was something ominous about the way she said this.

We had booked an apartment in Montparnasse which Erica had found on Airbnb, and which at her insistence had two separate bedrooms because she told me that she hadn't had a night of uninterrupted sleep for three and a half years and warned that there was a medium to high probability of resenting me if I got in the way of this finally happening for her. But at the last minute, Erica's mother-in-law had tried to cancel their childcare arrangement, claiming that she couldn't look after the twins without her husband who had conveniently elected to have private cataract surgery in this same twenty-four-hour window. In desperation, Erica had struck a compromise which involved basing herself at her mother-in-law's apartment so that she could assist with childcare alongside us hanging out. 'I feel bad for you, but worse for me,' Erica had said matter-of-factly when she'd told me. 'When I imagine you all alone in that apartment I become physically sick with envy.'

The Airbnb was on the fifth floor of an old apartment block and had a very narrow staircase with a faded carpet that was only wide enough for one person. As soon as I let myself inside I knew that I had made the right decision to come here, and even felt oddly appreciative that Erica wasn't with me because there was something very liberating about being alone in Paris. I had gone to Paris three years ago with Barney and it had felt a bit ridiculous, as though we were walking around inside a film. I had got into my head he might propose – not for any reason other than just because, well, you know, Paris – and as a result all my movements became quite performative and staged, and he'd told me I was doing weird things with my hands and said it looked like I'd forgotten how to walk.

I chose the bedroom I liked best and unpacked my clothes into the pine wardrobe. There was an enormous bookcase in the living room filled with lots of novels and plays and poetry, mainly in French and Italian and Greek – none of which I could read but nevertheless enjoyed their presence in the room. This was the same way I felt about the old-fashioned school desk in the corner. I didn't intend to do any writing at it but it was pleasing to look at and sense the possibility of some great work within me that I was yet to produce.

The tall shutter windows had an iron balcony railing and looked out onto a square cobbled courtyard. Someone was cooking chicken down below; I could smell it wafting up through the floor of the apartment, so rich and comforting – and I didn't even eat chicken. The sky was probably grey but to me seemed silver. Yep. This was joy. I distinctly remembered the feeling. So sharp and palpable and momentary.

Erica had instructed me to meet her at a bar in the Marais at seven o'clock and when I arrived punctually, she was already there, tucked inside a red leather booth in the corner, halfway through a glass of beer.

'I was going to message to say I was running early but decided I'd be on better form if I had ten minutes of me-time,' she said, standing to hug me. She was wearing a black velvet hat that was shaped like a mushroom and looked like she belonged in another era. 'Chic, no?' she said, pointing to it.

I had none of the criteria for chicness, which I felt required a height and a composure I couldn't ever hope to obtain, but it was fun to be in close proximity to Erica's.

'Irresistible.'

'Such a charmer,' she said, grinning.

As I sat down I looked around and tried to work out the theme and style of the place, which seemed to be many conflicting things. There were neon strip lights and square plastic tables but also old wooden chairs and an abundance of mirrors.

'I know, right? It's like a cross between *Blade Runner* and a fifties diner,' said Erica, responding to my face. 'And you haven't even been to the toilet yet, it's like a child's vision of the future.'

'That's what I think about the Pompidou.'

'The French are awful at being modern; they should just stick to old-school.'

'Why is everyone so obsessed with the future anyway?' I said, leaning in towards her. 'I want paper money and pens back. Not even fountain pens; at this point I'm even nostalgic for biros.'

'You'll take any ink you can get.'

'Genuinely, though,' I said, watching a man walk through a mirrored door that I had thought was a wall. 'Like when people bang on about Space. Is it wrong that I just don't care?'

'Oh, same. I have zero time for Space.'

'It really seems that some basic fundamental stuff hasn't been sorted on Earth and we're bothering with Mars. I mean, why?'

'I guess because poverty and childbirth and the housing chain don't directly affect Elon Musk.' She drank from her beer and asked, 'What are you drinking, by the way?'

'Probably wine. Do I need to go to the bar or is it table service?'

'You need to go to the bar, and you should go now because the queue's getting longer.'

I nodded and said, 'I'm just thrilled I don't have to order on an app.'

'They don't really do that here; they're quite behind with technology as a nation.'

'Maybe I've found my people.'

'No,' she said definitively. 'You're way too warm to be French.'

When I got back to the booth, Erica was grinning at something on her phone.

'I feel like you won't know about this, or possibly even care, but there's this group of middle-aged women who don't understand the internet and are watching all these spoof conspiracy videos and now believing in the conspiracy theories because they don't realize the videos are parodies designed to mock the people who actually believe in the conspiracy theories. How good is that?'

'Oh no I can't.'

'Can't what?'

'I can't laugh at them because I'd be one of them.'

Erica rolled her eyes and said, 'Fine, laugh at this instead.' And she told me how on the way here she had passed a discount antique store and had spent a considerable amount of time, like a whole five minutes, describing a green velvet sleigh sofa that she had seen in the shop window several months earlier to the shop assistant who swore no knowledge of such a sofa until Erica remembered the place she'd seen it wasn't inside the shop but inside her dream.

'Now that's funny,' I said.

'Funny-annoying-waste-of-everyone's-time-funny.'

I asked her how the mother-in-law situation was going, and she replied that it was objectively preferable to being a single parent, but that she feared this ratio may tip over the course of the two days if Adrienne's mother continued to comment on Erica's 'unorthodox' parenting style. 'Which is just another way of saying un-sexist,' said Erica, taking a long sip of beer.

Clement and Aurore – although different sexes – when clothed, looked identical. Both had a mane of straggly red curls and were predominantly dressed in navy romper suits. Erica had been determined to raise them without any reference to their sex or gender, wanting to prove that their reproductive organs at birth didn't have any relevance to their character, but had forgotten that this would essentially mean raising them away from society in an incubated room so that people couldn't tell Aurore how nice she looked or remark to Clement on how much energy he had. She had deliberately swapped their name badges over when she'd taken them to a party and had witnessed her point being proved when she'd watched the mother of the birthday girl take Clement by the hand (assuming him to be Aurore) and lead him over to a quiet corner to 'play nicely away from the boys', which had riled Erica no end.

'She keeps telling me to cut Clement's hair because he looks like a *petite fille*. I told her, if anyone's getting their hair cut, it's me.' Erica permanently wrestled with the decision to cut off her hair, which she felt had been weighing her down for years, both literally and in terms of her identity, but was also concerned about chopping off her USP and the back of her neck being cold in winter.

We stayed in the dated futuristic bar for another hour until Erica looked at her watch and announced it was majorly time to leave or else we would miss our restaurant reservation. It was relaxing to be in her assertive company and not have to make any decisions.

I went to the loo on my way out and got what she meant. It had a transparent cistern in the shape of a large test tube so that I could see the water filling back up again when I flushed. My calves felt fettered watching it.

When I joined Erica out on the street the light was violet.

'Is that as dark as it's going to get?' I asked.

'Yep. That's Paris la nuit.'

For some reason I felt unreasonably happy about this and announced, 'I feel like collapsing just for fun.'

'OK but don't actually,' said Erica, striding off into the purple night. 'I'm not remotely committing to catching you.'

After dinner we took the pale green Metro line together going west but when it got to my stop, Erica suddenly announced, 'I'm not ready to end the night. Let's have one final drink,' and so we surfaced arm in arm onto Boulevard Raspail.

'Somewhere super close by,' said Erica, 'I'm already regretting this decision.'

'Our apartment's literally there,' I said, pointing up at a block of flats lit by an old-fashioned streetlamp.

'I love you for saying *our*,' said Erica, holding her hand over her chest. 'This will be painful for me but OK, yes.'

As soon as we were inside she immediately made a beeline for the bookshelf, exclaiming, 'Our host has excellent taste,' as she pulled down a large hardback of Norse myths from a shelf too tall for me to reach. I didn't share Erica's passion for Nordic mythology and found the epic nature of it too childlike and unbelievable but Erica said the bigness and implausibility of it was the whole point, that that was what made it epic.

I left her liquidizing under the bookshelf like a pool of butter and went into the kitchen.

'I don't actually have any wine or any alcohol,' I called through to her, but by this point I had lost her to dragons and giants.

On the counter was a box of Nuit Calme left by the host or a previous guest. I opened two teabags from their sachets and began boiling the kettle.

'I think if someone was tasked with designing the most boring tea ever, it would be this,' said Erica when I brought the mugs into the living room and she examined the tag of the teabag.

'Maybe there's some whiskey or something in the back of a cupboard.'

'It's fine. At least my head will thank me in the morning,' she said, rising from the floor beneath the bookcase and walking over to the window, its shutters still open.

'Not a star in sight,' she said, peering out into the night. 'How vexing.'

I curled my feet up underneath me on the sofa and asked, 'Did I ever tell you about the woman who walked in off the street when I was doing that creative writing class a few years back?'

'Start, and I'll stop you if I remember or just get bored,' she said, still looking up at the sky.

'OK, well, it was a weird layout, as in the door to the classroom was directly accessed via the street, so there was no formal reception area or anything, and the door wasn't locked while we were inside having the class.'

'Is this bit relevant? Should I already be listening?'

'Yes. So, one week about halfway through the session, this woman just walked in off the street and said, "Please can I sit with you?" She asked it really gently and reasonably and she didn't seem drunk or on drugs or even homeless.'

'How old was she?' said Erica, reaching for her Nuit Calme and wincing as she attempted a sip.

'I'm bad with ages but maybe forty- or fifty-something? Anyway, one of the people in the class, not the teacher because she found authority deeply uncomfortable, said, "I'm afraid we're just in the middle of a class right now." And the woman said, "That's OK. I just want to sit with you. I won't say anything." And then another person in the class joined in and said quite firmly, "Sorry, I'm afraid it's a private class and we need to get on now." And the woman off the street said, "OK, I'm really sorry to have bothered you," and then left. And after she shut the door we carried on with the class but all our stories made even less sense than before.'

When I'd told this to Barney later that evening he'd said, 'But short stories aren't meant to make sense, at least not obvious sense on first-read,' which I'd felt had missed the point of the anecdote in quite a monumental way. I wondered if this would also be Erica's response and suddenly regretted mentioning it, because it somehow felt as though I was testing her without her realizing.

'What?' said Erica, peering out of the window again and frowning at the sky. 'You mean because the point of writing is to engage with life and you all just ignored that woman who was real and lonely?' I beamed at her then as if we were the only two people inside Paris, rather than just that starless living room.

'OK, I vitally need to leave before I just stay,' she said, standing abruptly and walking swiftly towards the door, her undrunk tea steaming on the table. Her hat was slanted at an angle.

Erica's son hadn't slept so she hadn't slept. She told me this in a WhatsApp the following morning shortly before I was due to meet her for brunch near her mother-in-law's apartment.

Fyi I don't want to talk about my tiredness on arrival, I just want to give you a heads up that if I seem exhausted it's because I am.

It was still quite shocking to me that Erica was a parent. I think because I had spent so little time with her in the presence of the twins they were almost fictional to me, and so when she talked about them or sent messages like this and I was suddenly reminded of her reality, I was filled with admiration for her capability and overwhelmed by my own inadequacy. I felt the weight of responsibility just walking around all day making sure I didn't get myself hit by a car or choke on a grape, while Erica was doing this not only for herself but also for two other people, which was quite unfathomable to me.

She was wearing a tote bag with the Walt Whitman quote *I too am untranslatable.* I complimented her on it and she raised her eyebrows. 'So snowflakey, right? Like ew to carrying around an unironic author quote.'

I always felt one step behind her, as though my sincerity was a handicap or at the very least a deficiency.

As we walked the pristine neighbourhood a woman in turquoise Lycra jogged past us, reminding me I also used to run; these days even small gradients alarmed me, as though it felt imperative to tread deliberately.

'Are you more worried about stuff like climate change since you had the twins?' I asked as Erica gestured for us to fork left.

'No, if anything less so.'

'Less so? How come?'

'Fine, the same so. I just don't have time to dwell on it. Also, I don't want to get too het up about it because I'm not willing to change my life in a massive way so it's better if I just blot it out and plough on through.' Erica seemed to be particularly skilled at blotting stuff out.

I asked if she remembered the time a few years ago when she'd visited me in London and we'd got drunk to go and watch *Cats* at the cinema and it was as bad as we'd hoped.

'SO bad.' She grinned. 'I still can't assimilate Prufrock with that giant mess of a film. Surely Eliot is just rolling in his grave. Then again,' she added, 'aren't we all?' I didn't really know what she meant by this last bit and wasn't sure if she did either, but I liked the sound of it hanging in the air.

Inside the café, Erica scanned the menu, rolling her eyes. 'France makes a total mess of brunch. Who wants a set menu starting with a soup at ten a.m.?'

'I guess the French?'

We played it safe and both ordered a croque madame and a Perrier. After the waiter had left our table I told Erica that I wanted to remain open to the world, unlike my mother, who, somewhere along the way, had cast her opinions in stone.

'I think she's so steely because she had to be. It's a progressive thing to do, especially back then, choosing to be a single parent.'

'But by that logic, shouldn't she be more fluid and less judgy?'

'Not necessarily. In fact, it's probably easier to be fluid and open if you're more conventional because you can afford to let go of stuff and change your mind without it costing you anything. But if the way you're living is constantly butting up against society then no wonder you develop a fixed stance. You can't afford not to.'

Erica and my mother had only met a couple of times but they were always sticking up for each other behind the other one's back. I secretly believed that my mother would have preferred Erica as a daughter to the one she had got; someone who held it together more and wasn't moved to tears at the sight of a child wearing glasses. Then I thought how funny-odd it was that I had chosen a friend who shared a sizeable number of my mother's traits. In many ways, Erica represented the middle of our mother-daughter Venn, where my mother and I didn't seem to overlap even faintly.

I poured my Perrier into a glass and looked at the tiny bubbles shooting up to the surface. 'Overall, would you say parenthood's given you more of a hardness or a softness?'

'Hard, soft, medium, whatever. I don't have time to review my personality these days.'

'Do you reckon self-reflection's an equally valid part of living, though? As much as, you know, just living.'

'Maybe. I don't feel I'm hugely missing out either way. Like, I think if I had any extra time I'd rather do something practical like learn how to mend my own clothes or fix my bike rather than assess my personality, which, to be fair, is already excellent.'

She looked at me in earnest for a second before we both burst out laughing at her audacity. But it was true; she did have an excellent personality and why shouldn't she acknowledge it among friends?

Erica often joked about the vastness of her ego, but really hers was one of the smallest out of everyone I knew. What

Erica had was a very strong sense of her own self-worth while accepting her ultimate irrelevancy. It was the opposite to most people, who were outwardly self-deprecating but privately believed they were exceptional. One of the ways in which Erica embodied her irrelevancy was allowing her boss at one of the companies she temped for to call her Eliza for the entire five months she worked there.

'But why didn't you correct him?' I'd asked, aghast, when she told me.

'Why does it matter? It's just a name.'

'But it's *your* name.'

'So what? He doesn't care and neither do I. Erica, Eliza, what's the difference?'

I couldn't at all relate to this, but I was really much more precious about this kind of thing and would even correct a barista if they wrote *Kirsty* on my cup, which they did, not infrequently.

But hang on, now Erica was telling me about the village cat who came to the chateau at lunchtime every day and ate an omelette complète she was expected to cook for it.

'Stop it.'

'It's true.'

'But that's so extravagant.'

'It's outrageously extravagant but the old housekeeper's set a precedent and now the cat's got expectations and I'm so exhausted that it's easier just to chuck the eggs in the pan and stop it miaowing than try to change its behaviour.' She pulled at the hair tie on her wrist and in one swift motion drew her thick mane into a ponytail.

'So does someone bring it or does it find its own way there?'

'It finds its own way.'

'At the same time every day?'

'Well, not to the exact minute; I mean, come on, it's a cat.'

'I really can't get over this,' I said, opening and closing my mouth to catch imaginary snowflakes; my tongue felt hot and intangible. A young boy who was watching me started opening and closing his mouth too, which felt like a fun but maybe slightly inappropriate game either one of us might get in trouble for and so I stopped and turned back to Erica.

'That expression about children being cruel . . .'

'What about it?'

'Isn't it really just that they're honest?' I watched Erica's neck tighten as she stifled a yawn. Looking at her shadowed face the word that sprung to mind was *crepuscule*, but I couldn't remember what this even meant. 'I think if I had a child I'd make a list of all my flaws and continually update it so I couldn't be caught off guard. Like, that way if they turned to me and said, "You're quite self-involved," or, "You're overly sensitive," or, "Why don't you know more stuff?" I could say, "Yes, correct, these are deficiencies of mine." But the thing, the thing that would make me want to crawl into a hole or at least go into the bathroom and not come out again for several hours, is if they announced, "You're very un-self-aware." That would just crush me.'

'Sure, for like a minute, and then you'd just have to get over it because they'd need something from you.'

As the waiter brought our plates over to the table a single stream of sunlight appeared at the exact same moment Erica clasped her hands together as if in prayer. I thought she looked so lovely and weary in the grey light.

'Is that a figurative thanks?' I asked.

'It's a literal *I'm so tired I can't pick up my fork* thanks.'

'I'm sorry. I'd offer to feed you but I think it's too weird.'

'Yeah, I wouldn't accept the offer but it's sweet you half made it.'

'How many eggs, then? For the cat. If it's an omelette then presumably minimum three?'

'OK, you're obsessed.'

'Yep.' And then I repeated something my grandfather had told me before I left for Paris, that when King Louis had tried to escape during the revolution he'd attempted to disguise his identity by wearing peasant clothing and was taken in by a farmer for the night who was none the wiser, but then Louis had blown his own cover the next morning at breakfast when he'd asked for an omelette with *sixteen* eggs. Erica enjoyed this so much that she bit down on her teeth and threw back her head like a whinnying horse, and even the waiter looked over and smiled. I thought of that other Walt Whitman quote about containing multitudes and how Erica was so many things: friend, mother, wife, daughter, deviant, and now horse. Here's what I wanted for her – to keep gurning majestically.

'Of course, you know why I ordered this?' she said, pointing at her croque madame. 'For the egg.' And she was off again: teeth, head, stretched neck. It was the best. From now on, I was solely going to picture her rearing upwards in a plume of dust.

All too soon it was early evening and we were sitting inside a brasserie in the Latin Quarter, still wearing our coats. Erica had ordered us a bottle of Beaujolais Nouveau because she said it was all the rage thanks to their highly successful marketing campaign and even though she could see through the gimmick it was fun to get in on the hype. I looked up at the roof that had vast sloped panes of glass like a greenhouse, and then down at the floor which was covered in black-and-white chequered tiles, dotted with potted palms.

There's a stoicism to palm trees in March, don't you think? I wasn't sure if I had said this aloud or just thought it, and Erica's non sequitur left me no clearer.

'Apparently there's a quiz you can do that will make you fall in love with anyone you do it with.'

'I don't believe you. How is that even possible?'

'Right? Like, it's really hard to fall in love. Or at least medium-hard. But anyone, sorry no, I draw the line at that, for love's sake.' She frowned, topping up our glasses. 'It would just completely undermine it.'

'I agree. I am also intrigued, though. We could find it online and try it now?'

Erica raised her eyebrows and said in a sultry voice, 'With you, I wouldn't dare.'

I threw back my head and cackled. The air felt icy and valiant. 'Do you think our platonic infatuation is normal? I don't think I have it with anybody else.'

'Me neither. But given we only see each other approximately five days a year, I'd say yes.'

'It really is the wildest thing, though, to be sitting across from you and stomping the streets with you and just having a wine or a Perrier with you.'

'Cool it, Frank O'Hara,' said Erica, picking up the pepper grinder and shaking it liberally like a maraca. 'Maybe all my relationships need this level of absence. I'd be such a better wife if I only saw Adrienne one week a year.'

'No you wouldn't because you literally wouldn't be there.'

'Fine, but I'd be a better me.'

'I'll give you that.'

I hadn't directly mentioned Christopher up until now, which I felt was testament to our friendship that we had too much else to talk about, but suddenly I needed to speak my thoughts aloud.

'I think if things keep going with Christopher I'm going to end up changing in a way that's both painful and potentially risky, in terms of losing things I won't be able to get back, like even my wants which used to feel much clearer and safer. But I'm still going to keep seeing him anyway.'

'OK. I think that's fine. I mean, maybe not ideal, but definitely fine.' How I loved her in that moment for allowing me to love him.

'And maybe that sounds self-sabotaging. But it's not that. It's more that desire and curiosity are these huge driving forces spurring me on, and panic and doubt are just these annoying by-products I have to suck up because I'm too far in to turn back now. I have to see it through.'

'You're in the thick of the woods.'

'Exactly.'

She looked at me sharply and then said very matter-of-factly, 'The way I see it is it's very unlikely his situation is going to change so the most likely change would have to be your feelings about the situation.'

'Agree.'

'Well, as long as you know that then it sounds like you're not deceiving yourself and you can keep going and see where you end up. And maybe you'll decide that it works for you – this current set-up – and you'll go on being in a relationship with him.'

She made it sound so possible, but hearing it also felt jarring: the idea of years of my life spent with someone I could only ever share part of it with. 'And at least this way the relationship can focus on pleasure and quality time and not get weighed down with mundane obligations like finances and parenting and housework.'

But I wanted the conventional mundanity of everyday life with him. I wasn't craving excitement in a tired, stale marriage which was dominated by domesticity. It was domesticity I was craving. Erica's own predicament made me envious, and I told her this, to which she replied, 'You're deranged.' But then added, 'Well, in that case, maybe you could also end up being in another relationship additionally to your one with him, and having a family with someone else like he does.'

Could I imagine this? Having my own primary partner and child alongside Christopher? It was so far from where I was currently at – investing in anyone else – that the image was hard to summon.

Erica rewrapped her scarf around her neck and took a sip of wine. 'I'm on the cusp of entering them too, by the way. The woods.'

'How do you mean?'

'With Suze. But I probably won't.' She said this so casually that at first I wasn't sure if she was being serious. 'Not least because we don't live in the same city, or even country.'

'But wait. I knew it was weird when you said you two were back in touch but I thought things were over-over between you, as in beyond-resuscitation over.'

'So did I. But now I can't stop thinking and fantasizing about her and every time she messages me it's just the most thrilling feeling.'

'What about the dust? Can't you use that as a turn-off?'

'She's not into that any more. She makes these rustic hand-carved wooden bowls. They're all over her Instagram. I mean, trust her to go and get all tangible *after* we break up.' Erica held her phone up and showed me a photo of a bowl that looked impressively bowl-like but did nothing for me aphrodisiac-wise.

'Also,' she continued, 'I know this isn't a very acceptable thing to say but I don't actually want to be turned-off. I'm enjoying having something to obsess over that's just for me, and to be honest, it seems relatively harmless in the grand scheme of betrayal. Like, if anything it makes me a better wife and mother because it's lifting my mood for everyone, and it's not like I'm planning to act on my feelings.'

I wasn't sure whether Erica was lying to herself or to me with this statement, or maybe even telling the truth. I felt there was more I ought to say but didn't want to offer direct advice because who was I to claim to be an authority on the situation when she was the one living it? That said, I felt a responsibility towards Erica's integrity and fulfilment, but also to her long-term happiness and that of Adrienne and the twins. And currently these things were at odds.

'I guess my question is: where does it end? The messaging. Because it seems as though it either has to fizzle out or, you know, spark and catch alight.'

'I think that's probably right.'

'Well, in that case, and I'm not going to tell you what to do, but I think you should really try and aim for the fizzle-out option because I think it will serve you and the people you really love and care about best overall.'

'I agree,' she said, without emotion. 'I really don't think I'm going to do anything about it. And it's not like I don't have a great life with Adrienne and the twins. I'm horribly in love with the three of them. Plus, I've made my bed already, you know? Even if sometimes I increasingly wish I hadn't.'

This seemed to me to be an understandable predicament for Erica. I hadn't made my bed, though. Mine was still vastly open and lacking any form of definition, not just its interior but now I didn't even know what it looked like structurally.

We paid the bill and left the restaurant with sudden haste, realizing I was in danger of missing my Eurostar. We had already agreed not to do goodbyes – me because I cried too readily, and Erica because she said she didn't have the energy to be theatrical on three hours' sleep.

'Thanks for all the thoughts, the facts and the fun,' I said, reaching up to hug her.

'Thanks for this weeny slither of bliss,' she said, stooping to receive me. 'Come again soon.'

As we broke apart I nodded and locked eyes with her. 'Be good, won't you,' I said firmly, wanting to teleport into her the weight of what she had just told me about Suze, but she didn't want to go there, to that more serious energy.

'Urgh. I'd rather be sly.'

'Oh, you're already that.'

She grinned. I blew her a kiss and watched her mime catching and pretending to drop under the weight of it. She was still a performer in her bones. As she started to walk down the street I called out, 'Wait, though. Should I come back in summer or autumn?'

'Summer's sooner, autumn's cooler,' she said with customary directness. Yes, it was this I would most miss.

I headed towards the Metro with the Panthéon lit up behind me like a giant toy temple, and considered at what point did anyone start to owe anything to anyone? People divorced and broke off engagements and had affairs and left each other quite a lot of the time. And all of these actions, although far from aspirational, seemed to be acceptable and relatively ordinary things to do. How could a person be expected to buy into love and trust in it with all of this in mind? No. I still could not get my head around what love meant if it wasn't the promise to stay. I thought how useful it would be if there was a book that could give a definitive answer to this question, but suspected this was the kind of thing that had to be understood through living, not through reading. One–nil to life, then.

That night, as I boarded the Eurostar, I thought how when I got back Dan would ask, *How was Paris? What did you eat?!* And how it was easier just to bang on about cheese and croissants (neither of which I'd eaten) than to try to explain how full and multitudinous the last twenty-four hours had been – how they had both validated and challenged my life choices and left me so invigorated that sleep currently felt impossible. But even as I thought this I could ironically feel my eyes becoming heavy and drooping. I thought of Christopher (no surprises there) and wondered what he was doing right now back in London. Rowan would likely be asleep. Would he and Sara be reading on the sofa next to each other, her feet stretched out on his lap?

Our last exchange had been a photo I'd sent him from St Pancras yesterday afternoon of Tracey Emin's neon sign – a call-back to our first date. He'd replied,

I want mine with you too.

This wasn't technically true, since he also wanted it with Sara and Rowan, but in fairness to him and to quote Erica,

I want (some of) my time with you didn't quite have the same ring to it.

The last thing I remember before falling asleep and waking up at St Pancras was watching a couple with silver-grey hair and tanned skin uncork a half-bottle of Montrachet, and how I liked the woman immediately because she was reading a book by my favourite author. Not a lot happened in these books plot-wise but there was a truthfulness to them that often left me holding my breath, and this powered them in a different way.

As I waited for the Brighton train at St Pancras I received a text message from an unknown number saying,

Hi Misty, it's Sara. Would you be available to meet next time you're in London?

That's literally all the message said.

I had read on poly online community boards about relationships blossoming between people sharing the same partner, and even scenarios in which the 'me equivalent' ended up moving in and living with the primary couple and them all being one big happy family. I briefly wondered if the purpose of our meeting would be for Sara to suggest this, but based on the brevity of her message, decided it was unlikely. Nor did I want this level of welcome. My preferred MO was to, not pretend that Sara didn't exist, but to keep our worlds distinctly separate.

I didn't reply until the following morning, trying to match her tone as I wrote,

*Hi Sara, yes, sure.
How is this coming Saturday afternoon?*

I'd been expecting her messages to get longer rather than shorter and tried not to read into her abruptness when she replied,

2pm?

OK

I wrote and then added,

Just let me know where.

She didn't reply to this; presumably now the date and time had been agreed, this detail was irrelevant to her.

I wasn't due to see Christopher until that Saturday evening and wondered whether I ought to mention my meeting with Sara in advance to him but decided against it; the fact he hadn't given me a heads-up that she would be messaging me suggested that she hadn't told him about making contact, and I could therefore assume he wasn't privy to the content of whatever she wanted to discuss. I did wonder how she'd got my number, though, and considered the fact that if she knew his passcode then had she also read the entire correspondence of our messages? This made me uncomfortable, and then physically squirm when I thought about the partially nude photograph I had sent him.

In the same way that you might not hit it off with your best friend's friend, I had low expectations of our meeting, based on my understanding that we had nothing in common aside from Christopher. Where I was physically cowardly, she was brave; where I was moved daily, she was unsentimental; not to mention the fact she was also a mother to a nine-year-old and almost a decade older than me.

I timed my arrival at the café she had selected exactly for 2 p.m., so as not to perform any kind of offensive manoeuvre by being either early or late. But when I got there she was already sitting with a porcelain cup of something and reading a journal of some kind. Presumably neither she nor Christopher would ever be caught without hardcopy reading material in their possession.

She stood and said, 'Misty?' I had thought about wearing a yellow hat as an in-joke to her earlier comment about me but the sternness of her energy made me glad I hadn't.

I nodded and said hello. She made a movement as if to initiate a handshake but then touched the back of her neck instead, so I was left to imagine the feel of her skin, which was in excellent condition and so pale it was almost translucent. She wasn't wearing any make-up, or if she was, it was too subtle to register. Her height and thinness, paired with her oversized linen trouser-suit, emitted chic-Scandi vibes. I felt proud of her attractiveness, as if it reflected well on both of us, and wondered if she felt the same way about me.

'What would you like to drink?' she asked.

'That's OK, I can get it.'

'If it's OK with you, I'd like to.' She said this without a rising inflection, making clear it was a command rather than a request. I told her I'd have a herbal tea of any kind, assuming that was what she was drinking, but on closer inspection, hers turned out to be just hot water.

While she was at the counter I glanced at her journal, titled *International Affairs*. I'd half expected her to defy the cliché of herself by reading a best-selling novel or drinking a mocha, but nope, so far she was in every way as erudite and puritan as I had imagined.

She wasted no time in getting to the point once she sat back down. *What did you expect?* said the voice, chidingly. *Pleasantries? You're in a relationship with her long-term partner and the father of their child.*

But in fact, what she had to say did surprise me and wasn't what I had been expecting, which was to be in some way chastised.

'I don't know how much Christopher's told you about our

relationship but the fact is, I'm away a lot and you seem to be making him happy and fulfilling his needs. As far as I'm concerned this is working, but I wanted to check it's working for you too?'

As I said, this is not what I had been expecting and my face clearly showed surprise because she continued, by way of justification.

'I suppose I feel an ethical obligation to make sure you don't feel used in all of this.' I understood then, in that moment, she wasn't privy to the intimacy that Christopher and I shared. She may have understood it was about more than sex, but her wording implied she felt no threat from my presence.

'I don't feel used, no.'

She smiled then and it suddenly occurred to me that perhaps she was threatened by me but was using her age and maturity and position of power as the primary partner to exert her authority by claiming to be looking out for me while actually staking her claim and establishing her turf by belittling what I shared with Christopher. Because I didn't know her, I didn't know if I was being cynical or accurate in my interpretation.

'Good. Well, in that case, the second thing to say is that I'd feel more comfortable if you were dating concurrently to Christopher.'

At this, I felt she'd overstepped the mark, which she anticipated by saying, 'I thought about this maybe sounding patronizing but then decided even if it did, it was better still to say it.'

Perhaps sensing she had nothing to lose at this point she added, 'You may think you're happy with this set-up but you also won't be this young and attractive for ever and I don't want you to feel caught out later down the line.'

I felt temporary and expendable then, but didn't want to

show her that she had rattled me, and so said, 'Sure, I'll think about it.'

'I think that would be good, for everyone's benefit.'

I thought she might try to speak about something unrelated to Christopher, but she seemed to have no problem whatsoever with us failing the Bechdel test as she reached for her jacket on the back of the chair, signalling an end to our meeting.

'One other thing,' she said. 'I'm not comfortable involving Rowan in any of this. I've already made that clear to Christopher but I'm just saying it to you too: I don't expect to come back to a stepmother situation.'

I forced myself to hold her gaze as I replied. 'Understood.'

Sara certainly seemed to be implying my relationship with Christopher wouldn't last but did she really believe this or was it a manipulative tactic? And if she did really believe it then was it because Christopher had led her to believe this while leading me to hope we had some form of a future together? But what was this hope of mine even based on? And I realized he had never given me concrete cause to believe in a long-term future with him. I had to acknowledge that we were still in the heady early stages of our relationship; presumably it would fade. Wasn't love, at least at the start, mainly hormones anyway? And if and when it did fade, surely he wouldn't stick around to make it work. He already had his serious relationship with Sara. He would only continue for as long as it was good for both of us. He'd even said this himself.

As she stood to leave, I registered our meeting had lasted for all of thirteen minutes. 'I think it's unlikely we'll meet again,' she said. 'But you've got my number, in case you need it for some reason.'

I nodded and said, 'You've got mine too,' which I thought sounded pretty ridiculous considering how unlikely it was I would ever have anything to offer her. As she was leaving, her phone lit up with a message and I caught a flash of her screensaver. The three of them looked so much happier than I had allowed myself to imagine and I felt like a child, like a fool.

'So how was Paris?' asked Christopher as we lay on the bed, still clothed. It was later that evening and we were in a hotel room, which was where we spent our nights since Sara had returned.

'Paris was great but I won't bore you with how great.'

'The best of times makes for the dullest anecdotes.'

I smiled but gave him no more than this, feeling guarded and protective over myself.

'Are you OK?' he asked, stroking my arm.

'You mean because we haven't slept together yet? Presumably this feels like a waste of your time just lying here together.'

Christopher tilted his head and said, 'I wasn't thinking that at all. I like lying here with you.'

He continued stroking my arm and I asked, flatly, 'Did Sara tell you we met this afternoon?'

'She did mention it, yes.'

'What else did she say?'

'Nothing.'

I waited for him to ask how it went and when he didn't, said, 'Aren't you curious to know what we talked about?' I tried to ask this alluringly but heard the sullenness in my voice.

'I am. But I also think it's reasonable if neither of you want to tell me.'

'And because you don't think either of us will tell you, you don't want to beg?'

'Something like that,' he said, smiling. I didn't know how

to respond to this and felt frustrated by his lack of probing and my lack of skill in eliciting his probing.

'I do like the idea of her and me having something that's just between ourselves since you have that with each of us. But, well, I also want your opinion on something she said, so I probably am going to tell you.'

I paused long enough for him to say, 'Is this the bit where I have to beg?'

I smiled, weighing up how much longer I could extend the moment without it getting annoying.

'She said she thought I should be dating alongside you. Is that what you think?'

'I think if you want to you should.'

'You mean you wouldn't mind?'

'I suspect I'd be a bit jealous actually, but I certainly wouldn't be in a position to stop you.'

I was not satisfied by the second part of his answer. I wanted more. I wanted proof of his level of investment in me.

'I think Sara thinks I'm just a child in all of this,' I said. 'And I know I don't understand the intricacies of your relationship, partly because you don't really talk about them, and partly because, well, I'm obviously not inside it. But she kind of insinuated that I was being used.'

He frowned and said, 'She's wrong about that.'

'Is she?'

He seemed less sure now that I'd queried this.

'Isn't she?' he asked. 'Using would imply that you somehow get less from this exchange, that it's predominantly for my benefit that we're seeing each other.'

'I don't think it's just for your benefit that we're seeing each other. I definitely get as much as you do, if not more, from that bit. But I get less in that I don't also get the other stuff you get. I mean, you've got a child and a house together, and

I don't have either of those things, and I won't get to have them with you.'

He kept his face very still so that I had no idea what he was thinking or what he was going to say next.

'We won't be able to share a lot of the traditional milestones, no. So, if things like getting engaged and married are important to you then, well, we ought to end this. But people do make it work long term with more than one partner, even raising two sets of children, splitting their time more evenly between two different homes. It's not impossible that if we keep going we'll find a set-up that reflects this, if that's something you want.'

Was it? I hadn't even allowed myself to consider this as a possibility. Hearing it, I felt as though I'd been filled with helium but was still tethered to the ground rather than shooting off into the sky.

'Something tells me Sara wouldn't go for that.'

'Well, that's a discussion I'd have to have with her, further down the line. If and when we get to that point.'

I felt light enough then to get up and go to the bathroom, bolstered by this turn in the conversation. But as soon as I sat on the loo, I immediately deflated again. Sure, I was more encouraged about the future now, but it didn't change anything about the immediate situation. I still lacked enough of him in the present. It ultimately came down to this: I was alone without him but he was not alone without me.

When I came back into the room, Christopher was sitting upright against the headboard not doing anything, just looking at the wall in front of him, which was odd because he was normally reading something from a book.

I got back onto the bed and said, 'You never just do nothing.'

'I'm thinking. Does that count as nothing?'

'It depends if you're daydreaming or trying to work something out.'

'A bit of both.' He paused and then said, 'The late May bank holiday weekend. Sara reminded me this morning she's taking Rowan to a family feminist festival in Lea Valley. I was thinking you and I could go away together for a couple of nights. If you'd like that?'

I beamed by way of response and then asked, 'You don't fancy the feminist festival, then?'

'I did actually propose joining them but was told it wouldn't be my scene.'

It suddenly occurred to me very strongly that Sara might not just be attracted to men. I didn't know whether I was thinking this for the first time now or whether I had previously suspected this and was only now in this moment articulating it.

'Is Sara bisexual?' I said.

'She sometimes sleeps with women, yes.'

I paused and then asked, 'Do you ever sleep with people together?'

'Not for a while. Not for quite a long while, in fact. Why? Are you interested in sleeping with a third party?'

Was I? I wasn't sure. 'Maybe, but not with you and her. That would be too weird.'

'Don't worry, I wasn't suggesting that.' He scratched the side of his head and then said, 'There are nights we could go to, though, if you wanted to do that with strangers?'

'What kind of nights?'

'Organized play parties, that kind of thing.'

'Is it something you want us to do?'

'I'm not fussed either way,' he said, stretching his arms above his head.

'Can I think about it and let you know?'

'Of course.' He glanced at his watch as he brought his arms back down and asked, 'Are you hungry?'

'Not for food,' I said, my appetite for him returned now I

felt more secure again. I began unbuttoning his shirt and he allowed himself to be submissive. Afterwards we fell asleep and when we woke it was 11.35 p.m. We picnicked on the floor with peanuts and crisps from the minibar and Christopher added a box of mini raisins into the mix he kept in his satchel as an emergency snack for Rowan.

'Will he mind?' I asked.

'He won't know. I'll replace them.'

I felt a sting of sadness at my being kept away from him but also hopeful, based on what Christopher had said, that one day I may now get to meet him.

Because neither of us were tired enough to go straight back to sleep and we were sore from sex, we took turns reading to each other from the Old Testament in the Bible on the nightstand. But it wasn't as good as people harped on about it being, plus I felt too energized just to lie there, so I taught him a couple of gymnastics moves instead, which turned out to be way more fun than the Bible. But when we lay back down in bed and I listened to Christopher's steady breathing as he soon fell asleep, my doubts began seeping out again, burning holes in my stomach like splotches of acid.

I couldn't see the point in dating anyone because I didn't want anyone other than Christopher. Was I meant to deliberately cultivate this want? It seemed perverse, given I had so many organic wants, but was I tricking myself into no longer wanting the things I'd previously wanted – marriage and monogamy – in order to stay seeing Christopher or because I really no longer wanted them? Was it an act of great delusion or a genuine character transformation? I was evidentially due another appointment with my imaginary therapist and made a mental note to book myself in at my earliest convenience.

In the meantime, I decided I would go on one date to confirm to the three of us (myself, Christopher and Sara) that I had no interest in seeing anyone other than him. This way Sara couldn't hold it against me for not attempting to fulfil her request. She didn't need to know it was just a tick-box exercise, and besides, maybe I'd be proved wrong and end up being really attracted to this stranger; my body loved to work in opposition to what my mind wanted.

I couldn't be bothered to re-download the dating apps I had deleted and create a new profile for the sake of a single date, and so that afternoon when I left Christopher I messaged Dan,

Is your friend Tom still single?

Tom was someone Dan had mentioned to me a couple of times since breaking up with Barney, telling me I ought to go on a date with him. But at no point had he, me or this Tom guy cared enough to make it happen. I didn't know anything about him other than that he was a school friend of Dan's and, according to Dan's biased judgement, 'a lovely guy'.

Last time I checked, yes!

I waited to see if he would send me his number and when he didn't I wrote back,

Can I have his number in that case?

It really was like tugging at teeth, or whatever that expression was.
    I felt bad that my weekly coffees with Dan had dropped off and that I didn't really know what was going on in his life right now and so added,

Also. How are you?!

He sent back Tom's number with the crossed fingers emoji, followed by a photo of himself and Shiv in hiking gear with the peak of a mountain behind them. They were smiling and his caption said, *We're good!* Which told me that either things really were good between them or he had no interest in discussing the fact things were not good. I signed off,

Happy to see/hear this!

Wanting to avoid lengthy correspondence, I messaged Tom immediately, cutting straight to the point.

Hi Tom, I'm a friend of Dan's and wondered if you'd like to go for a drink? Misty ps. Yes. I actually am called Misty

The message showed as read seconds after I'd sent it. He started typing and then stopped and then started again until after another minute or two my phone pinged with his reply.

Hi Misty. How do you know Dan?

Climate protesting. I'll try not to blind you with my halo . . .

I waited by the entrance to the Tube to see if he would reply but this time the message stayed marked as unread, and so I descended underground where I presently lost signal.

Sitting across from me inside the Tube carriage was an old woman and a teenage girl who I assumed were grandmother and granddaughter but never got this confirmed. The old woman kept asking the girl lots of questions about her life and technology and really buying into her feelings and experiences and trying to understand what was important to the girl and her friends. Several times she repeated things back to the girl to check she'd understood correctly. And listening to her, I thought: When I grow old I want to be this woman. More than anything, more than even becoming a novelist, I want to be like her. *Yeah right*, countered the voice. *I don't believe for a second you want to be some random old woman more than a published author.* OK, so the voice was right. But after having a book in print, after that, it was this old woman I next most wanted to be. So curious and engaged. So un-old!

When I surfaced at King's Cross, I saw my phone was in low battery mode and that Tom had sent two replies.

That's cool you do that. I get panicked in crowds ;-)

Oh and yeah to the drink.

Why the winky face? Was he saying he didn't really get panicked in crowds and that this was just a line he used to avoid protesting? And if he really did get panicked, then what was wink-worthy about that? I feared he might be one of those people who substituted actual humour for emojis, which would make for tiresome conversation and regrettably I wouldn't have the skill to turn it around on my own; I wasn't clever or sharp enough to produce wit out of a blunt stone. Still, he was all I had to work with at this present moment, and at least Dan had vouched for him being a nice person, albeit likely a dull one.

Aware I wasn't due back in London until the following weekend and that my phone would soon die, I abandoned any attempt at repartee and wrote,

> *I don't suppose you're free now? I'm about to head to Brighton but could delay if you're about?*

I watched it say 'Tom is typing' multiple times and then went offline to try to minimize the pressure for him, which presumably worked because seconds later he wrote,

> *Sure, I can meet. What are you up to in Brighton?*

I didn't want to tell him that Brighton was where I was currently living in case it put him off meeting me and so kept my response vague but still honest.

> *Brighton = my mother's house. And great to our mutual levels of keenness/availability . . .*

He sent back the crying-laughing emoji. At the very least, he would be a generous audience.

We arranged to meet at a pub in London Bridge and when I

entered and saw how busy it was, I realized I didn't know what he looked like (his WhatsApp photo was of a space helmet) and was concerned about us finding each other as my phone was kaput by this point.

I did a loop of the interior, trying to scout him out, but the only men sitting alone either looked too old to be him or had their heads down absorbed in their phone or a newspaper, unreceptive to my eye contact.

After two more loops I was beginning to lose hope and wondered if it was possible he hadn't arrived yet (even though I was seven minutes late) and whether I ought to bagsy the last remaining table in the corner by the door, when a woman covered in tattoos walked in from a side entrance I hadn't spotted.

I went through it and found a small courtyard populated by smokers since it was otherwise too cold to want to sit outside. The only person who wasn't smoking was a small tanned-looking man who was sitting at a picnic bench table with his hands clasped together, looking hesitantly at me. His dirty-blond hair was woven into a topknot bun thing high on his head, giving him the air of a professional surfer, or at least someone who worked remotely from Thailand half of the year. He did an awkward wave, confirming it was him, and simultaneously the absence of any attraction I may have felt towards him.

'Sorry I'm a bit late,' I said as I approached. 'There's an empty table inside, by the way.'

'That's OK. If it's not too cold for you I'd rather stay out here.' He paused and added, 'It's part of my getting-panicked-in-crowds thing.' So his winking emoji had been in lieu of wit.

I nodded and told him that was fine even though I was surprised because a busy pub was nowhere near a protest-level of people. He didn't have a drink yet and so I asked him what he wanted and went back to the bar to order us two orange juices with soda water.

Because of his remote-working-surfer-vibe, I was pleased to be corrected when he told me he was a children's magazine editor for a publishing house based in Kent. I had lots of questions and enjoyed him explaining how he always 'printed up', which meant kids would send in their drawings and he'd pick a few to print but he could never pick ones done by a five-year-old cause if a ten-year-old saw it they'd think, Oh my God, this comic is for *kids*.

He was quite sweet and nerdy and also a real over-thinker (which was rich for me of all people to say). He told me he'd got into a bad headspace last year so that his mother had got worried about him and had bought him a wetsuit so that he could swim in his local lido because she kept reading and hearing everywhere that cold-water swimming was good for mental health. And I was glad he'd told me this because it meant that when I got tired towards the end of our first drink and wanted to leave when he suggested another, I persuaded myself to stay, reasoning: Misty, this is someone's son – whose mother cared enough to buy him a wetsuit because she thought the cold water would be good for him, which means the least you can do is stay for the duration of two drinks so you don't knock his confidence and squander the benefits of the swimming and the literal cost of the wetsuit.

And so I stayed and we ended up having a nice time, even though I wasn't fractionally attracted to him. But he told me something that I knew, as soon as I heard it, I would go on to think about a lot, definitely for days and weeks, and probably months, and possibly even years. It was this: he told me that he didn't want to be surprised any more, even with good stuff. His justification was that there were so many unpleasant surprises in life that if something good was going to happen, like a present or a party or a trip, he'd like to know about it in advance and derive the extra enjoyment from the build-up to the good thing. 'I want the knowledge of the treat that's to come,' he said. And then he told me how when he had said this in passing to his mother she had taken it very literally so that she came home the next day and told him, 'I've bought you some goggles and I'm going to give them to you next week, OK?' And he said he spent three days trying to imagine what the goggles might look like, and even though they turned out to be pretty standard goggles, he'd enjoyed the three days he'd spent trying to imagine them. I guess, in many ways, I felt he really knew how to live.

When I got back to Brighton, the lights were all off downstairs and my mother called down that she was already in bed.

I entered her room and found her sitting upright under the duvet, still clothed, tapping on her iPad.

'Are you ill?' I asked.

'Just cold.'

'Then how about turning the heating on?' I said, moving towards the radiator, but she cut me off sharply.

'There's no need to be excessive.'

'It's not excessive; it's just reasonable if you're cold.'

'I was cold and then I got into bed and now I'm not cold,' she said. 'And when you start paying the bills you can decide what's reasonable.'

I turned my palms upwards in a gesture of exasperation and said, 'Fine. Goodnight then.'

'Goodnight.'

I was almost out of the room when she announced, 'By the way, I've booked to go to Mexico at the end of May, with Jennifer.'

'How come?' I was shocked by this, having never known my mother to willingly go on holiday, let alone a long-haul flight, unless under duress from either me or my grandfather.

'I've never been and I want to go. Is that reason enough for you?'

'I guess so,' I said, not wanting to let on how unsettled this made me. 'What about Grandpa?' I asked, thinking also, What about me?

'What about him? I think you'll find I do more than enough for that man. And you'll be here in case of an emergency.' I felt uneasy as well as excited by the prospect of this responsibility.

'I approve of the trip,' I said, trying to sound encouraging.

My mother pursed her lips in what looked like an effort not to smile and asked, 'How was London?'

'Good,' I said, perching on the edge of her bed. 'But I'm increasingly wondering if it's a place I'd rather visit than live full time.'

She looked alarmed, presumably by the prospect of our co-habiting long term, and said, 'You could have fooled me. You're there an awful lot these days.'

I hadn't planned to tell her about Christopher but the moment seemed too opportune not to. I wanted to share my life with her; I was fed up with hiding this whole vast aspect of it as if it was something to be ashamed of.

I pressed my fingers down into the duvet and said, 'I'm actually seeing someone who lives there.' I paused before adding, 'He's in an open relationship with his long-term partner and they have a child together but we're serious about each other.'

'And tell me how being serious about you manifests when he's already with another woman?' Her tone was immediately judgemental; she was breathing hard through her nostrils, steaming up for a confrontation.

'I don't know why I bothered mentioning it. I knew you wouldn't understand.'

'Oh, please, don't make out your generation invented open relationships. I lived through the sixties. The women I knew invented free-love.'

'Well, then don't make out that I'm the other woman, like I'm some kind of whore.'

My mother looked stunned at my use of this word and said

very quietly and sternly, 'I'm not even capable of thinking of you in that light.' I realized it was the first time I had ever heard her admit to being incapable of anything. 'But I do think you're belittling yourself.' She brought her iPad up to her face then, signalling an end to the discussion.

Inside my room, shaken by this conversation, I messaged Christopher asking if he was around to speak. I so rarely called him, as I was conscious of not infringing on his time with Sara and Rowan, but tonight I needed his reassurance, to hear his voice, and so when he didn't reply I tried phoning him anyway but he didn't answer. Of course his priority was to Sara and Rowan. I only got his time when it was scheduled; no allowances were made for my impromptu requests. How foolish to think any exceptions would be made in my hour of need.

I lay on my bedroom carpet and considered what kind of a life I would be realistically signing up to by staying with him. In the very best-case scenario, he had said we may get to a set-up where he was splitting his time between two homes, but how was this even affordable? He and Sara seemed financially comfortable, but presumably not to the extent he would have money to co-own a separate place with me and to go on holiday together and do all the other expensive things couples did. I was not materialistic but a base level of money felt contingent to a base level of happiness. And even if we did stay together, I would never get the status Sara had. I would never get him for occasions like Christmas and Easter, or even my birthday as it was cruelly the same day as Rowan's. I would be fated to spend it with my mother and grandfather for the rest of my life, to never grow up and move beyond this. But no, it wouldn't even be for the rest of my life because they would die before me and then who would I spend it with?

Alarmed, I messaged Erica,

> *Would I hypothetically be able to spend Christmas with you if I'm single when we're middle aged and my mother and grandfather are dead?*

But it wasn't just that Sara would get him for all the major occasions. She had all the privileges that came with being his primary partner. She could no doubt end my and his relationship, if she wanted to, at any time she chose. The moment it ceased to be acceptable to her, she would simply stop us seeing each other. Christopher cared about me but surely not enough to insist on keeping seeing me, to sabotage their twenty-year history and the family they had. It was an impenetrable bond – two decades of life together, owning property and sharing a child. How could I possibly compete with this? *You can't*, confirmed the voice. *You might as well give up now.*

My phone pinged and I lurched with hope that it was him, but it was Erica.

> *It's a routinely horrid day. Adrienne and I fight, the twins cry, her mother criticizes, and her father drinks too much. You are welcome to enjoy all of this with me every year!*

I replied with the prayer of thanks emoji, barely registering her response. My message to Christopher was still single ticked and it suddenly occurred to me that something bad may have happened to him which was preventing him from contacting me, that he wasn't ignoring me but lying in intensive care somewhere.

As I contemplated this scenario, I was forced to acknowledge how in the instance of a fatality it would of course be Sara contacted as his next of kin, her called in to view the body, and left to arrange a funeral. This felt like an absurd thing to be envious of, but oh! I was. If he died, nobody except for

Dan and Erica (and now my mother) would be aware I'd even known him, let alone loved him. This hurt so strongly I felt it even in my hands.

I spent the next few minutes awash with panic, placing my head between my legs and squeezing my fists, wondering if I ought to call Sara, given I now had her number, but was thankful I hadn't when he messaged,

We're having some rare family time.
Can I call you later?

I was relieved at his aliveness but ached when I pictured the three of them, under the soft warm glow of the lamp in their living room, reading aloud to each other or playing a game of Scrabble with all their impossibly high word scores. I wanted this set-up too, and felt a pang of fear at what I stood to lose by continuing to see Christopher. But when I tried repainting the scene with myself in it and replacing the man's face with someone who wasn't Christopher, I didn't want it at all. It had lost all its allure. It was no use; I would take the fraction of what he currently had to offer me, and bank on it increasing, in exchange for the utter completingness of his company.

Determined to persist in battling against my doubts, when he called me back a couple of hours later I resisted telling him about the conversation with my mother and said instead, 'I've been thinking and I do want to go to one of those play party things with you.'

'You do?' I felt his voice contained surprise and a definite note of attraction.

'I do.' Or rather it was not that I actively wanted to sleep with lots of people but that I wanted to continue to push and stretch myself, to keep growing so that I could become the version of myself that would allow me to go on being with him. 'But only if it's not too much admin for you,' I added.

'It's the fun kind of admin. Leave it with me.'

'I'm excited about our trip, by the way.'

'Where would you like to go? You can choose anywhere that circumnavigates the M25.'

'I don't really have any preference.' This was true, while unusual for me in a non-food capacity. 'You choose.'

'I have a university friend with a holiday cottage on the Norfolk coast. I can ask him if it's available? There's no electricity, though, so it would be candles and wood fires if you're up for that.'

I told him I could think of nothing I was more up for. Then he said it was time for him to get off the phone and so we said goodbye and I went downstairs to graze on the contents of my mother's cupboards.

The sex party turned out to be inside a new-build apartment in Elephant and Castle. The flat had lots of broken features, like the tap in the bathroom had come loose and the wiring of the flush was visible, and inside the kitchen the hinge of the fridge door was on the opposite side to normal so that people kept trying to open it the wrong way.

There was picnic food laid out on a table and each of our names was written on a paper cup, which I thought was a cute touch. It had the feel of a house party, except for the huge jigsaw of mattresses spread out over the floor. The light in the room was orange and hazy from the coloured air purifier, and there was an ambient soundtrack playing from an iPhone hooked up to a speaker in the corner.

The host encouraged us as much as possible not to use verbal communication, which felt like removing the main aphrodisiac for me, and I was intrigued to see purely what my body was attracted to without language there to turn me on. It turned out I was much more shallow than I realized, in that I was drawn to classically aesthetic bodies – specifically that of a Mediterranean-looking man who looked to be about forty-something, who had come with a Mediterranean-looking woman who looked about the same age. When they saw me glancing at them, they approached us to ask if we wanted to join them. Christopher looked to me to respond and I nodded and so the four of us moved across to a corner of the giant mattress by a potted yucca plant.

I think the couple could tell I hadn't done anything like this before and that I felt – not nervous – but incapacitated, because they were very gentle and kind with me. They smiled encouragingly and asked, 'So what brings you here?' Their accents were thick and soft and I decided either Italian or Spanish. I said, 'You know when you think your life is one thing and then it suddenly occurs to you it could be a completely other thing?' They said they did know and smiled to each other about my answer as if they were sharing a private joke.

The woman asked if she could remove my underwear and I said yes, and then the man moved so that he was sitting behind me with his legs open on either side of me. He eased me backwards so I was almost lying down, and touched my breasts while the woman very slowly took off my knickers. She kissed the surgical scar on my knee and I wondered if she had a fetish for them or was just being sweet and showing me she wasn't grossed out by it. Then I felt her fingers start to stroke between my legs.

The two of them kept checking in with me to make sure I was happy and I nodded each time, feeling very looked after and taken care of. Christopher was lying stretched out next to me, watching, and he placed his hand across my stomach and held it there, which made me feel protected. I wondered if he minded not being actively involved but he looked content to be a spectator, even though I would have preferred him to be the main player.

Every so often the couple spoke to each other in Italian, but I didn't feel excluded; I liked that they had their own shared language. After a while the woman's strokes got firmer and I felt the softer texture of her tongue combine with her fingers. I tried to climax from the sensation alone, but couldn't. When I eventually came, I thought of Christopher entering me and considered it my own personal failure to have to resort to this.

I sat upright again and smiled and thanked the woman. She kissed me on the lips, which I didn't mind but which also ignited nothing in my groin, confirming my theory that I was predominantly, or maybe even exclusively, attracted to men. She placed my hands onto her breasts, and I said, 'I've never touched breasts that aren't my own before and well I guess my mother's when I was a baby.' Her partner nodded encouragingly and said, 'Look, you're smiling; you like them.' I was actually quite indifferent but didn't want to offend the woman by not appearing charmed and so was giving off more enthusiasm than I intrinsically felt.

Later in the night, I watched Christopher being massaged by a woman with pierced nipples, feeling awkward and left out. I approached the couple again who were lying on the floor and this time the woman took my hand and guided it onto her partner's penis and we rubbed him together until he came. As he did this, he threw back his head and laughed so that his teeth became fangs and she did the same, dropping her head down so close to his that their noses were touching. Grinning wildly like that, they looked to be so completely in love that I burned with longing for what they had. 'I love your love for each other,' I said, but by this point they couldn't hear me or had chosen not to.

I looked around to make eye contact with Christopher but he had his eyes closed as the woman with the pierced nipples stroked his inner thigh with a large feather. I wanted her to get out of the way so I could have sex just with Christopher but knew this was contradictory to the purpose of a sex party. And so I left the main mattress area and went across to the picnic table where I ate an abundance of wine gums because I hadn't eaten dinner and was now starving. Looking around at all the naked writhing bodies I felt more emotional than aroused. *You're at a sex party. You're not meant to be moved.* But there was something so humbling and levelling and beautiful about it, all the bodies in all the different colours and sizes and ages. But I didn't know how to describe it without making it sound like a Jesus song. Really, though: never mind knowledge and growth, wasn't pleasure pretty much the point of life? So long as it wasn't harming anyone in the process. Had I been doing this living thing all wrong?

Afterwards, on the Tube ride home, I felt myself crashing from all the wine gums. My hands were jittery and clammy and there was cold sweat at the base of my spine.

'So what did you think?' asked Christopher.

'I liked it as an experience but I still think I prefer it just the two of us. Even though I know that's not a very fashionable thing to say.'

He laughed and said it was nonetheless perfectly valid.

Then I told him I had wanted to cry at one point but had stopped myself, as I often did when I felt the urge to cry in public, because it wasn't really socially acceptable just to go around being moved for no real reason.

'You don't strike me as someone who's particularly concerned about social acceptability.'

'I don't want to annoy people, though, when they're just trying to get on with their day or their evening. They might think they have to stop and ask me if I'm OK and I'd be embarrassed not to have any real reason for crying other than, "It's all just a lot, in a big and primarily wonderful way."'

He paused and said, 'I think they'd find it more intriguing than annoying.'

'Most people find it a bit awkward.'

'Most people don't buy into life the way you do.'

I thought about this and considered he was probably right. 'It doesn't alarm you, then? How much I feel stuff.'

'No. I find it incredibly appealing.'

As we exited the station, he put his arm around me as if to provide shelter, only this time there was not even any rain.

Something shifted in him after that night. I felt his – well, if it wasn't love by this point, what was it? – inching upwards, like a shoot pushing through tangled roots and rocks to surface above ground.

We now saw each other two or three times a week and I had stopped claiming that I was even contemplating my course without him. I was still seeing my imaginary therapist but with much less interest and vitalness than I had been before. That morning, I registered it was the beginning of May and that I had missed several weeks of sessions, which my therapist had emailed to say she would still be billing me for. I transferred my outstanding balance to her inside my head, along with the note, *Of course; I completely understand you've got to make a living.* I even added a tip for my delayed payment. It was so much easier to be generous with fake money.

The following Wednesday I went along to my session, curious to find out what we would discuss, as I felt positive about where things were presently at with Christopher.

'Because you're in a relatively secure state,' she said, the moment I sat down, 'I think this would be a good opportunity to use today's session to do some difficult work we've been putting off.' This was so typical of my imaginary therapist – or of any therapist, for that matter. Why couldn't she just let me sit with my brief contentedness?

'I'd like to begin by coming back to your mother.'

'Really? I'd rather not. It seems a bit clichéd.' Unfortunately, she wasn't deterred by this insult to her originality.

'I'm sensing a strong resistance to talk about her, which implies there's something there to discuss,' she said. 'It may be so buried that you aren't even aware of it yourself.'

'Are you married?' I asked her. She didn't answer. It looked as though deflection wasn't going to work either.

'Perhaps you could tell me what she's like, as a mother and as a person?'

I thought of a string of adjectives to describe her – strong, capable, selfless, proud, hardened, joyless – and said none of them.

'Do you think she's happy?'

'Not hugely, no.'

'And why do you think that is?'

'Because she's alone, obviously.' She had me and my grandfather but it wasn't like having a partner to take care of her. And she seemed to resent us for this.

'Why would she resent it?' I had obviously said this last bit out loud. 'It's something she chose, isn't it? To be a single parent.'

I took a tissue from the box on the table next to me and began pulling tiny bits off it until I realized this was creating unnecessary mess for my therapist (imaginary though she was). I stretched it out on my lap like a square white napkin and stroked it instead, remembering the spa hotel my mother had taken me to on my sixteenth birthday. She hadn't wanted to go but I had banged on so long about being taken that eventually she'd relented, declaring it would be my sole present and that she wasn't going to go through the rigmarole of shaving; that both the spa staff and I would have to accept her yeti look.

The day had gone well. We'd read on teak sunloungers by the pool in white waffle dressing gowns and slippers with the hotel logo, which was exactly how I had imagined and wanted it to be. My mother made a serious dent in her unread stash of

*BMJ*s while I read women's magazines like *Elle* and *Vogue* that epitomized the glamorous adult life I hoped to have. (If I *had* to become an adult, I would at least do it in style.)

But things took a turn when it got to the evening meal part because my mother didn't have the right kind of trousers for the hotel restaurant (by that I mean she was wearing jeans, which went against the restaurant's dress code) and so the hotel manager apologetically told us he would have to seat us in a separate side room. My heart broke a bit for my mother because she had tried so hard but it was not her . . . her domain, and that wasn't her fault, but I was also cross with her because I had wanted the full, proper experience, and was annoyed and embarrassed that she had not read the hotel website's small print, which was so unlike her because she was normally so officious and thorough. But mostly I just felt angry at the hotel for putting us in this situation where she had lower status than she deserved or naturally carried, and we didn't know how to behave with this weird reversal of roles where I felt protective over her. Watching her get on with dinner as though we were inside the dining room and not inside a separate side room made my chest ache and break a bit.

I found out a couple of years later from a comment she made in passing that, leading up to the spa day, her mammogram had come back showing an abnormality and she had been waiting for the results of a biopsy, which had turned out to be fine – hence why I had never heard anything of this at the time – but it explained her not reading the website small print, how distracted she must have been. When I found this out, I felt my chest ache and break a bit all over again.

'You told me in a previous session,' said my therapist, interrupting my reminiscence, 'that your mother hadn't ever tried to initiate a relationship with your father.'

'That's what she told me.'

'And do you believe her? Or do you think it's possible she's telling you a different version of the narrative?'

This was getting a bit intense. I needed time to think, or rather to not think – to shut this whole thing down. I pointed at the abstract painting on the wall that looked like a swollen testicle and asked her how she'd acquired it but she ignored the question, and asked again, 'Misty, do you think your mother lied to you about not wanting to be with your father?'

'No.' *Yes you do*. I told the voice to butt out and go and find someone else to inhabit. *No can do; I'm tied to you*. So now it rhymed? This was getting intolerable.

'Do you believe that in actual fact he rejected her?' And now my therapist was back for another swipe. Between the two of them, I couldn't catch a break. 'Leaving her alone to raise you?'

I'd had enough of listening to this. I got up from my chair and began walking towards the door.

'Which would mean your fear of being alone stems from—'

I slammed it shut before I could hear the end of her sentence and terminated my imaginary sessions with immediate effect.

Did I think this? Of course I did. But I hadn't known I thought it until now. Or if I had known, then hadn't wanted to admit to knowing, because it felt so wrong and appalling to view my mother in a rejected light. I was not used to seeing her with any form of weakness. How could I look her in the face when she got back from Mexico, with this newly acquired knowledge? Even thinking about her suspecting that I knew made my skin feel as though something small and teethy was crawling underneath it.

I was due to meet Christopher that evening at one of our regular hotels, but in the afternoon he messaged to tell me that Sara had gone away for the night to stay with a friend in Lincoln, which meant I was able to sleep over at their place for the first time since we had begun seeing each other again.

It was a weeknight and I waited until shortly after 8.30 to arrive, when Christopher had told me Rowan would be asleep. I was worried about him waking but Christopher had told me he was a heavy sleeper and when I got there he had a French record playing relatively loudly and didn't seem to be worried about us being all that quiet.

I watched while he poured us each a large glass of wine. We always drank when we were together. Sara didn't like alcohol and this was one of the things I knew Christopher enjoyed doing with me and which was unique to us, but tonight I didn't want it – I wanted the evening to feel as little like a date as possible. I was lusting after the everydayness of herbal tea and told him this. He obliged and immediately began boiling the kettle.

'What would you like to do?' he asked. 'Sit and read together?'

'I think I'd find that pretty thrilling, yes.'

I lay on the sofa with my feet on his lap and it was peaceful with the record playing and the lamplight, as well as extraordinary in its ordinariness.

After a while I unzipped my trousers and slid them down my thighs. 'You could also touch me. Providing you keep reading.'

'I think I can manage that,' he said, smiling as he put his book down on his lap and held the pages open with one hand while placing his other hand between my legs. As things got more heated I pulled my trousers down to my ankles and then off my feet, leaving only my underwear.

'I'm just making sure you have easy enough access.'

'That's very considerate.'

I dropped my book onto my chest and arched my neck back, looking up at the shadow of the lamp on the ceiling as I let out a moan and then another one, which I cut short as I heard a creak and the sound of a door opening. We both froze and I tilted my neck forwards to look at him in panic.

'Dad?' said a child's voice, followed by the pad of light footsteps. Immediately, Christopher pushed my legs off him and moved quickly off the sofa. I jumped up and ducked behind the arm of it, crouching next to the indoor fig plant. The leaves were brushing my cheeks and I felt so silly and undignified, squatting in my knickers and socks from a child, in fear.

I listened as Rowan told Christopher he'd had a nightmare about being made to ride an enormous bicycle and being squashed by cars on either side. His voice was quivering and I could hear it breaking as he spoke. I heard Christopher say, 'It's OK. It's not real. Let's get you back to bed.'

Waiting until I heard the creak of floorboards as they went back inside Rowan's room and closed the door, I crept out from behind the sofa and put my trousers on, burning from shame and disappointment. I ought to be relieved, I thought. *But you're not*, said the voice. And then I was ashamed of my disappointment; that I had wanted to be seen, to be caught, to have interacted with Rowan, even if it had meant adding to his distress. But then I thought, That isn't true, or else I would have made myself known to him. Instead, I had crouched there, exposed from the waist down, in order to protect him. Or had I done it to protect myself? Knowing that Sara would likely force Christopher to end things with me if Rowan found out about us?

I sat upright on the sofa and waited for Christopher to come back. It was quite a while before he returned and I tried reading my book again but wanted to be close to him and so picked up his book instead and began reading from where he had left off, even though the sentences were out of context. In the bit I read, the writer was making a case for socialism by arguing that one of the things we lose from market capitalism is a sense of community because our experiences cease to be relatable to each other, if one of us can, say, afford to get a taxi when the train is cancelled but their neighbour has to sit on a very slow rail replacement bus. I thought about how excluded from Dan and Erica's experiences I currently felt, sitting here inside Christopher's living room while he put his son back to sleep who had no knowledge of my existence. But that wasn't anything to do with capitalism. It was just my choosing to be with someone who was already with someone else. The feeling of loneliness was the same, though, like lying ill on the sofa on a summer's day and hearing music and laughter coming up through the open window.

'Sorry about that,' said Christopher when he returned. 'It's a recurring nightmare he has. He hasn't had it for almost a year now.'

'That's OK. Is he all right?'

He nodded but looked concerned. 'Also, just to clarify, we haven't ever given him an enormous bicycle to ride.'

'I didn't assume you had.'

'Though I'm sure a therapist would do a deep dive into his subconscious and interpret it as fear of abandonment.'

'I'm not judging your parenting.'

'That's kind of you. But I think I am.'

I wanted to distract Christopher from feeling bad and so told him about the recurring nightmare I'd had as a child and which I was embarrassed to admit had lasted all the way up to my teenage years. It consisted of me dying peacefully as an old woman in my bed. I'd wake up beside myself with grief and call for my mother, who would come into my room, sit on the edge of the bed and place one of her cool palms on my forehead while I said the thing I said every time, 'I'm just so not ready to die. I mean SO not ready.'

'And the thing is, she couldn't even comfort me by saying, "It's just a nightmare, it's not going to happen." Because it literally was going to happen, and actually of all the ways to go, this way was probably even the most ideal.'

I glanced at Christopher to see if he was bored by my dream talk but he looked invested and asked, 'What did she say?'

'Oh. She'd say the same thing every time. She'd say, "You're not meant to feel ready at your age. But the older you get the more tolerable death becomes." And I'd make her promise this was true and then eventually I'd fall back to sleep again.'

'That's a good response.'

I nodded, not bothering to mention that when I'd reminded her of this on her seventieth birthday, she'd shuddered and said, 'I take that back entirely. If anything, I'm even less ready to go.' And I had felt my stomach lurch and couldn't eat even the tiniest mouthful of cake. Even now, when I remember that I'm not always going to be here – that none of us are – it takes my breath away in a very physical way, like the shock of getting into cold water, even though death is such a predictable and unsurprising thing.

Christopher moved to the counter and took one of the full wine glasses he had poured and drank from it. I waited until he was sitting back down next to me and then asked, 'Do you think Rowan suspected anything? About me being here?'

'Quite possibly.' He paused and then added, 'He asked me if there was someone else in the room. He said he heard me talking.'

'What did you say?'

'I said that I was on the phone to his mum.'

'But you don't think he believed you?'

'I don't know. He didn't seem to want to not believe me.' Christopher scratched the back of his head and left his hand there, cradling his scalp.

'What would have happened if he'd seen me, do you think?'

'I suppose I would have said that you were a friend . . . of sorts.'

'Is it bad that I kind of wish that had happened instead?'

'No, it's not bad. Come here.' He moved his hand to put his arm around me, as though really registering me for the first time again since coming back into the room. 'I think part of me wished that had happened too.'

'And yet . . . well, neither of us made it happen.'

'No. Because I think that would have felt deceitful.'

'To Sara, you mean?'

'To her and to Rowan, but well, also to you, to have let you meet under unintentional circumstances.'

I rested my head on his shoulder and felt incredibly sad.

It was so melancholy, being hidden away. Whoever thought secrecy was exciting must never have experienced it.

'I wish I could meet him under intentional ones.'

He stroked my hair in silence and then said, 'Sara and I, we . . . had an argument before she left. Quite a big one. I broached the subject of you staying here when she's next away and she got upset and said she wants us to see a couples therapist.'

I brought my face up to look at him, not hiding my surprise. 'How come you didn't tell me this until now?'

'I suppose because I was worried it might make you want to stop seeing me.'

I thought I was probably not a very wholesome person when he said that, because it didn't.

'It probably ought to but it doesn't,' I admitted, nestling myself back into him.

He kissed the top of my head and said, 'I realize I haven't even asked you if it's something you'd want. Ideally I wanted to come to you with it as an offering rather than something that's still under negotiation.'

'It is something I want.' I pressed the heel of my palm into a cushion and, without looking at him, asked, 'Are you going to see the therapist, then?'

'I don't feel inclined to, no.'

'Why not?'

'Are you sure you want to talk about this?'

I looked at him then and said, 'Yes. I mean, it's not stuff I want to hear but I want to understand it.'

'All right.' He ran his fingers across the top of his leg and back down again like he was doing a quick piano scale. 'Well, she's right that we agreed not to involve Rowan and that nothing was meant to impact our family unit. But from my point of view, she's . . . already impacted it. She's been impacting it for the last fifteen years while I've been here, holding the metaphorical fort.' He did the piano scale thing again and said, 'And now I think she's experiencing what it feels like to be on the other side of things because it's the first time I've felt this way about someone, and so it suits her to suggest that this is the moment to actively work on our relationship, and well, I'm afraid I don't agree.'

Listening to this, it sounded legitimately complicated and hard to work out who was the victim and who was the perpetrator. Didn't rules and initial terms of conditions become redundant when love got involved?

'I've told her I don't have any intention of she and I separating, nor am I suggesting a kitchen-table polyamory set-up where we all live together, but I am serious about you and continuing to see where we might end up, and that means you meeting Rowan and starting to put your needs more in the foreground.'

I felt such gratitude and fondness for him for saying this but then wondered if his conversation with Sara was really prompted by my needs or by his own. It didn't ultimately matter since our needs were aligned but I was still curious whether his own desire or mine had precipitated their discussion.

'So how have you left it?' I asked.

'I said I'd agree to therapy if she agrees to discuss you living here while she's away, which she's currently saying she doesn't want to do. So, I suppose we're . . . at an impasse.'

There didn't seem much more to say after this, nor did it seem appropriate to just keep sitting there reading about socialism and so I initiated going to bed and he readily agreed. It suddenly occurred to me his face looked very tired, as though he had aged – only slightly but distinctly – during the conversation.

Inside the bathroom I tried to work out what would happen

now. I was pleased that Christopher had shown me this sign of commitment but couldn't see a clear image of a satisfying ending; when I tried imagining the future my mind filled with static and then cut out like that old VHS of *Cinderella*. I brushed my teeth overly hard so that I spat out small amounts of blood and heard the voice chiding me for being needlessly careless with myself.

Erica's father was recovering from a small stroke. When I asked on the phone, 'How small?' she said, 'Not in any way life-threatening but life-shaking. Enough to make you reconsider stuff, you know?' I said I did know, and that I didn't even need health scares to daily question my life choices.

The doctors were confident he would make a full recovery and as an upshot he had also been given a hearing aid while he was in hospital so that for the first time in three years he could experience the full chord sequence in Led Zeppelin's 'Stairway to Heaven'. As a further upshot, his minor stroke had prompted Erica to come back to the UK for a fleeting solo visit without Adrienne and the twins.

She was taking the Eurotunnel shuttle through the channel crossing – using the opportunity to pick up the gargoyle from her parents' house, which she had successfully acquired (declining to pay international shipping) – and had asked if I could meet her for brunch in Folkestone before she headed north. I readily agreed before realizing this involved a three-hour train journey for me, but considering Erica had driven from the outskirts of Paris that morning and had a further five- or six-hour drive at the other end, I didn't feel I could retract my offer.

We had arranged to meet at a fish shack on the harbour and spotted each other as we approached from opposite ends of the promenade. She was wearing a trench coat and sunglasses, and as she walked towards me she took on a dramatic sleuthing air as though she was in a detective spoof.

'Do you think I'm the campest lesbian in Folkestone?' she asked, raising her sunglasses archly.

'I think you're the campest lesbian, period.'

She smiled gleefully as her coat blew out behind her like bat wings.

The fish shack had brightly coloured deckchairs overlooking the seafront which reclined so much that we were essentially lying next to each other. Erica was dressed in leggings and a smock under her coat as well as open-toed sandals with thick socks. I didn't follow fashion so wasn't sure if this was a trend that was about to hit the high street and Erica was just ahead of the curve, or whether she was simply rocking her own look.

I thought she was in excellent spirits, which I attributed to her father's recovery and, conceitedly, to my own presence.

'When did Kent get so zhuzh?' she said, turning her head, her hair whipping her face in the wind.

'I think some parts of it are still pretty rundown but they've gone all out with this bit.'

'At least it still has real people in it.'

'What do people even mean when they say that?' I was thinking how it was something I had once heard Barney (or was it Tracey Emin?) say about Margate and it had made me picture lots of fake robot dolls walking along the seafront.

'People who aren't like us, aka tucking into lobster rolls metres away from a council estate.'

'Should we not be here?' I asked, concerned. 'Presumably we're helping tourism, aren't we?'

'Helping tourism, yep,' she said. 'Pricing out the locals, also yep.'

It was confusing to try to live well and do the right thing when nothing seemed to have a clear-cut answer. Was part of the problem that I never stayed in political conversations long enough to get any further to a conclusion? We would have a five-line exchange about gentrification and then swiftly change topic. I could sense it about to happen now. Then again, people spent years debating inequality and it never seemed to change anything in terms of actual policy. Also, there was something hypocritical about discussing social housing while eating lobster. *Then stop eating lobster,* said the voice.

'How's your writing going?' asked Erica.

'It's not going. I just wish I could want to do something else.'

'Can't you?' she said casually.

'Can I?' I posed this as a question but my tone made it clear I thought this was a fanciful suggestion.

She shrugged and said, 'I've deliberately cultivated an interest in *Peppa Pig* since the twins demand I read it to them every night. It's just better for all of us if I get on board even though I hate the lack of narrative arc.'

I mused on this and then remembered something not unrelated I had read in an article several months earlier.

'Apparently one of the eminent anti-free-will scientists – as in he's basically proven it doesn't exist – says he gets death threats from people saying, YOU'VE RUINED MY LIFE. And that's not even the worst part. The bit I found saddest was when he said if he could go back and unlearn what he's learnt that he would, that he wouldn't have chosen to dedicate basically his entire life to proving a theory that hasn't made him or anyone else happy. How sad is that?'

'Well, duh. I could have told him as much before he even started.'

I watched three old men sit down on a bench in a row and smoke, and felt nostalgic but I had no idea even what for.

'Do you know the mad thing is, even after I'd finished reading the article and felt completely bereft with existential despair, I still walked home telling myself, Misty, stop it. Stop choosing to dwell on this piece of information.'

'Oh, that's funny,' said Erica, smiling wickedly. 'I honestly think knowledge is overrated.'

I thought this was an unhinged viewpoint and told Erica that knowledge was the best thing you could have to equip you for living, which was why I permanently wanted more of it.

'For what purpose?' she asked. 'You've just said yourself it doesn't equate to happiness.'

'Maybe not happiness per se, but isn't growth a kind of happiness? It's preferable to denial, at least.'

'Is it?' she said, scrunching up her face. 'And anyway, I'm not even talking about denial; I'm just talking about detail. Like, bad and awful things are happening all the time but why do I need more than a broad overview? Unless I'm going to do something extra with that information, like give more money in correlation with my knowledge of the situation, then why bother? There's no point knowing stuff if it makes you sad.'

'Maybe that's the fundamental difference between you and Socrates.'

'I'd say there are numerous other more substantial differences,' she replied, tightening her coat as she did a visible shiver and segued into what she said next. 'By the way, I'm still having crazy strong feelings for Suze so I've decided it's best just to act on them and then go back to France and get on with my life.'

'What do you mean act on them?' I felt alarmed, and then further alarmed by what she proceeded to tell me.

'She's exhibiting her bowls at some gallery shop thing here next week and I've arranged to see her on my way back to Paris.'

I felt duped and aggrieved that Erica had not only kept this from me but that the whole trip had presumably been planned around their meeting. Her deceit made me want to come down quite hard against what she had just told me, but I also thought I had a stronger chance of getting through to her if I stayed open, and so did my best to push my pettiness aside.

'You seem quite detached from what you just told me,' I said. 'Like, you've kind of rationalized it but you don't actually sound very persuaded by your own argument.'

'That's because it holds no logical or moral weight,' she said, looking out to the sea forlornly. 'God, I want to have sex with her so badly, though.'

'More badly than you want your life with Adrienne and the twins?'

'No. I mean, yes, in terms of sheer want. But I need Adrienne and the twins.'

Did need trump want? Films and books were always telling us it did, as though want was a superficial little degenerate. But why was wanting something less valid than needing it? Who had decided that?

'I genuinely don't know how I'd fill my time without them,' she concluded.

'But wait, you're always saying you're desperate to be free and have more time to yourself.'

'Well yeah, but that's only because I don't currently have any. It's like you saying you want to be trapped with a child and a partner and a house. However much you claim not to want your solitude, subconsciously you fight to protect it.'

Was Erica right about this? It was either a very astute observation or a completely inaccurate one. It was rare for me not to have a handle on my motive, and I wondered if I had been too hasty in cutting off the services of my imaginary therapist, resolving to make enquiries about her next available appointment.

'I don't think you're going to dissuade me at this point,' said

Erica, turning my attention back to her. 'So I wouldn't worry about even attempting to.'

'Then why did you tell me?' I asked. 'Do you think you're looking for my permission?'

'No, I don't think I want that either.' She paused and looked concentrated in thought. 'I think it's just that it's a sizeable life moment and ordinarily I'd share those with Adrienne. But for obvious reasons that's not appropriate this time around.'

We parked Suze as a discussion and Erica said, 'So go on. Tell me about you, then.'

'OK, well, this maybe isn't going to seem like much of a big deal now after what you just said, but things are developing with Christopher to the extent he's asked Sara if I can move in with him next month while she's away.'

As previously mentioned, Erica was unshockable and so it unsettled me to see surprise and possibly concern flash across her face before she regained her default composure.

'And that's presumably something you want, is it?'

'Massively. But Sara's not keen. We're still hoping she'll come round to the idea, but . . .' I paused, unsure whether I ought to say this next bit, worried that Erica, as a married person, would take her side. 'She said she wants to work on their relationship and see a couples therapist. And he's only willing to do that if she agrees to his request.'

'He's kind of got her in a bind then.'

'Yes and no. She's also got him in one, in that he doesn't want to do the therapy but will do it if she bends on the moving-in thing.'

Erica suddenly shrieked with laughter so that I jolted in my deckchair.

'What's possibly funny?'

'It's just weirdly comical when something lives up to its stereotype. Like, polyamory is obviously going to be messy and end up with these impossible situations but people present it as this uber-chill option that eliminates the mess of affairs and stuff.'

I felt oddly defensive as I replied, 'It's not as though the alternative's less messy. I mean, you're in a so-called monogamous relationship and that's just as complicated.'

'Totally,' she said. 'It's messy whichever way you do it. I just thought that stuff like this didn't happen in open relationships, with the other partner feeling aggrieved and threatened. Like, basically, non-monogamous people are just as human and flawed as the rest of us, and that's the bit I find funny and reassuring.'

I didn't think there was anything funny or reassuring about my situation, but if Erica wanted to take solace from it then that was a positive by-product of what I personally considered to be distinctly un-funny.

'So, what's the long-term plan if you do move in?' she asked. 'Would you be some kind of thrupple?'

'No. Definitely not. But later down the line, it's possible he could end up living with both of us. I mean, separately but with each of us, splitting his time between two homes.'

She frowned and asked, 'What about the child?'

'Rowan.'

'You haven't met him yet?'

I shook my head. 'That's the bit Sara's most against and Christopher's pushing for.'

'What about you, though? What do you want? I mean, you'd be a kind of stepmum figure if it kept progressing.'

I nodded and said, 'I've obviously thought about that and I don't think I'd mind. I'm pretty undecided about wanting children anyway and this would take the question out of my hands.'

'Actually, you'd probably be entering parenthood at the best bit. Bypass the birth and the sleepless nights and the toddler tantrums and just get in at the point where they start getting interesting.'

I didn't tell Erica that it was also possible Christopher and I might have our own child in the future, if we stayed together. I wasn't sure if this was even something I wanted, but wanted to know that it was hypothetically open to me if it turned out I did. How much of wanting was desiring the option of something rather than the thing itself?

'So you'd be satisfied enough with that as a set-up?' she asked, twisting her whole body to face me.

'Right now I think I would be, yeah. But . . .' As I tailed off I saw Erica's face flash with concern again.

'What?' she asked.

'What if I'm wrong and I regret it in the future? I mean, do I make a decision based on what present-me or future-me wants?'

At this point she looked entirely sure of herself again and sat back in her chair.

'Obviously present-you. If you knew already what you wanted in the future it would be a fairer debate, but you're guessing what you might want versus what you know you currently want. It's pointless to even deliberate.'

'Hang on, you're saying you never make decisions based on what you might hypothetically want?'

'Supremely rarely and only ever in the tiniest and most insignificant ways like when I'm not hungry and I'm in the supermarket deciding what to buy for dinner, but big life stuff? No, never.' I found this relatively mind-blowing.

'So, just to be clear,' I said, sitting upright and swivelling to face her, 'you're telling me that when you got pregnant with the twins it was because at that moment in your life you actually wanted a baby?'

'Yeah.'

'Wow.' I leant back again, my mind blown.

'*One* baby,' she quickly added. 'Not two.'

I left Erica and went back to Brighton to pack for my weekend away with Christopher. The house felt strangely odd and lonely without my mother there. I called my grandfather but got through to his answering machine. *You've reached Stanley Watson. I'm likely on the golf course. If you have bad news then break it to me on the twelfth hole. Otherwise leave a message.*

My grandfather and his friends always delivered bad news to each other on the twelfth hole when they were furthest from the clubhouse to give the receiver time to process and digest the information. One year, three separate diagnoses of prostate cancer had been announced in the space of four months, and everyone's swing had started to seize up around the twelfth. And so they'd abandoned this rule and adopted a free-for-all approach before realizing that this made everyone's entire game out of whack, and so had promptly returned to the rule of the twelfth.

'Hi, Grandpa, it's Misty. Just checking in. I'm going away tomorrow for the weekend but I'll come over and see you when I'm back.' I paused and stopped myself signing off with any reference to loving him. He would find it distasteful, and some things were best left unsaid, however much I hourly and minutely went against this ethos.

I didn't feel tired enough to sleep yet and so changed into my running clothes while drafting my therapist an email inside my head, trying to strike a balance between humility and also letting her know that if I were to return to our sessions, the topic of my mother would have to be off-limits.

Apologies for leaving so abruptly last week. I'm happy to start up sessions again providing we leave my mother out of any further discussions. It'll give us more time to focus on the pressing issue of Christopher and what I want from my future with him. Let me know what you think. Best wishes, Misty. But before I'd had a chance to even press send, she'd already fired off a reply.

Hi Misty, thanks for your message. If you'd like to return to our sessions then I have a slot opening up next month. However, I'm afraid it won't be possible for me to agree to the terms of not mentioning your mother. I believe this is where most of our work together lies. Kind regards, Anya.

Yeesh, was I riled. How dare she claim to know more about me than I did? And what did she mean she wasn't free until next month? Who else was she possibly seeing? This was some serious power-play she was enacting. I would hold off replying while I contrived to get what I wanted; hopefully my silence would make her reconsider. *Good luck with that*, the voice piped up. *She's one step ahead of you, remember.*

Yeah, well, I'm one step ahead of her too, I reminded the voice as I double-knotted my trainers.

That's just called being in sync.

I shut the front door on the voice, forcing myself to jog slowly down to the seafront, desiring the day when I would be able to run fully again, not quite believing this day would ever arrive. Looking out at the water, at the burnt pier silhouetted against a backdrop of pink and orange light, I thought the sky looked fake with its loveliness, as though I was running inside a painting.

On the promenade I passed a woman on a bench with a speaker system drinking from a bottle of Smirnoff, pulsing her head and neck in time to the music. Was she waiting for anyone? Or just having a Friday-night party by herself? I smiled as I jogged on, keen not to be invited but wanting to show my respect. When I got back to the house, I stood outside the front door for several minutes and watched the clouds change from marshmallow pink to burning red and then turn gold against a backdrop of deep royal blue. A flock of seagulls were flying overhead, all in the same direction, and each time they turned, they stayed in formation. For some reason they looked pale brown in the light, like sycamore seeds pulled by a gust of wind.

Christopher didn't own a car and so he had hired one from a company with a green logo on the side, the interior of which was very clean and smelt of cinnamon. As we drove out of London that Saturday morning and joined a strip of motorway, I told him about the time I had crashed the barrister's car, and he laughed and said, 'That's good copy.'

'No but wait for it, that's not even the punchline,' I said, sitting up straighter and telling him Erica's response, 'Who *drives* to breakfast?'

And this time he did his big full laugh, and I sat back, pleased with how I had told the anecdote.

'I sometimes wonder if I ought to relearn. What do you think?'

'I think you quite suit being a passenger.'

'I do take it seriously as a role.' I wound down the window and placed my arm on the ledge so that it was lit by a strip of sun.

'What does that entail?' asked Christopher. 'Good map-reading?'

'Ah. No, that's the other thing I can't do.'

'In addition to driving,' he said, smiling.

'Correct. But I have lots of conversational topics and I'd never let myself fall asleep, at least not without asking your permission first.'

'You don't need to ask my permission to fall asleep.'

'OK but I'm not going to fall asleep, and I don't think you should either.'

'Deal,' he said, taking his eyes off the road to glance at me.

'I can also feed you grapes with my right hand,' I said, picking one from the punnet wedged next to the gearstick, and putting it into his open mouth. 'As well as do this with my right hand.' I began rubbing my palm over his crotch, feeling him immediately go hard.

'If you did that then I might have to pull over at some point.'
'You could do. It depends how good your driving is.'
'Comfortably better than yours but that's a pretty low bar.'

The cottage was old and dark with stone walls. It felt like entering a monastery. Even though it was May, it was cool inside and so Christopher set about making a fire while I watched how to make one. Then I realized I wasn't really watching how to make one, I was just watching him make one. I thought about how much I had relied on Barney, who was very practical, especially for a poet, but even just for a person. He had been naturally skilled in the kitchen and was also resourceful around the flat and out and about, say if a bike chain broke or we had to remember directions. Watching him finely chop a shallot one evening, I told him I'd been thinking about the fact that I outsource most things to other people – that my predominant life skill is persuading people to do things for me – and so in the hypothetical scenario of my being stranded alone on a desert island I'd die incredibly quickly. He'd asked if this realization made me want to become more self-sufficient and I'd told him, not hugely no, following which he had accused me of being lazy. I had jokingly refuted this, making it sound as though it was actually true, but all the while knowing, deep down, that it wasn't laziness that made me continue to go on being useless; it was fear.

I had tried to let Barney know, on a daily basis, how much I needed him so that he wouldn't be able to leave me. I hadn't even minded being an invalid. Yes, I'd hated not being able to run and my lack of mobility but not the dependence it gave me. When Dan had said, 'I wouldn't be able to stand people having to do everything for me,' I had agreed, too ashamed to admit that this part of being injured I had liked. I had felt safest in the relationship when I'd been on crutches and had even kept wearing the leg brace after I had to on days when I felt particularly insecure because it made me feel more protected.

But now, watching Christopher, it suddenly felt distinctly preferable and almost vital to know how to fend for myself so at least the option of this was there, even if I chose not to call on it. And so, for the next three minutes, I really concentrated on what he was doing and made a mental list of instructions for myself that I planned to write down later when I had access to a pen.

In the early evening Christopher and I walked down to the beach at low tide. The dunes were bowing with their wild grass and the setting sun was bouncing off the water, blinding me in a good way.

'Sometimes I envy my own life,' I told him, treading over grooves in the sand that looked like the surface of the moon.

'Can you envy something you already have?'

'As in I envy this current version of me walking along the beach with you because in two days' time I won't be walking on the beach with you. Like, I think this, right now, is the very best of my existence.'

'You've reached your zenith.' He said this with a smile but there was something a bit mournful about it.

'Exactly. Whatever that is.'

'The opposite of your nadir.'

'OK, you're doing that thing where you use another word I don't know to explain a word I don't know.'

He frowned and said, 'It's still confusing to me what you do and don't know.'

'It's like a game,' I said, doing a small jump over a thick rubbery strand of seaweed. 'Guess the gap, in my knowledge.'

'Do you really not know zenith and nadir?' I shook my head and he looked surprised and maybe a bit embarrassed but I wasn't sure if the embarrassment was for me or him.

'Is that really bad?'

'No. No, it's just, well, Rowan used them in a sentence the other day.'

'Of course he did, he's got you as his dad.'

'There's an insular logic to your argument I won't refute.' I didn't fully get this but took it to mean I'd won the point, and took hold of his hand as my reward.

'Do you know what Apolo Ohno said about winning Olympic gold?' asked Christopher, swinging our arms.

'Firstly, do I need to know who Apolo Ohno is?'

'A retired speed skater.'

'Also secondly, no.'

Christopher laughed and said, '"It's gold, and then what?"'

'Oh, that's good. And by good, I mean terrifying. I mean, literally my worst nightmare, having nothing to aspire to.' But if this was true – which it was – then why did I believe that if I got the things I was striving for that were currently out of my grasp, I would feel a sense of arrival and calm? Surely I would only go on to replace them with other things that were out of reach? Because it was partly the reaching I was enamoured with. *Duh, because you're human?*

We stopped walking then and watched a couple paddleboarding towards the horizon; two silhouettes ploughing into tons of coloured sky.

*

When we got back to the cottage Christopher opened a bottle of wine and relit the fire and we lay on our sides on the rug in front of it, even though there was an empty sofa right next to us.

'I've got an update on our . . . situation.'

I felt panic funnel up through my stomach and into my throat. He must have seen it in my face because he smiled quickly, only a small one, but a smile it was.

'It's good news. At least, relatively good news.' He paused and then said, 'Sara's agreed to you moving in while she's away. Providing . . .' He paused again and looked hesitant, making me nervous about what was coming. 'Providing we're not romantically involved in front of Rowan.'

'As in . . . I'd be, I mean, we'd be . . .' I tailed off, not attempting to hide my confusion.

'She doesn't want to upset or disturb him and says a reasonable first step is to introduce you as a family friend who's staying to help out while she's away.'

'So, how would that work?' I asked, adjusting my position to sitting upright. 'I mean, where would I even sleep?'

'You'd sleep in our bed,' he said, still lying on his side, propped up on his elbow. 'We'd just make sure the sofa bed looked as though it had been slept in.'

'But what if he wakes in the night again and I'm not there?'

'I posed that same question to Sara, and she didn't have an answer, so I can only infer that's a risk she's aware of and willing to take.'

I turned away from him, holding my knees, and stared down at the diamond of rug between my legs, trying to work out why I felt so dissatisfied with the proposal. It was a generous offering on her part; even I could see that.

'So, does this mean you'll agree to the couples therapy?' I asked, turning back to look at him.

'I think she's upheld her part of the bargain, so yes.' He sounded willing, even keen perhaps, about the prospect of this now that she had conceded to his request. 'I know it's not exactly what we wanted but it's a very sizeable step.' He placed his hand on the bottom of my spine, drawing me back down to the floor.

'No, I know it is. I'm grateful to her, I really am. I'm just thinking . . .' I rested my head on his shoulder, draping my upper arm around his chest. 'I'm just thinking about what happens when she comes back. I mean, presumably I'd move out again, right?'

He didn't answer straight away and I felt him holding his breath before he released it and said, 'That's my current assumption and understanding, yes.'

I was quiet for a bit while I considered this. 'I'm thinking about how hard that would be.'

'I think you're right to consider that.'

I thought about how, in spite of their relationship's openness and freedom, he and Sara did in fact have a non-legally binding contract, not just in the form of Rowan but in the fact it seemed impossible, or at least highly improbable, that they would ever leave each other.

He paused and then, sounding sorrowful, said, 'I may never be able to offer you enough. And only you can know the answer to that.'

But how could I answer that even for myself? How could anyone? What was a reasonable amount to want and when did you have to call quits on wanting and say yes to what was being offered? Another ripe question for my imaginary therapist, whom I was still holding my ground against replying to. But later that night when Christopher was in the bathroom, I caved and drafted her an email – this time sending it before she had a chance to reply.

Understood re my mother. I'll see you at our regular time next month?

Hi, Misty, it's nice to hear from you. I've actually just had a last-minute cancellation so we can do next week now if that suits?

How convenient, I wrote back, playing along with myself, which turned out to still be amusing but only moderately.

The next morning, Christopher and I went for a walk across a stretch of common down to the staithe. The sky was cool and overcast with a thin drizzle and the air smelt strongly of wet coconut. The greyness of the clouds was making the yellow flowering gorse look particularly rich and buttery. Everything – including my desire for Christopher – felt vivid, as though I was playing out the scene in high definition.

On the bend of the road I almost trod on a deer head lying on the path. It had been cleanly severed and the body was nowhere in sight. Its glassy eyes and the bits of pink flesh hanging from its neck made me recoil but also want to keep looking, less out of morbid curiosity, and more out of obligation to seize the experience. Come on, Misty, this might be the only chance you ever get to inspect a dead deer head, etc., made for quite a compelling argument. It smelt of leather and had emerald flies buzzing around the flesh of its neck that looked like shiny beads. There was a tiny tusk coming out of either side of its mouth, like fangs.

'It looks like a vampire,' I told Christopher.

'It's a muntjac,' he said. 'But they're colloquially known as vampire deer.' It really was like walking around with a permanent encyclopaedia to hand. Then again, I had Google on my phone, didn't I? Why were the facts so much more engaging coming out of a live person than a machine? I didn't want to sleep with a machine, but was that really the major selling point of humans?

I thought we ought to move the head off the path in case a

child got frightened or someone accidentally tripped on it. I didn't want to touch it with my hands and so tried kicking it like a football but it was heavier than I'd anticipated and just rolled slightly. I tried again and, with a series of harder kicks, managed to roll it into the trees. The big toe of my left foot was throbbing as though I'd stubbed it on a rock.

By the time we reached the staithe I could hear the tapping of light rain as it hit the stack of empty lobster pots outside the boathouse.

'Is it really a working fishing village, then?' I asked. 'Or just a set constructed for tourists like us?'

'Real. Unless we're unwittingly in *The Truman Show*.'

'I haven't seen it.'

'Of course you haven't.' He looked approving of this – much more approving than when I hadn't known zenith and nadir.

'But I do get the reference because I know the premise.'

'Rowan watched it last year at his friend's house and then became fixated on the idea that he was in it, that Sara and I were playing a big trick on him.' I loved these nuggets of personal information he occasionally offered up.

'That's very funny and sweet. How did you persuade him he wasn't?'

'I told him we didn't have the time, energy or inclination to stage such a major operation.'

'Punchy. Plus, presumably it would go against your values of an "authentic life".' I was expecting this to land like a joke but as soon as I said it, I felt a spark of energy coming off him.

'What made you choose that word?' he asked, looking at me curiously. 'Authentic.'

'It was the word you used when we first met, when I asked why you're in an open relationship.'

He frowned and then said, 'I'm not so sure I do live one of those.'

We carried on walking and I didn't know if he was going to expound on this or whether I would have to probe, but after a few more moments of silence he said, 'One of the arguments in favour of non-monogamy is that it allows for deeper intimacy and more transparent communication, but, well . . . it also allows for avoidance of these.' He swallowed very visibly and pulled at a tall piece of dried grass. 'When Sara and I opened up our relationship we agreed it was because we wanted to not be bound by the restrictions of monogamy that felt false to us. But we didn't admit – or even consider, I can't remember which now – that authenticity, that kind of deep connection, was lacking from our own relationship, and that's something I've been reckoning with lately.' He turned to me then and said, 'I guess this is a roundabout way of saying that in the same way it's possible to lead an authentic monogamous life, I've been leading an inauthentic non-monogamous one.'

We had reached the coastal path by this point, which was overrun with nettles. My ankles were exposed in my cropped trousers and I could feel myself getting stung already but wanted the conversation to continue more than I wanted to turn back.

'What would an authentic life look like, do you think?'

'I don't know exactly. Perhaps one in which I own a microwave.' I smiled but refused to laugh; for his own sake I would not let him off the hook so easily. He breathed in and then biting his bottom lip as he breathed out, said, 'Or one in which I see Sara more than six months of the year and we're honest about our wants and insecurities. One in which I'm able to express generic terms of endearment towards Rowan.'

'You could always preface your "darling" with "here's a generic term of endearment",' I said glibly, as a reward for his earnestness.

He laughed but also looked a bit pained.

'Sara and I have been together twenty-two years and I've never told her any of this. I'm not even sure she'd be that interested. She doesn't have much time for first-world self-analysis, hence my surprise at her suggesting therapy.'

'I kind of admire that.'

At that moment I spotted a bunch of dock leaves and pulled the two largest ones from the batch, tying them in a knot around each ankle.

'Very inventive,' he said, looking impressed.

'I think they look like sushi wraps,' I said, surprised by my own resourcefulness.

As we looped back over the common, I told Christopher, 'Do you remember the first time we were seeing each other and I asked what you got out of our exchanges? Well, actually, I kind of thought I knew the answer already: sex and being looked up to. But you actually seem to prefer it this way around, with this version of me who's more of your equal. It's like the stronger I get, the more you seem to like me.'

'Well, yes, that's true,' he said. 'But it's also because of what you're doing right now.'

'Assessing your character?' I asked, confused.

He laughed and said, 'Being honest. That's the bit I find so arresting. You don't have a facade and that's incredibly rare for adults.'

I waited, enjoying his praise, before admitting, 'I do, though.'

'Do you?'

'It's that. My honesty.'

He wrinkled up his face in dismissal of my claim. 'How can honesty be a facade? Surely facades are deceitful in some way.'

'But my honesty is deceitful because it stops me from having to confront the thing I don't want to be, which is alone.'

'I'm not sure I understand.' Had he ever said this phrase before?

'Basically, for as long as I go around openly admitting how scared and useless I am at looking after myself, I pretty much won't have to because the people in my life who are more capable and less self-serving than me – i.e., everyone – will likely just keep taking care of me. Which is what I want but probably not what I need.'

He stopped then and looked at me, his eyes narrowing with interest. 'And what is it you need?'

'Ugh,' I said, disgruntled by what I was about to say. 'Probably to learn to do life by myself.'

'Hm. You may not have knowledge per se, but you have self-knowledge in spades.'

'It's just a shame there's no pub quiz category for that.'

He laughed and said, 'You'd be cleaning up in a big way.'

By the time we got back to the cottage it had stopped raining and the sun was out in force, sending beams of light over the ploughed field opposite.

Christopher checked his phone and said, 'I've got three missed calls from Sara. I better call her back.' I told him I would make lunch while he was on the phone, and he kissed me three times in quick succession before he left the room.

As I retrieved the various items we had brought with us from their wrapping and laid them on the table, I felt my knee twinge. Alarmed, I told myself not to panic – that it was just a side effect of all the walking I'd been doing and would settle down as soon as I rested it. It twinged again in disagreement but I pushed my concern aside, determined not to tarnish the weekend.

I was slicing bread with a sharp knife and getting very in my head about accidentally cutting my thumb off when Christopher re-entered and said, 'I'm afraid we need to leave. Rowan's in hospital.'

'What?' I asked, hoping but knowing I hadn't misheard him.

'Apparently he was complaining to Sara about his stomach hurting yesterday but she thought it was just trapped wind and Rowan said he felt a bit better in the evening but then this morning the pain got worse and so they took him to A&E and the doctors think his appendix may have ruptured. They're preparing to operate on him now.'

'So, it's serious?'

'Yes.'

I wasn't sure what to say or do. I made my way to hug him, but he stepped back and said, 'I'll go and gather up my things.' Nodding, I said I would quickly pack up the lunch stuff and then do the same. He didn't look at me or touch me as he left the room. It felt as though a dark cloud had just appeared inside the kitchen even though sunlight was streaming through the window above the sink turning half of my arm golden. A faint rainbow had now formed in the sky, the colours and timing of its arrival absurd.

'My friend Beth had appendicitis,' I said as we drove back to London in tense silence. 'When we were in year five. They ended up taking out her appendix and she missed two weeks of school but she made a full recovery.'

'They think Rowan's has burst,' Christopher said, gritting his teeth and gripping the steering wheel.

'Let me know what you need. I can do silence, conversation, sing to you; whatever you want, I can do.'

But he didn't answer or maybe he didn't even hear me. I stared out of the window and willed Rowan to be OK. Please, more than anything, please be OK. Even more than wanting to be with Christopher and wanting to get a book published, I wanted this for Rowan. I could hear the voice on the cusp of piping up to reject the sincerity of my claim, and then silence itself when it discovered I was being sincere. I would give up both of these things if it meant this nine-year-old I had never met whose father I was utterly in love with would be OK.

Around Stansted I realized I badly needed to wee but couldn't bear to ask Christopher to stop driving and so focused on counting the trees in sets of three. At some point he turned on the radio and a song came on about loving and dying. We both reached to turn it off and our fingers touched for a second before he pulled his hand away as if my skin had scalded him. I tried putting my hand on his shoulder but he tensed up and so I took it off and went back to my tree-counting.

At the hospital there were no empty parking bays and

Christopher looked despairing as we waited in a queue of cars for a space to free up.

'Leave me to do it,' I said.

'Are you sure?' I could see him remembering the incident with the barrister's car.

'I can do it. Really. You just go.'

He looked so relieved and thankful that it made me feel momentarily strong and capable, but the moment he got out and disappeared into the entrance of the hospital I felt flooded with dread. I couldn't park this car. What was I thinking?

As I got out of the passenger seat my knee twinged sharply from the sudden movement, having been stationary these last couple of hours. I walked tentatively around to the other side of the car and got into the driver's seat, congratulating myself on having completed step one. But after that I couldn't remember anything. My brain completely shut down. *What's the point of having a driving licence if you can't even park a hire car?* Shut up, I'm thinking! But I couldn't even do that; I was too busy being furious and ashamed at myself. A car behind started honking at me to move into the space in front that had just become available and I was so panicked and desperate that I wound down the window and pleaded with a passing woman to do it for me. She saw the state I was in and agreed even though she was reluctant because of the issue of insurance.

I still needed to return the car key to Christopher and so steeled myself and entered the reception. I didn't like being inside the hospital. *You and everybody else*, said the voice, chidingly. It brought back all the feelings of loneliness and of being left behind while my friends got on with their big and brilliant lives. 'They only seem big and brilliant on the outside,' my mother had said. 'On the inside they're just as mundane and disappointing.' But that had made me even sadder, that if I got through my period of recovery, mundanity and disappointment were all that was waiting for me on the other side. What kind of a milestone was that to aim for? I had wanted to believe that there was something big and brilliant around the corner for me too. Did this count as that? It felt big but very unbrilliant.

I didn't know which section of the hospital Christopher was in, and disturbing him to ask his whereabouts seemed trivial and so I started to walk down a corridor that had an arrow sign with the word 'Paediatrics' above it, but felt an even sharper twinge in my knee so that I had to stop and sit down and wait for it to pass. Why was it acting up right now? The timing couldn't be worse. *Don't you mean better?* challenged the voice. *You really don't want to see them together.* This was not untrue; Sara alone had been bad enough but the two of them – three of them, even – all as one family. I didn't want to witness this; the voice was right. What would I even say? I pictured lamely holding out the key to Christopher, him barely registering me as he took it and turned back to Rowan and Sara, feeling myself shrivelling even imagining this. No, I didn't want to do it. Please don't make me, I said to myself.

Fine, then. Be weak and post it to him. Yes! That's what I would do. I knew the car didn't need to be returned until Tuesday at midday, which meant as long as I sent it special delivery first thing tomorrow morning it would get there in time. Before I could convince myself to change my mind, I ordered an Uber to take me to St Pancras, and left the hospital to the voice's chant of, *Weak weak weak.* But I let it have its little moment as a reward for being useful for the first time in its life.

On the train back to Brighton the twinges became more frequent and I had to hobble from the platform to the taxi rank outside the station. By the time I let myself back into my mother's empty house, I couldn't stand without wincing.

That evening I lay on the sofa icing my knee. I kept looking at my phone to see if Christopher had messaged, wanting to call him but knowing I couldn't. I wanted reassurance that he had not forgotten my existence but how could I possibly ask that from him when his son was life-threateningly ill? The only permissible reason for making contact would be to offer him comfort, but what could I say or do to provide that? In the end I decided the only thing of use would be to give him practical information and so sent a message saying,

> *I've paid for parking until Tuesday morning. I can post the key to you first thing special delivery or I can drop it off in person tomorrow.*

I felt bolder making this offer from the distance of my mother's sofa.

> *This goes without saying but I hope more than anything Rowan's OK. xx*

I tried calling my mother on WhatsApp but she didn't answer even though I could see she was online. She was due back from Mexico tomorrow and I sent her a message,

> *How's your trip going?*

She sent back the smiling emoji with the sunglasses. She really had checked out. I phoned Erica but she didn't answer either. She was probably with her ageing father or driving on her way to meet Suze. I couldn't call Beth because she had an eight-month-old baby to look after. I thought about trying Dan but then remembered he and Shiv had his nephew staying with them this weekend – a 'trial run', he'd called it, suggesting Shiv was coming around to the idea of children. Either way, he had an actual child to be taking care of and didn't have time to field a call from a small-sized adult who felt very alone and was experiencing shooting knee pain. Everyone had their own bigger and more important things to deal with.

I waited for another shooting pain to pass, calculating I had at least a couple of minutes respite before the next one, during which I would force myself to go in search of some stronger painkillers. I had optimistically thrown mine away after the second operation – naively hoping that by not having them in my possession I would no longer require them. But my mother had recurrent bursitis in her hips brought on by her hunched posture, the pain of which when it flared up kept her awake several nights a year.

Crawling up the stairs I entered her bedroom, still on all fours, and made my way over to her bedside drawers, pulling myself up to standing by balancing on my good leg. I found the box I was looking for almost immediately but when I opened it, the foil packet was empty. In desperation I rummaged deeper, pulling out my old items of artwork and homemade cards I had made her on birthdays and Mother's Day, stopping abruptly at the sight of an opened airmail envelope. The thin blue paper looked worn and the handwriting of my mother's name and address was faded. It was the postage stamp that caught my eye, though. Red and white. The Indonesian flag. I knew what it was right away, or at least suspected what it was. It would be the letter from my mother's old colleague telling her my father had died. I'd never seen it before, and when I'd asked to read it as a teenager she'd said, 'You're welcome to but it's not a pleasant read,' making me frightened of the gruesome details it might contain. But now it was in my hand, my curiosity and desire to know exactly what it said overrode my fear.

Sliding the letter out, I opened it from where it had previously been folded three times leaving ridged crease marks. The address at the top confirmed it had been sent from Jakarta but the thing that threw me was the date on the other side of the page. *March 1998.* The year I was seven, the same year we had met my father in the BHS café in Glasgow. But that didn't make sense. He hadn't died for almost another two years.

I sat on the bed and began reading. I read it through and felt sick and then read it again and felt more sick. It still didn't make sense but now for a different reason. If this letter existed – which it did – then how come my mother had turned out the way she was? I heaved myself up and tipped out the drawer onto the bed, searching for a reply or follow-up correspondence but found none. I tried calling my mother but this time there was no reply at all, not even an emoji. I started typing a message to her, furiously demanding an explanation, but at that moment I felt another one of the sharp shooting pains beginning and braced myself, but this time it didn't stop. It just kept going.

The pain was extraordinary. I tried to stay calm and breathe steadily but my breath would only go in and out in sharp judders. I bit the neck of my jumper, pulling on it with my teeth, like a cat mauling a bird. What was happening? Why was it suddenly doing this? I took hold of my own hand and squeezed it, pretending it was somebody else's, and said aloud, 'It's OK, it's OK, you're OK' lots of times in a row in the kindest voice that would come out, the kind I imagined I'd use if I ever met a lost child to try to make them less afraid, but the words came out more like a hiss. I wanted my mother (treacherous though she was) to be here holding a wet flannel over my forehead, or have my grandfather recite a poem to me, or feel Christopher's massive palms, but none of these things were available. Nobody, not even the people who loved me, could help. I quite literally had nobody but myself.

I thought I'd known pain like this before, but the absoluteness of it was like nothing I'd ever experienced. Not just the pain, but the panic of how long it might last was terrifying.

You just have to get through the next minute, I told myself. And when it turned out I couldn't do that, I said, All right then, the next second. And when even that was too much, I bargained, OK, fine, just the next breath; that's your only task – like I was capable of no more than this, because I wasn't. I didn't dare ask for more than just to keep breathing. As I did it, I cheered myself along, thinking, Yes, Misty, keep going, you're doing it, you're doing such good breathing.

Praising yourself for breathing now, are we? said the voice. *Things really are bad.* But yes, that was the whole point; they really were that bad.

There were seven and a half minutes of this acute pain. When it finally subsided, I felt high and elated, as though I had birthed something. And the fact that I had done it all alone, without leaning on anyone, made me feel enormously powerful, even though physically I felt extremely weak.

I hobbled to my mother's bedroom window, where it was now dark outside, and opened it, breathing in gulps of cool air and shivering. *Stop acting like we've been reborn,* said the voice. Stop denying us this moment, I said back to it.

I thought about how I'd expected Barney to make me feel totally safe and protected – but from what? Being alone? Christopher couldn't even protect his own child from actual death. How absurdly unrealistic to expect love to offer safety, either emotionally or physically. Barney had broken off our engagement, Erica was about to embark on an affair, Sara and Christopher lived with the knowledge that at any moment either one of them might fall in love with someone else and change the parameters of their relationship, and as for parents and children – they eventually abandoned each other either by growing up or dying or even just going to Mexico. No kind of love could give a guarantee – not parental or romantic, monogamous or polyamorous. There was a freedom that came with this realization, but the flip side was a loneliness which I knew I would have to live with, at least in bursts, for the rest of my life. This was strangely comforting to acknowledge, to stop trying to fight against it, and to just accept: I could join myself to someone again, but I would ultimately still be alone. What a discovery! Even though this was exactly what my grandfather had told me, I hadn't known or felt it to be true until now.

All those years I'd clung to my relationship with Barney because of the false belief that he could protect me. Had I known this truth earlier I likely would have ended things myself, but instead, all that time I had been chasing after something that didn't even exist. It was actually enormously comical. *We need to work on your definition of humour.*

Taking in one last mouthful of the night, I closed the window and sprawled out on my mother's bed, too exhausted to move into my own. I fell asleep listening to a podcast about blue – the colour, the feeling, the mood.

When I woke at half past seven I had a message from Christopher, sent at ten past five that morning.

Thank you for being so understanding yesterday. The operation went well but they're running further tests for signs of infection. In terms of the car key, are you OK to come to the hospital? Otherwise, I'm sure it would be fine to post. x

It was a longish way to go but I wanted or needed – or both – to see Christopher, to tell him that armed with the knowledge of my new-found discovery, I could now truly accept what he had to offer; yes, I would choose to live with the bitty, rich uncertainty of being with him, because what was the point of choosing safety and security when they were only fallacies anyway?

I felt giddy with clarity as I showered and dressed, testing out my knee, which seemed to be stable, albeit stiff and sore, and so replied to Christopher saying I was happy to come, and he wrote back saying,

Thank you x

Taking a crutch with me for back-up, I emailed my consultant on the train explaining what had happened. I was impressed when I received an almost immediate reply from her, cc'ing her secretary with a request to schedule me for an appointment. *You will see patient has history of prolonged issues around the joint. Probably just small glitch but would like confirm in person when back from annual leaf.* At the bottom of the email it said, *This email was dictated using voice recognition software.* Just like her new-looking trainers, there was something endearing about her grammatical errors, even if an AI rather than her own poor spelling and grammar was at fault.

At St Pancras, I bought a bunch of yellow roses from a flower stand and then decided to buy Rowan a book to read when he was well again. I wondered if this was presumptuous, to assume he'd make a full recovery, before concluding it was a good and necessary level of presumption.

Inside Hatchards I browsed the children's section for books about old musicals but couldn't find any and so, based on the iPad game I had once seen him play, chose a book called *The Pirates of Pompeii*, which was part of a larger Roman mystery series also being sold as a boxset, but the woman at the till assured me they could be read as stand-alone stories and that her eleven-year-old nephew had found this one to be particularly good. I didn't write inside it because I assumed it would be easier for Christopher and Sara to pass it off as their own gift rather than have to field questions at this present time about who I was, especially as Misty wasn't a very brush-overable name.

When I got to the hospital, I messaged Christopher telling him I'd arrived and he replied with Rowan's ward number. I took the lift up to the second floor and walked along the corridor, feeling violently nervous at the prospect of seeing Sara again, but as I approached the ward, Christopher was waiting alone outside it, sitting on a blue plastic chair holding a polystyrene cup.

He stood up when he saw me and said, 'Sara's in there with the doctor at the moment.'

I nodded, holding out the book and roses, and said, 'This is for Rowan and these are for you and Sara.'

'Thank you. That's very kind.'

He gestured to the crutch I was holding as if to ask for an explanation but it felt inappropriate to discuss my own medical condition rather than Rowan's and so I said quickly and lightly, 'My knee had a bit of a relapse. But it's basically fine now.'

I handed him the car key and he took it from me and said, 'Sorry our trip got cut short.'

'Please. Don't even think about that.' But I was a tiny bit pleased he had.

He opened his mouth to say something but then a doctor came out of the ward along with Sara. I stepped back as Sara looked at me without comment – not in a way that was actively rude, just in the way that I was irrelevant. I thought in that moment how if she had shown even a flicker of hatred towards me I would have found that more bearable than her indifference. She and Christopher turned towards the doctor as the doctor began speaking and confirmed that Rowan's blood test results were showing no further sign of infection and that he was out of the danger zone.

Their faces broke into relief as they thanked the doctor who shook their hands before walking off. I watched them take hold of each other's heads in their hands and start to do a kind of spluttering laugh. Or were they crying? It sounded like gasping, like they'd been holding their breath under water for a very long time and had finally pushed up to the surface. Watching them, I started to cry too but didn't feel I had a right to do this in front of them and so turned to leave as quietly as possible, aware of my shoulders shaking as I walked. I thought of the relief I felt and then multiplied it by as many zeros as I could visualize to try to imagine their level of relief, and even then I felt it probably didn't touch the sides.

I was about a third of the way down the corridor when I heard Christopher call my name. I turned and saw Sara had gone back into the ward, and I stood and waited while he walked towards me.

'Are you OK?' He put his big right hand on my shoulder as he asked this, and it felt unbearably comforting.

I was wrong. I had thought that knowing I didn't need to keep looking for safety and protection meant I could now be with him, but watching what he had with Sara, I now knew I couldn't. I wanted more than he could give me – not security or a guarantee – just more of him in the present. Even if my life didn't have marriage or children or monogamy in it (I still wasn't sure if I wanted all or any or just some or none of these things), I did know that I wanted to be someone's main person, and he already had that with Sara.

'I will be,' I said, still crying. 'And I'm really happy and relieved about Rowan. I really am.'

He nodded and smiled in a way that showed sadness and understanding.

'I . . . I'm sensing this has the feel of an ending, but it doesn't have to be that, unless you'd like it to be.'

I didn't like or want it to be, but I also knew I was choosing for it to be.

'The thing is, you're someone I'm always going to want more of. And you can't give me any more of you. You're already maxed out. And for as long as I keep seeing you, I don't think I have a chance of finding that main thing with someone else. But first, I'm going to need to be by myself for a bit.'

He chewed the side of his mouth as his shoulders rose up. When they came down again he breathed out a sigh, one of longing and of resignation.

'I admire your self-reliance.' He said this with a smile, as though we were sharing a secret.

I opened my mouth to refute him but then realized, he

was right. I was finally looking after myself instead of trying to get someone else to do that for me. Maybe I would survive on the desert island of life, after all. *Don't get carried away; we still can't light a fire.*

Christopher and I hugged without kissing and then stayed looking at each other until somebody came to get a Coke out of the vending machine next to us. When the can wouldn't come out, they started pressing the button repeatedly and shaking the machine, and I hated them – for robbing me of this final moment with Christopher – until I remembered I was in a hospital and that maybe someone they loved had just died or was very ill, which made me hate them fractionally less.

As I opened the front door to my mother's house, the familiar sobering voices of the *World at One* travelled through the hallway from the radio in the kitchen. Not knowing the precise timings of her arrival, I had left the letter from my father on the kitchen table in full view. As I entered I saw it had now been removed and that my mother was midway through unpacking shopping items into the fridge.

'I see you've taken care to restock for my arrival,' she said curtly.

'I haven't been here. I went away.' I didn't move to hug her as I normally would have done and instead stood my ground inside the door frame.

'Well, in that case, let's hear all about *your* trip.'

'No thank you.'

'Suit yourself.'

'I assume you saw the letter,' I said, trying to sound calm as I jerked my head towards the table.

'I also saw you left quite a mess on my bed. I'm not sure what prompted your rummage but I'd appreciate you clearing up next time.'

'I went looking for your strong painkillers. My knee locked in the night.'

'That sounds painful.'

'It was agony, actually.'

'But you're walking again now. That's good. Have you had lunch already?' she asked, tipping tomatoes into a colander and rinsing them under the tap.

'Are we going to talk about it?' My words were clipped with fury.

'About what?'

'The letter.'

'I'm not quite sure what there is to talk about,' she said offhandedly, placing the colander on the draining board.

'You're not sure what . . .' I couldn't even finish my sentence I was so incensed.

She stayed facing the sink and with a forced casualness I didn't buy, said, 'Well, I'm making myself a salad if you'd like one.'

I was used to her denying me moments of emotion, of underplaying anything that went on in my life, but no, she would not deny me this.

'You lied. You lied to me all these years.'

'I didn't lie to you.'

'He wanted to be with us. We could have been a three.' I was raising my voice now. 'We could have been a family.'

'We are a family.'

'Hardly,' I snapped back. 'What right did you have to turn him away?'

'Every right. I didn't want to be in a relationship with him. We already had a perfectly good life together, me and you, the two of us.' She took a knife from the drawer and began slicing the tomatoes rhythmically.

'Really? Is that why you made the two of us living together so miserable?'

'Oh don't be so dramatic.'

'Why don't you ever listen to music?' I asked.

'What's that got to do with anything?'

'Just answer the question.'

'I prefer to hear about what's going on in the world,' she said sharply.

'So you prefer not to be happy?'

'I prefer to be informed.'

'You're allowed to be both!' She stopped chopping, startled by my shout. I marched over to the window, shaking my hands, scared I would hit her. 'You denied me a father!'

'I didn't.' She said this firmly, with a shake of her head.

'You did. You didn't even *try* loving him. You punished yourself and you punished me by shutting yourself off and pushing him away.'

'I don't deny that I didn't try loving him. But I never denied you a father. I made sure I never did that.' She closed her eyes and then opened them again and turned so that her back was against the sink. 'I replied to him saying I had no interest in pursuing a romantic partnership but that of course if he wished to move back to the UK and have a relationship with you then I'd facilitate this.' She paused, looking resistant to continue. 'But he never wrote back.'

The line bounced around inside me like a pinball before dropping and landing in my chest with a thud. So my father had rejected *me*, not my mother. I pressed my palm to the glass of the window, which felt cool and sturdy.

'I never told you because I never wanted you to feel unwanted. I was trying to protect you.'

'But you did the opposite. You made me terrified of being alone.'

'What are you talking about?' She sounded cross and defensive now. 'I set you an empowering example – choosing to be a single parent.'

'That's what you said, but I never believed you. How could I have believed that you'd actually chosen it when you were so unhappy about it?'

'I wasn't unhappy about it.' She sounded genuinely confused, which enraged me all the more.

'Yes you were! You were always showing me how hard and tough it was by how hard and tough you were. I just thought you were too proud to admit that you'd wanted a partner but that nobody had wanted you. And this made me terrified because I was so scared that being alone, that nobody wanting me, would . . . would . . .'

'What? For God's sake, just say it.' She spat out the words with impatience.

'Make me like you!'

'And what exactly is wrong with me?' she asked, rising up defiantly to her full height.

'You're bitter and cold and never let anyone in. And I don't want to be those things. And now I'm scared that if I end up alone, even by choice, I'll end up being them anyway.'

My mother opened her mouth and I assumed she would reason with me logically. But instead she began jumping up and down, shaking her arms and letting out a wail. It was more frightening than when she'd cried from *The Railway Children*.

'Mum, please stop. Please. I didn't mean it. I take it back.' But she went on wailing and jumping and throwing her arms about until eventually I moved to grab hold of her and gripped her tightly, my arms wrapped around her torso. I was considerably smaller and weaker than her and she could easily have kept thrashing, but she accepted my lock hug and stayed there, breathing furiously like an angry animal caught inside a trap. When she spoke it was through gritted teeth, trying to hold back the break in her voice.

'I'm the way I am, not because I don't have a partner but because my mother showed her dislike for me every day of my childhood and made it clear she'd never wanted me. If I cried or complained I got smacked with a steel ladle and made to drink from a glass with vinegar in it. But most of the time

I was largely ignored. My mother's moods were completely erratic, so I never knew if I was about to be stuffed in a dress to be shown off to someone she wanted to impress or sent to my room and hit around the head for not sitting in a way that was "ladylike". If you think I'm hard on Grandpa it's because I'm resentful that he didn't stop his wife, my mother, from bullying me. Where was all that love when I was growing up that he's shown you?'

'I'm sorry. I'm so sorry—' I said, but she wasn't done.

'All I've tried to do – all I have ever tried to do – is pump love into you since the day you were born and let you know how wanted you are. And yes, OK, I may not have done it with fanfare and the mushy way the other mothers did it but I did it the only way I knew how, rigorously and consistently. And if I didn't prioritize making you feel special and unique and turning the house into a disco every night, it was because I was too busy making sure you felt safe.' Her voice cracked then. 'So, my apologies if I didn't provide you with the template of a mother you wanted, but it's a hell of a lot better than the one I got.' Exhausted, she finally crumpled in my arms and allowed her head to hang down so that her hair touched my face.

'It's OK, it's OK,' I said, soothing her. I felt her ribcage going in and out within the circumference of my arms, like a ball expanding and deflating.

'You don't need to fear becoming like me because you're so entirely different to me.' She pulled back to stare at me through her red blotchy eyes and said, 'Look how open you are. I cannot understand how I bred a creature as open as you, but I did and I marvel at it.'

I reached up and placed my palm onto her forehead and held it there, the way she had done to me all the times I had been upset. I had always thought I wasn't strong enough to comfort her but as we stood there, I realized that in reaching out and comforting her, I had become strong enough; yet another miniature revelation to add to my ongoing list of them.

'How come you never really told me about your mother?' I asked her that evening as we sat on the sofa with mugs of chamomile tea. 'I mean you kind of did, but you mainly didn't.'

She shrugged and said, 'Again, wanting to protect you, I think.'

'She'd already died by the time I was born, though.'

'Not from her, specifically, but from the knowledge of the . . . abuse, if you can call it that.'

'You can,' I said firmly. 'Because it is.'

She looked lost and childlike for a second and then found her steeliness again and said, 'God, that woman was a battleaxe.'

I didn't know what to add to this and so sat there in silence, listening to the small gold rectangular clock ticking on the mantelpiece, trying not to think about my mother's fear as a child. It really was the most unfair thing you could do, wasn't it? To bring someone into the world without their choosing and then make them afraid of being in it.

'I suppose I was also protecting you from resenting Grandpa,' she said. 'I wanted you to go on feeling the same way about him.'

'I don't think I can, actually. How could he let that happen to you?'

'He worked so many hours that she was left largely to raise me by herself. I think that might have been part of why she resented me so much.'

'That's not a good enough excuse.'

Her mouth twitched into a quick smile at my allegiance before going back to straight again.

'No, I'm not absolving him, he knew what she was like, but I don't know whether he knew all of it. She was a bit more restrained when he was around.'

'Have you ever asked him?' I said.

'I got rather drunk the night of her funeral and accused him of turning a blind eye.'

'What did he say?' It felt as though we were talking about a stranger and not my lovable grandfather who I had only ever admired.

'He didn't deny it. He apologized for not standing up for me more. And I do think the way he is with you is his way of trying to make up for being a shitty parent.'

I couldn't fathom how my mother had kept this secret from me all this time. Only I could; she had done it to protect me, as she said. But now we both understood I didn't need to be protected any more, or rather to be given the illusion of protection.

'I don't know if I can go on feeling the same way about him,' I said. 'But I'll try. If that's what you want.'

She paused before replying, 'It is, yes.' I took hold of her hand and it felt oddly but not uncomfortably intimate.

'You haven't even told me about Mexico.'

'Enjoyable. Lots of Hacienda architecture. Far too many tacos. Overall, a very successful trip.' I smiled, enjoying her version of effusiveness.

'What about you? You said you'd been away. With . . . ?' She tailed off. 'Actually, I don't think you ever told me his, your – boyfriend – partner's name.'

I wanted to cry then, at how much it took from her to say this and that she'd said it anyway.

'We're not together any more. It's all horribly sad at the

moment but at least this way I think I have a chance of being ultimately not sad.'

'Well, in that case, I think that's very brave.' There was that word, being applied to me again; how odd and exciting to hear it. She brought our conjoined hands up to her face and kissed the back of my palm. 'I'm going to read in bed.'

As I was cleaning my teeth that night a videocall came through from Erica. I answered as I continued brushing, curious to know what had happened in Folkestone. Presumably she was calling to atone for her adultery.

'I'm going through the Chunnel if the signal cuts out,' she said.

'And I'm about to spit out toothpaste if you want to call back.'

In typical Erica-fashion she didn't respond to this, but cut straight to the beating point.

'So it turns out I don't actually need to blow up my life, even though it feels as though I want to, pretty much all the time. I just needed to know I could.'

'Wait, you mean nothing happened with Suze?' I spat and began rinsing my mouth.

'No. Well, I mean, we masturbated in front of each other, but I don't think that technically counts as cheating since we didn't physically touch—'

'Mm. Debatable.'

'And then we lay down on the bed together fully clothed and I told her I was leaving, and I left.'

I waited, wondering if the line had cut out or if I had accidentally missed some key information.

'So, yeah, that's it,' Erica concluded.

'No, wait, I don't get it. You're saying you were attracted to her but not enough to sleep with her?'

'The opposite. I was insanely attracted to her. So much

so that I felt myself falling in love with her all over again and that's when I realized this is ridiculous. When it was just sex it made sense to me, but if it's love as well then what's the point? I already have that with Adrienne. I'd just end up leaving Adrienne to build a life with Suze, then feel trapped by it, and have to blow it up all over again by falling in love with someone else. That's not freedom, that's another trap. It's more fun and less work to just keep it going inside my head.'

'That's wise. That's very wise.'

Erica grimaced. 'Ugh. Such a ridiculous word for anyone under seventy. Either to say it about someone else or have it applied to you.'

'Which adjective do you want instead?' I asked. 'You did something semi-noble today so you can have your pick.' She grimaced at noble as well.

Pressing her palms together she twiddled her slender fingers, looking playful and witch-like. 'Cunning.' She raised her eyebrows as she said it, and I felt my appreciation of her was unlikely to ever diminish.

'It's yours, my friend. Indisputably yours.'

I started to ask how her father was but the signal cut out and she froze on my screen, grinning manically.

The next day I called in at my grandfather's house. He was midway through lunch, finishing off the reheated remains of a roast duck, which he was eating directly from a Pyrex dish. He asked if I was hungry but the sight and smell of the duck were immensely off-putting and so I said no and got myself a glass of lemon barley water.

His dining-room table was cluttered with newspapers and the various bottles of tablets he was required to take, so that it was a challenge to find any surface area left uncovered. I moved the Dignitas forms (which he had filled in and ready, saying that when the time came he would not accept a slow and degrading decline) and as I did this, looked down at the headline in the local paper spread out across the table: *Pensioner Stabbed by Granddaughter*, as though showing me there was a quicker, more direct and less expensive route than his going to Switzerland, should we dare. This was the greatest act of love, was it not? To end someone's suffering even if it meant heaping more of it onto yourself.

'So you've been away, have you?' he asked, bringing me out of my murderous thoughts.

'I went to Norfolk for a night.'

'My friend Arthur knew a Norfolk farmer who got diagnosed with pancreatic cancer,' he said, sucking the remnants of meat off a thin bone. 'He went straight home and shot himself with his rifle.'

'Grandpa, do you think we could not talk about death?'

'What would you like to talk about instead?'

I thought about answering, How you failed to protect your daughter; how you let me think of you as this kind, loving and decent man when actually . . . *But he is all those things too. Our fault was thinking he was infallible.*

'Maybe we can just sit and listen to the radio,' I said, which had begun playing some old crooner track.

'Your grandmother loved this song. It was the only record she ever asked me to buy her.'

So even my battleaxe grandmother had swooned about two strangers falling for each other in the night.

As I listened to the strings underscoring the sight of my grandfather devouring the leftover duck, a wasp flew in and began circling the table. My grandfather made occasional attempts to swat it by waving around the bone in his hand, and each time he did this the sweet fatty smell of duck flesh pervaded the air. This is such a distinctly average moment, I thought. And still, I do not want it to end.

We continued to sit there until the song finished and the presenter switched to someone whose voice my grandfather said sounded as though he had swallowed gravel. And so he turned it off and gave me a tour of the garden, reciting the Blake poem as he pointed at the patch of soil where he had recently sown his sunflower seeds. As I watched the ball in his throat do the choking-up thing, I felt the urge to tell him I still loved him. But it would have been redundant, like pointing at a pouring sky and saying, 'Look, it's still raining.'

By the time I left my grandfather's it was almost two o'clock and so I went directly to my imaginary therapist's office, not wanting to be late for my first session back. I saw she'd had a refurb since I'd last been and that the picture of the swollen testicle had been replaced by a large black-and-white photograph of sand dunes covered in wild grass – identical to the ones lining the beach in Norfolk where Christopher and I had walked just three days ago.

I felt exhausted by the sheer quantity of stuff that had happened since I'd last seen her and enormously relieved when I remembered she knew everything already and I could just sit there and field her questions.

She was smiling, in a way that I could tell she was proud of me for making good and hard discoveries and hard and good decisions but would never say all this because it would be breaking some impartial ethical code of conduct.

Didn't we say she was allowed to offer her opinion? I let this comment wash over me, deciding the voice would have to get used to being a lot more rhetorical from now on.

I kept waiting for her to say something but she didn't and neither did I. It wasn't a stand-off silence where each of us was waiting for the other one to break it. It was the still kind of silence after a storm where everything is done blowing. Just like with Christopher, I was sensing my time with her was about to come to an end, at least for now, for this next chunk of my life.

As the clock approached the end of our session, she said, 'It's been a pleasure working with you, Misty. I hope you know my door is always open.'

'Thanks. I appreciate that.' I uncrossed my legs to stand but then crossed them the other way again and said, 'Before I go, I could tell you why I chose you, if you like? Out of the other therapists. Just in case it's useful for, you know, marketing purposes.'

'There were others to choose from?' she asked, surprised. Had she been living under a rock? Didn't she know that her industry, along with yoga, had as many qualified instructors as it did clients?

'Quite a few,' I said. 'I mean, actually loads.'

'OK.' She sounded a little nervous for the first time, a slight quiver in her otherwise smooth voice.

'All right, well, it was just how you were smiling in your profile picture.' She was looking at me expectantly and so I continued. 'I mean, you still looked pleased to be here, like whatever you'd been through – to get to this point – you'd come out the other side, more up than down on life. Whereas lots of the others looked quite bitter and sad. And I couldn't see the point in therapy if I was going to end up looking like that.'

She made a strange contorted face as she tried not to smile, and I realized that I had now made her feel awkward about doing this in front of me.

'Thank you; that's useful to know,' she said.

I hoped I might hug her on my way out but she kept her distance at the door and shook my hand; her professionalism really was outstanding.

As I left her office I checked my phone, hoping Christopher might have messaged, but also knowing and hoping he wouldn't have done. I had no WhatsApps – only an email from the library notifying me that the Henry James novella I had reserved had now arrived and was ready for collection. When I'd told Christopher about my failed attempt to read *The Golden Bowl* he'd said, 'You could try *The Beast in the Jungle* instead. He wrote it around the same time so it's still late Jamesian in style but, well, much shorter.'

'What's it about?' I'd asked.

He'd paused and then said, 'Stuff not happening.'

'But how can that be interesting?'

'Read it and see. It's oddly gripping, and well, quietly devastating.'

I had decided that this was as near to an overt instruction or piece of advice as I was likely ever to get from him and so had reserved it from the library catalogue but because the nearest copy was in Eastbourne and was currently on-loan it had taken several weeks to arrive.

On the way to the library I got a message from Erica.

Mother in law has cut ONLY Clement's hair!!
I AM RAGING

But that's outrageous!
What will you do?!
Cut Aurore's so they still look the same?

That's what I want to do but she doesn't want short hair!
It doesn't feel fair to cut it anyway
MIL is going to get my unleashed wrath when I see her

With good reason!
How's your dad by the way?

Glued to the cricket
Barely noticed my presence at his bedside
How was your weekend away?

Eventful
It will need a phone call
I could speak now?

Sadly this will have to wait
Adrienne and I have a solicitor coming to revise our wills

How thrilling
But also genuinely envious you have anything of value to leave behind

If I go it's just a hard-drive of unpublished manuscripts

Ah . . . The unbearable lightness of freedom

Inside the library I collected the book from the front desk, surprised by how skinny it was, just seventy-five pages. I sat down and began reading it then and there. At the start I found it overly verbose and thought I'd end up abandoning it as I'd done with *The Golden Bowl*, but after ten pages or so I got into its style, and ended up reading it from beginning to end.

In short, it was about a man who spends his whole life with the underlying belief that he's going to suffer from some catastrophic fate that lies in wait for him – aka the beast in the jungle. Because of this, he lives in a way that's timid and afraid and stops him committing to loving his life-long friend – always expecting the beast to jump out at any moment. And only when this friend dies does he come face to face with the beast, understanding that it had already come for him – that his fixation on his fate had made him miss the opportunity of loving her, so that the beast had become self-prophesizing, in that he'd lived his life half-fully. It was just as Christopher had said – a gripping and shattering read. And essentially, zero stuff had happened. I was so confused. How could basically nothing happening provide this much tension? *Because of the underlying question of what the 'beast' is, duh.*

I thought how if Henry James had told someone that he wanted to write a story about a man to whom nothing happens, people probably would have told him, 'But you can't! That will be really boring and impossible to write because a story is made by stuff happening.' But he had ignored the voices of doubt – both his own and other people's (that's if he'd had them) – and had found a way to do it anyway.

That evening, with *The Beast in the Jungle* still pulsing inside me, I sat at the kitchen table and opened up my laptop. As I clicked onto a new Word document, for a second I felt the despair and fear and fatigue of starting all over again, but also the hope and excitement of getting to begin again. This time I wouldn't try to second-guess what other people would find dramatic or interesting, or work out what was trendy or zeitgeisty. Nobody was a complete authority anyway. Not literary agents or scholars or Christopher or maybe even Henry James, so what was the point? I might as well just follow my instincts and write whatever was interesting to me – and even if nobody wanted it, I would presumably only keep getting better the more I did it. There was no guarantee, of course, because however good I got there was still Georgia O'Keeffe's point about timing. But I couldn't control that bit so it was a moot point. I would just go on doing it regardless. I would go on falling in love and writing stuff down and probably go on doing both of these things again and again and again even if each time they didn't work out, because as Christopher and now Henry James had said, 'What was the alternative? Nothing happening.' And that was an even more intolerable and frightening option. How dull and wasteful of this one life. I started to write.

It was sixteen months later when I saw him again. I had moved back to London by this point and felt explicably high – from all the good things that were happening to me – but also from the September air which churned me with adrenalin. Those shorter evenings and golden leaves got me whipped up every year.

I was running in Highbury Fields when I spotted him sitting on a bench, reading. Yes, I was running – something I wasn't sure I'd ever do again, but there I was, doing it. I had finally sold a book as well – something I also wasn't sure I'd ever do, but I had done it. It felt too happy and neatly tied up as an ending, but it *was* a happy and neatly tied-up ending. Or rather, a happy and tied-up next bit.

The editor who had bought my book had taken me to lunch to celebrate at a restaurant in Marylebone that was so light and airy that everything looked dreamlike, as though it had been purpose-built to reflect my mood. She kept saying throughout the lunch such lovely things about my writing that my jaw hurt from smiling. 'It's just, the thing is . . .' I said. 'The thing is, when I started writing this one I'd already decided I was going to keep doing it anyway, even if nobody wanted it. And so now to hear you say all these things, it's well . . . this enormous extra.'

'And the money,' she said. 'Don't forget you get paid to do it now, too. I mean, not a lot – it's publishing, not television – but still something.'

I smiled some more until my jaw shook and I had to bring my knuckles up to my face to massage out the tension.

*

Christopher happened to look up as I ran towards him, but I think I knew I would have stopped anyway.

He smiled, looking pleased to see me. 'Hello,' he said.

'Hi,' I said, smiling too.

'This is a nice surprise.'

'It is, isn't it?' I meant this and was almost disappointed to mean it, that I felt no more than basic pleasure to see him. Where had it gone? All that longing.

'You look well,' he said.

'I am well.' I paused and then added, 'I sold my book, so I'm actually very well.'

'I know. I've read it.'

I was shocked by this. 'But how? It hasn't come out yet.'

'A publishing friend sent me a proof copy along with a Post-it saying, IS THIS YOU?!'

Of course he had a friend who worked in publishing; he'd been to Oxford. I felt myself go hot and said, 'Sorry. I kept umming and ahhing about emailing you but chickened out.'

'Don't worry. I found it a rather generous — albeit square — portrayal, so I won't be taking umbrage.'

'Phew. Although I was more concerned about you taking me to court.'

He laughed and said, 'I won't be doing that either.'

I waited and then asked, 'So, what did you think of it? Aside from your thinly disguised characterization.' I pulled at the edge of my shorts, nervous to know the answer.

He picked at the spine of the book in his hand before looking up and saying, 'I found the ordinariness of it surprisingly gripping.'

'Really?' I asked.

'Really.' He said this in such a way that I knew he was telling me the truth and not just what I wanted to hear. 'You didn't even put the sex party or burst appendix in.'

'True. Pretty much everything else made the cut, though.'

He smiled knowingly at this, and said, 'It felt very real. To the extent I forgot I was reading fiction.'

'The highest praise coming from you. Thank you.'

He crossed his legs, angling himself towards me, and asked, 'And what does it feel like? Now you know you're going to be published. Like Apolo Ohno winning Olympic gold?'

I laughed and said I hadn't got to the 'what's next?' bit, not yet. That I knew I would probably get there eventually, even though I couldn't currently imagine it, but that I was trying to hold on to this bit for as long as possible.

'Good, and so you should.'

I asked after Rowan, and Christopher said he was well and pointed to a boy in the nearby playground area hanging upside down on a set of monkey-bar rings. I could see his appendix scar where his T-shirt had ridden up, his wild curly hair fanning out below his face. I thought he looked just so lovely.

'And Sara?' I said. 'Are you two still . . . ?'

'Together?'

'I was actually going to ask if you were still open.'

'We're still that too, yes. She's doing more work from the UK office, though, so we have more time as a family.'

I smiled and tried to convey through my eyes my happiness at this.

At that moment Rowan came over and announced to Christopher, 'It's now nine minutes since you promised me an ice cream.'

Christopher touched Rowan's shoulder and said, 'I'd like you to meet someone first. Rowan, this is Misty.'

'Hi, I've heard lots of good things about you,' I said.

'What things?' he asked.

'Well . . . that you like watching old musicals and you like eating raisins.'

'I do like raisins but I prefer ice cream quite a lot more.'

I laughed and he looked at me quizzically and said, 'Are you one of my dad's colleagues?'

'No,' I said. 'Just a friend.'

He arched his neck back so that his chin jutted upwards before bringing it back down with a nod. 'You don't seem weird or old enough.'

I laughed again, and Christopher said, 'Sweetheart, why don't you join the queue and I'll be over in a minute.' Hearing Christopher call him 'sweetheart' broke my heart a bit, in a good way.

'OK, bye,' said Rowan, before running across the grass towards a parked ice-cream van.

'He's as brilliant as I imagined him to be. And by that, I mean very.'

'I agree. Despite my conscious bias.' I wondered if Christopher remembered coming out with this phrase on our first date. It seemed like an entire lifetime ago, which was a total cliché, but it really did.

'Well, take care,' I said.

'You too.'

As I left him I twinged with sadness for having lost the intensity of my feelings towards him, even though this was what I'd wanted for so long, but now I was nostalgic for it. The sky was lilac and amazing as it often seemed to be these days. As I ran I felt a yearning but this time the yearning wasn't for him, but for my longing. How I missed that too. We humans are such funny contradictory things with all our massive little wants and needs.

The following autumn I went to Paris to promote my book. It hadn't sold in France, where my foreign-rights agent had received the feedback from a French editor: *This is quite offensive to our nationality and also too chick-lit for our imprint.* But I was doing a reading at Shakespeare & Co. in an evening of English Language Debuts.

Entering that hallowed shop – looking up at the glass dome ceiling, every inch of wall lined with books – it was hard not to get swept up in the reverence of the place; so many iconic writers had passed through that I allowed myself a whispered, 'Misty, you did it,' hoping the events manager hadn't heard.

Erica came along to listen to the readings, and asked in the Q&A afterwards, 'I was just wondering if the protagonist's friend Eliza is inspired by anyone in particular? I found her to be extremely engaging.' I could see her mouth twitching as she tried to keep a straight face.

'Loosely, yes. A good friend of mine.'

'Cool. Well, tell her I'm a diehard fan,' she said, grinning.

Afterwards, there was a drinks reception put on for us upstairs, where the events manager pointed out the narrow beds that had previously been used by the 'tumbleweeds' – the writers who slept and wrote inside the shop in exchange for helping out – but who now slept inside the studio instead. 'Less romantic but more practical,' he said, touching the side of his glasses.

Erica sidled up to me while I was between conversations and said, 'I actually think it's great you waited until like your fifth attempt to get published, because now it feels too late for you to become a diva.' I loved her for this, for implying it had been my choice to be rejected for nine years. 'Plus, I don't think I can read books any more written by anyone under the age of thirty. I just find it cringe-worthy that a twenty-something-year-old thinks they have anything to tell me.'

'Don't you think by the time you're forty-something you'll feel that way about books being written by thirty-something-year-olds?'

'Quite possibly,' she said, plunging into the green velvet armchair that had just become unoccupied.

She seemed softer and slightly changed. She was still Erica – strong and witty and direct – but there was an underlying uncertainty she was also allowing in.

After the drinks had finished and we had left the bookshop and crossed the river, we passed a group of climate protestors who had chained themselves to the front of Hôtel de Ville and were currently being cut loose by two police officers. As we passed them she turned to me and said, 'I do think about it. I know I tell you I don't but obviously I do. I mean, I'd have to be an absolute psychopath not to.'

'What specifically are we talking about?'

'Climate change,' she said bluntly. 'Clement drew grass the other day and he drew it brown. Like, that's just normal to him. The sea is blue, the sand is yellow, the grass is brown, not green. It's completely terrifying. He'll be drawing the sky red next, and I have zero intention of doing anything about it other than continuing to do tiny insignificant things like recycling yoghurt pots. And that's probably all I want to say on it, OK?'

'OK.' We carried on walking and after a bit I asked, 'How's it going with Adrienne?'

'Better. Like, I still feel trapped but now it's more of a voluntary entrapment. I've also unfollowed Suze on Instagram.'

'That seems wise.' Erica rolled her eyes and I quickly corrected myself. 'Sorry, cunning.'

'How about you?' she asked. 'Are you currently dating?'

'I'm open to it but not actively pursuing it.' I had begun to feel so content and secure just having myself to rely on and pump good thoughts and warm air into, that I was reluctant to disrupt this dynamic by allowing another person to enter it. I was both helped and hindered by the fact that the woman I lived with set such a strong example of leading a full and varied life without a partner that I could go days and sometimes even whole weeks without remembering that I ultimately wanted to be with someone and so didn't want to cut myself off from that happening.

As Erica and I were saying goodbye I remembered something I had forgotten to mention earlier.

'Do you remember that guy Andy I dated for a bit with the favourite Pizza Express?'

'I probably think about that line on a roughly bi-weekly basis.'

'Well, I bumped into him in Hove when I was staying at my mum's a few weekends ago. He was coming out of a café holding hands with a woman he introduced as his girlfriend and the three of us ended up having a whole conversation, and they were both lovely – really warm and soulful – and for a second I wondered if I'd made the wrong choice and felt a pang of regret, until I remembered that I couldn't regret something now that I hadn't wanted at the time. I mean, that's not how regret works.'

'Not to burst your bubble,' said Erica, looking minorly concerned, 'but that's exactly how regret works.'

'Is it?' She nodded and hugged me, indicating the night was done. 'OK, well I think the bigger point here is that I didn't want his offering at the time and I still don't want it now. I just had a fleeting moment of wanting it, you know?'

'Oh, I know those fleeting wants. All too well.'

Later that evening I took the last Eurostar back to London. Those huge bronze lovers greeted me at St Pancras, turning my insides dust-like. I'd always assumed they were lovers but suddenly, walking towards them, I wondered if maybe they were just friends, having a go at a big tender kiss; now I'd had this thought, I really hoped I was right. I stared at the bright navy sky through the glass roof of the station, at the pink neon lettering below the giant golden clock. Yep. It still moved me. So much still moved me that sometimes I couldn't understand how I kept going. But why I did was easier. Even the bits that were sad and hard and anxiety-inducing, they too had left me achingly alive. I thought of the years I had spent with Barney, of the months with Christopher, of all those hours with my mother and grandfather and Erica. What might it have looked like, my time with each of them, had I skipped those bits instead of playing them out? And for a second, the loss of this made me forget to breathe –

But we didn't skip them, said the voice. 'We *had* them,' we said aloud. And out came air; oh ow, oh wow.

Acknowledgements

First and foremost, my thanks and appreciation go to Ceri Dunn and Abigail Butler. I could not have written this book without the time spent and conversations had with each of you. I'm hugely grateful to you both.

I'd also like to thank the following people:

My editors at Fig Tree – Helen Garnons-Williams and Ella Harold for helping me figure out what was needed to make this book work. It continues to be a complete privilege to get to collaborate with you.

My agent Cara Lee Simpson – and the team at SLA – for supporting me through the publishing journey again and for delivering such encouraging and useful feedback on an early draft.

My publicist Rosie Safaty for pitching the book with your signature enthusiasm and warmth.

The team at Penguin General: Alison Tulett, Leah Boulton, Natalie Wall, Josie Staveley-Taylor, Emily Moran, Autumn Evans, Lucy Keeler, Caitlin Knight, Emily Cornell, Sam Fanaken, Ruth Johnstone, Sara Granger and Savreet Virk, and designers Katie Smith and Emma Ewbank, for your much-valued contributions.

Sarah Jackson at Random House Canada for publishing me across the pond; I'm so happy we found each other through Misty's story. Also my extended thanks to the team at PRHC: Polly Beel, Megan Costa, Evan Klein, Talia Abramson, Sue Kuruvilla, Deirdre Molina, Catherine Abes and Madison Henricks.

Jonathan Lee and Keiran Goddard for your ongoing career advice, introductions and guidance; your generosity knows no bounds.

The staff at Hackney Central Library where I wrote and revised large chunks of the book (and my heartfelt gratitude for the existence of libraries across the country).

You, my readers, for buying copies of my books and enabling me to do this as a job; I'm extremely fortunate.

My friends and family – in particular Gemma Dunn, David Dunn, Natalie Orringe, Ted Wilkes and Patrick Wray – for your ongoing interest in and championing of my work.

Finally – and fundamentally – Jim Burke for your continuous love and endorsement, and for making our time together so immeasurably good.